THE ELEMENTAL STONE

A Mortaran Novel

Madelaine Taylor

I would like to dedicate this book to the memory of my nephew, Daniel. I miss him terribly.

CONTENTS

PROLOGUE

Dryad

T hree men stood around the great oak on the eastern edge of the Heartwood. They were no more than thirty paces from the retreating border of the woods yet the canopy above blocked all but the most persistent rays of sunlight. The pollen speckled beams reflected by the sharp metal of their axes.

"We'll tek it down in that direction. There's plenty room for it to fall and wi' any luck we'll knock some o' them there pears down an' we can have a snack for our way home.

"Yer mad you are! If we tek it that way it'll catch on them branches, and we'll be no better off than we are now! We'd be best tekkin' it over this way."

"What would you know? When was the last time you felled a tree this size?"

"I'll tell ye when, ye old..."

"Shhh. Ye hear that?"

"Hear what then?"

"That noise, I swear I heard a cry."

"A cry indeed, ye never heard nothing but the birds squawking o'er head."

"No, it was deeper than the birds callin'. More like a... well, a wolf or something of the kind... I reckon we should be on our way; we don't need the wood so bad as to be fighting' off wolves... or worse."

"Oh, 'ere he goes, 'there's Dryads in these woods'. Pfft if there were tree women roaming' about killing folk do you not think we'd 'ave seen them before?"

He started to laugh, a good, hearty laugh, that caused him to arch his spine and tip his head back directly into the path of the dark wooden staff. The sound of his skull cracking turned the stomachs of his friends as his knees buckled, and he collapsed to the ground.

The Dryad stood behind him. Her dark, braided hair framed the point of her ears and her deep, green eyes glistened with a mischievousness that was mirrored in the smirk on her thin, brown lips. She waited as the other men emptied their stomachs and then, in a panic, started to run for the tree line and the safety of their stead.

A second Dryad stepped out of the trees between the fleeing men and safety, a long, wood tipped spear threatened to pierce the flesh of the first man to run closer.

The younger of the two woodcutters stopped his flight sharply, grabbing the trunk of a small tree to break his momentum. He wrapped his arm around the tree and fell to the ground, facing back into the depths of the woods and the old oak he had hoped to fall. The dying scream of his older friend filled his head as he scrambled back to his feet. The Dryad closed in on him.

"You killed it." The Dryad's voice was soft yet full of accusation.

"It was old and ugly. No one would want it."

"It would have made an interesting hunt for the saplings. It ran well enough."

"My apologies, Princess Olerivia, I had not properly considered it's worth."

"No mind, it's death will serve as a warning to others. The saplings can hunt this one until it serves."

He considered trying to run again but thought better of it as the Dryad princess stepped aside, her smile wide.

"Run?" She gestured her invitation with a wave of her arm. He shook his head and dropped to his knees, the look of disappointment on her face was the last thing he saw before the staff struck his head and the darkness took him.

He woke on the floor of a willow cage, hanging two meters or so above the ground. His clothes were gone and his wrists were bound with vines. Below him the Dryad held a feast, a celebration of his capture. The food was plentiful, their wooden cups full of sweet wine. They ate and danced until the moon was high overhead, and then they disappeared, melted into the trees, leaving only the sound of their joy and their laughter to echo a moment in his ears.

His attempt at escape happened a week after his capture. He had been taken from his cage in order to feed him. A bowl of berries and nuts was placed before him alongside a cup of sweet, thick liquid which tasted like heaven but made his mind cloudy and his heart race. The Dryad assigned to guard over him was young and flighty, a group of rabbits playing nearby distracted her just long enough for him to get a minute's head start. They had kept him well-fed and healthy, although his legs were a little stiff from his lack of movement, he quickly found his pace. He ran from the small clearing and into the thick of the woods, jumping over ridges and raised roots, ducking and swaying around branches. He was used to moving through the trees, and he covered a good distance in the short time he ran.

Once he was sure he wasn't being followed he sat down at the base of a tree and dragged his wrist bindings over a rock protruding from the ground. It took a while to snap the vines that had held him and his wrists and forearms were badly scratched and bruised by the time he was free. He took a few moments to catch his breath and then started to move again. He wasn't sure which direction he was travelling in, but he knew he was moving away from the clearing in which he had been caged and that was good enough for now.

The woodcutter had been travelling thirty minutes or more when he heard the laughter. For a moment he thought he must have reached the edges of the wood and was listening to the sounds of stead children at play. That thought soon left him however when the stone struck his stomach. It was a small stone and hadn't been thrown with much force but it still left a mark on his skin. Another came quickly after adding a red welt to his thigh and a third marked his shoulder. He ducked behind a tree, looking more for shelter than to hide and was relieved as the stones and laughter stopped.

He darted to his right and ran for a moment or so, as fast as he could run through the trees, hoping to evade the Dryad once again. As the strength in his legs began to fade, he slowed once more to a walk. His breathing and heartbeat returning slowly to their usual pace he stepped carefully around the trees and the undergrowth.

Another twenty minutes passed and his heart dropped into his stomach as he rounded a thick tree. Standing just a short distance ahead of him were two young Dryad, each carrying short spears and nets. They looked right at him and laughed though they didn't move. He turned again and ran, half stumbling as his legs started to shake and buckle. In a few moments he stumbled over a branch and rolled to a stop on his back under an old oak. Exhausted, he lay in the undergrowth, his mind racing, his eyes darting from tree to tree as he waited for the Dryad to appear and drag him back to his cage. They didn't come. It wasn't long before the exhaustion hit his mind, and he fell into sleep.

He woke in the same place as he fell and was filled with relief as he realised he had not been recaptured. A sense of relief that turned to despair as he tried to move. His wrists and ankles were bound in vines once more and tied around the trunks of the surrounding trees. He was trapped, his limbs stretched wide like the branches of the trees that held him, the vines strong and tight. All hope of escape left him. Three Dryad appeared from the trees and sat around him.

"It's awake again. Can we let it go and play some more?"

"No, Erinia dear, your mother's seed is ready; it's time for it to serve us."

"I wish it had lasted longer, we hardly got to tease it at all and I never got a chance to practice my spear."

"We'll try to encourage the next one to escape its cage earlier. This one was as slow of mind as it was at running. Its body will serve well though, it is thick and strong. Are you ready Olerivia?"

"I am."

Princess Olerivia moved forward and sat across his chest. She took a flask of the thick, sweet liquid they had given him and poured it into his mouth. The liquid revitalised him. Rehydrated and stronger, he pulled at his binds, but they didn't move. He tried to move his body, to buck and twist enough to dislodge the Dryad sat across him but, though she was small, she was strong and forced him back down. The older Dryad grabbed his jaw and forced his mouth wide open. Olerivia took her seed from a small leather purse she wore, like a charm, around her neck. She placed the seed into his open mouth then poured more of the liquid from the flask into him. The older Dryad forced his mouth closed and held tight until he swallowed, they made sure the seed and the liquid had gone, and then they left.

He kept trying to escape, pulling on his binds, twisting them, scraping them across stones and roots, but they never broke and never loosened. Each day saw Olerivia come to him with another Dryad or two to pour more of the liquid into his mouth.

The woodcutter passed before the seedling pushed through his stomach and flowered. Olerivia came every day and tended to it as it grew into a sapling and, in time, into a young tree. Three years passed and all that remained of the woodcutter were his moss-covered bones, half buried under fresh topsoil. Olerivia came once more. She placed her hand against the trunk of the tree and merged herself with it. When she reappeared, she held a baby in her arms, small and delicate, her dark eyes wide, her skin a golden brown. She looked up into Olerivia's eyes and smiled, a gurgle of happiness broke the silence. A new life was formed, a new Dryad would grow within the heartwood. She would laugh and play with her sister, and, in time, she would meet a human child.

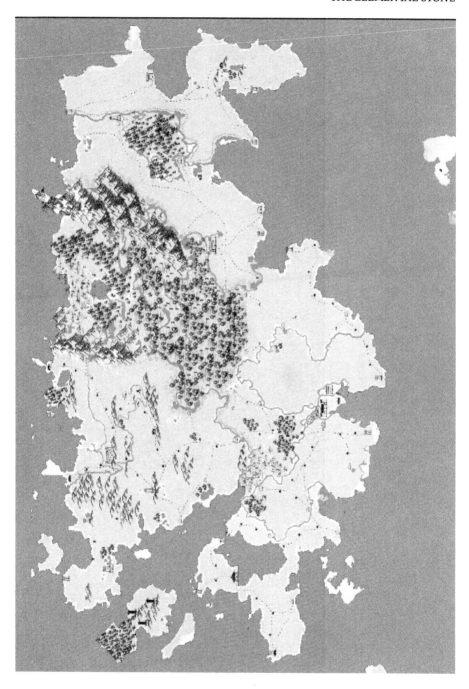

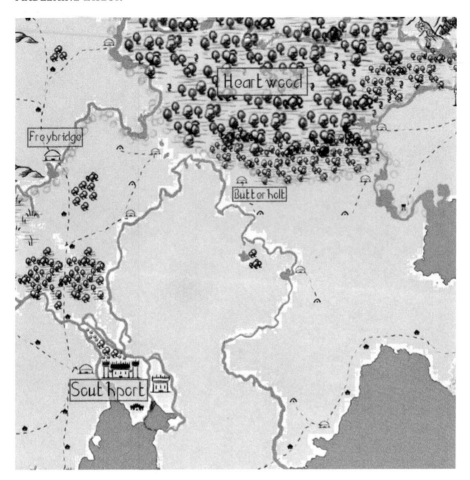

PART ONE
The Stead

1. BUTTERHOLT

Lana was sitting, crossed legged, on the grass under an old oak tree. Her mind was wandering, and she seemed lost to the world. She had a smile on her face and her fingers were fidgeting with a daisy she had picked. The sun was still low in the sky, slowly spreading its light and its warmth across the Stead. The warmth on her pale, freckled face made her happy. Geamhradh had been long and cold, but now it was earrach. The oak towering above her was becoming greener with each passing day and as the leaves grew so did her mood.

Watching her father work made her happy, he was herding calves and preparing them for their lives on the farm. Marking them with the Gesith's brand and their own number. She felt sorry for the young male calves though, having a band placed on them to remove their desires. She wondered if they had done the same with her older brother, and she laughed to herself.

Lana had grown up on the farm and lived in the stead, sharing a house with her parents and her brother. Her days had been free to pass as she wanted up to now, but that would end this year. At lùnastal it would be her birthday, and she would start working. She hoped she would be allowed to work with her father in the pastures and the open-air but feared she would be made to follow her mother's career. That seemed to be the way; girls followed their mothers and boys their fathers. It seemed odd and unfair to Lana; she was just as able as her brother to watch a field of cows. Her mother's job was to milk those cows that were ready for it, she spent her mornings milking in the shed and her afternoons churning butter and making cheese. She hardly ever got to wander in the fields or follow the tree-line of the Heartwood. She was concerned that her mother was missing the best of life and didn't want to be the same.

Lana stretched and yawned, realising her father had moved deeper into the pasture. She picked up her small bow and the quiver her father had made her. She only had two arrows and wasn't very skilled with the bow, but she often copied her father as he practiced and shot at critters that strayed from the woods. She liked to pull the string and pretend she was catching imaginary rabbits or shooting at foxes to protect the calves. The young girl walked the tree-line, her eyes darting between the ground, looking for fallen nuts or berries, and the woods, wary that a Dryad might jump out at any time and take her. She felt safer having the bow. Wandering slowly, she picked some berries from the bushes and trees to nibble on and followed her father, Hayal, east.

Lana passed the whole day in the pasture with Hayal, gathering food and flowers as she walked. She would give the flowers to her mother, Ellie, that always made her smile. Lana nibbled on some of her food throughout the day and gave some to Hayal when he came closer to see how she was. At the end of the day they walked hand in hand to the pasture gate and onto the path that led to the Stead square. Lana tugged on her father's sleeve and smiled up at him.

"Race me?"

Her father looked down at her sparkling green eyes and the grin on her face, and he laughed.

"You know you always win Lana!"

"Oh Please? I promise I'll stop at the crossroads and wait...."

"Very well... Three... Two... One... Go!"

She let go of his hands and ran, her red braided hair flailing around her head. He waited for a second, a smile on his face and then jogged after her taking care not to go too fast.

As evening drew in Lana sat in her house with her family, her mother had prepared food for them with their day's rations, cheese and bread with a thick, hot stew. Steam rose from her bowl as she slurped the gravy of the stew from her spoon. The warmth spread from her stomach to her fingers and toes as she ate. Once she had finished eating Lana ran to the corner of the room where she slept and picked up the flowers she had hidden by her bed. Running back to the table she kissed her mother's cheek, presented her the flowers she had picked and smiled.

"Thank you for our food mam, I feel full and warm."

Ellie took the flowers and smelled them with a smile then held Lana in a warm embrace and kissed her forehead.

"You're welcome sweetheart, and thank you for your pretty gift. Now go and wash up then get changed."

Lana went over to the bucket of water by the fire and washed her hands and face, then skipped back to her corner taking off her day clothes, a skirt and loose blouse. She pulled her nightdress over her head and sat on her cot, humming quietly to herself, waiting for her parents to finish eating and call her back to the fire.

Once everyone had washed Ellie gathered the bowls and spoons and put them in the bucket. Swirling the water over them and wiping them with an old wet rag before setting them out by the fire to dry. Her father pushed the small table to one side and set their stools around the fire. Once the room was set, he called Lana and her Brother, Andel, back over to the hearth where they sat a while as Hayal told them stories.

Tonight, he told them a story he had told them many times before, reciting the poem of the Dryad, describing how they sneaked into a stead in the North, taking the children from their beds.

When candles go out
and you're in your bed
Block your door
Or you might wake dead

The Dryad hunt
And you are prey
They take your bairns
They chase and play

They fix a bell
So they are heard
From tree to tree
Just like a bird

They run and hide
But ne'er go free
For Dryad spring
From every tree

They cage your child
Leash and cuff
They make them run
Til they've had enough

And then they're free
To roam the wood
They let them leave
If only they could

But the woods are dense
No path is found
Not by human
Not by hound

So they wander all day
And they wander all night
And never again
Will your bairn come in sight

For the Heartwood is death
The Dryad cause pain
Protect your bairns properly
Your prayers are in vain.

Although she had heard the poem many times before she was fascinated by it and hung on her father's every word.

The following day Lana went with her mother to the cowsheds and chatted as she milked cow after cow. She quickly grew bored and restless and started to pester her mother with games and questions. Walking back and forth across the dirt floor kicking up dust and singing little tunes to herself. Lana loved her mother dearly but spending days with her, watching her fill pails with milk wasn't at all interesting for her. The only upside, she thought, was that they were allowed to keep a bit more milk than the rations usually allowed, and she did like drinking that rather than the water the Stead folk usually drank.

She was trying to coax her mother into telling her a story, another one, about how she had met Lana's father and married. Ellie though found herself too distracted by the constant need for attention and decided she needed some peace.

"Lana pet, I'm busy and I know it doesn't seem it but I need to concentrate a bit more. Why don't you go and play in the field a while?"

Lana jumped off the fence she was sat on and ran to

her mother, flinging her arms around her neck and kissing her cheek, startling the cow her mother was milking in the process. She thanked her mother and ran out of the barn into the field next door.

The field was large and empty, the grass was quite high now, and she ran into the middle of it then lay on the floor next to a patch of daisies. The sun was climbing higher and warming the ground. She picked a handful of daisies and split their stems, passing one through another she made herself a daisy chain and then circled it making a crown for herself.

Lana lay a while in the sun imagining what life would be like as a princess with a real crown and that got her to thinking about what life must be like outside of the stead, outside of the hold; what a town or a city might be like or what the oceans might be? She had heard of the oceans from traders that would come to the Stead. It sounded fascinating, a place where the water was never still and you needed to travel in a ship to go anywhere. The stories she had been told made her smile, these ships were bigger than houses and had giant sheets hanging on posts to help them move in the wind. She was told of South-port and of how magical it was, big houses and streets of gold and gems. People wearing bright, wonderful clothes and talking with funny accents.

The queen of Mortara lived in the city, or next to it and would be seen walking the streets, giving wise advice and help to the people she met, giving out coins and food. It sounded so wonderful. She knew she would never get a chance to see these things for herself, she was bound to spend her life sitting next to her mother milking cows and churning butter. But she had her dreams and they made her happy.

Ellie finished her milking as the sun reached its peak in the sky, she came out of the barn and called for Lana to come back. At first, Lana pretended not to hear her, grabbing as many seconds of freedom as she could. She knew her mother was likely to send her up to the Manor House with the hand cart full of milk, and she really just wanted to lie in the sun. As her mother shouted a third time and her voice became sterner, she jumped up and ran back to her.

"I was beginning to think you'd fallen asleep Lana."

"I was just thinking, mam... I made you a chain, look."

She took the daisy chain crown from her head and gave it to her mother smiling far too sweetly and trying to look innocent.

"That's very nice, pet. I'd like you to take the cart up to the manor now though. Can you manage?"

Lana scrunched up her face at the thought of pushing the cart up the road, but she agreed and picked up the handles. She groaned as she lifted them exaggerating the effort it took and then walked slowly out of the barn and up the path.

The Gesith's estate was a mile up the path from the Stead. Surrounded by a wooden palisade his manor was the only building in the Stead made of stone. It had an upstairs floor and even a basement. The kitchens and storage buildings were off to the sides. He had a large staff, maids that served in the house, cleaning and attending to him and his Son Aeloth. A head cook and a team of younger cooks. Errands and pages, stablemen and a blacksmith; They all lived and worked within his walls in small wooden houses.

It seemed to Lana that the manor was a grand place so tall and big. She imagined the queen must live in something like this, probably a bit bigger because she was a queen, but in a similar style. She didn't understand though why The Gesith and his son needed so much room and so many staff members to look after them. She had never been inside the manor house itself though she imagined it was very rich and beautiful.

Lana walked through the gate, into the courtyard and toward the kitchen where she was greeted by Sera; the head cook. Sera was a little older than Lana's mother and had a similar nature, very happy generally but her voice had a stern edge to it. You never wanted to get on the wrong side of Sera as many a child could attest to. She pushed her hand cart up to the kitchen door and smiled.

"My mam sent me with these. She said there's a bit of extra cream in the big one. Are you baking something nice today?"

Sera laughed.

"Always thinking with your belly eh Lana? Did you bring me any flowers?"

Lana looked away a moment biting her lip.

"I'm sorry, I made a daisy chain but I have given it to my mam. She had shouted on me too many times and sounded angry."

"I see. Well, wait here anyway I'll see if I've something for you."

Lana smiled a big smile, there were some good things about coming to the manor. Sera often had something to give her by way of a treat, some jam on a piece of bread or a sweet pastry, often giving Lana a bundle to carry back home to her mother too, a bit of bread or cake, an egg or two she hadn't used. It all went towards a meal at the day's end.

Sera emerged from the kitchen a moment or two later carrying a piece of sweet bread lathered in honey. She handed the sticky treat to Lana who thanked her with a hug and a smile.

Besides speaking to the kitchen staff Lana would occasionally catch sight of Aeloth, the Gesith's son. He would often be training in the courtyard with a sword, his tutor teaching him to move properly, to defend himself and to strike properly. On occasion, she would take some time, sit somewhere inconspicuous and watch him. He was getting better at the sword and sometimes even managed a strike on the tutor. From time to time the training would turn into a practice duel, Lana enjoyed those days, watching the tutor and the young lord dancing around each other thrusting and parrying with their wooden swords. She thought it very elegant at times.

Today she wasn't the only one watching them practice, a small group of the Gesith's sheriffs had come to the manor and were watching the young lords progress. The sheriffs were men the Gesith trusted and held in regard, they had larger houses than most around the hold and made sure everything was done to the Gesith's laws and liking. A few were close to the Gesith and lived nearby, often riding through the farmlands with their longbows and swords on display, ready in case anyone decided to break the rules or in case a larger predator came out of the woods. They stood around in a circle as the tutor and Aeloth sparred, blocking Lana's view, so she went over to the storage hut and stood on a barrel to see better.

The duel was quite frantic, both the young lord and the tutor wanted to impress the sheriffs with their technique and stamina. At one point the young lord became too hot, so he stripped off his shirt and continued in his hose. Lana blushed deeply as he stripped, but she couldn't take her eyes from the young man. She never mentioned it to anybody, but after that day she would always try to be there as they sparred. Her thoughts and dreams contained more shirtless men duelling than she thought might be healthy for her.

As earrach went on Lana spent more time with her mother at the milking sheds and less with her father. Ellie would have her sit and learn, sometimes she had her calming the cows as she milked them. One morning her mother sat her down on the milking stool in front of a cow and told her to milk it.

"You've watched me often enough now Lana, give it a go yourself see how you get on. This cow's got a lot of milk to give and is nice and patient when she's givin' it."

Lana looked up at her mother

"But what if I do it wrong? What if I squeeze too hard or pull wrong?"

Her mother chuckled

"You'll be fine, pet, just warm your hands a little and use a bit of pressure, not proper squeezing like when you're ringing out clothes. It's not too difficult a task, but be sure the cow'll tell you if you do it wrong."

Lana sat a while and milked the cow without any problems, as she relaxed a bit, she found it quite soothing and started to smile a little. Ellie was happy with the results, and with the peace it gave her. She hugged Lana telling her how proud she was. Lana knew that spending more time with her mother was to get her used to being in the sheds, preparing her for her role as a milkmaid, and she wished she could wander the pastures near the woods more. Milking the cow wasn't as fun as watching her father and wasn't as satisfying as having a jar of pretty flowers by her bed or a pocketful of nuts and berries to munch on.

Still, there were always the treats from the kitchen and the chance to catch Aeloth train so it wasn't all bad, besides you got to stay indoors a bit more, and she supposed that would be nicer on rainy days.

The next few months were spent with her mother, watching her milk and then running the pails up to the manor. She did manage to spend some time with her father after three months of milking. It was samhradh now, and he was busy chasing down a young cow that had caught a burr and was looking a bit bothered. Lana enjoyed it but it could be a bit hazardous for a young girl to be chasing a cow if the mother or the herd decided to intervene. So she stood under the trees, watching.

She followed her fathers' movements along the edge of the forest, occasionally stopping to pick a flower or a nut from the floor. As she was walking the tree line, she heard a muffled sound not far behind her in the trees, she turned and stared but could see nothing. "It must have been a rabbit or something," she thought, and she went back to watching her father chasing cows. At one point he threw his rope to catch a young brown calf, it fell around the calf's back legs but the cow, startled, kicked and ran, the rope still attached. Her father lost his footing on a rut in the floor as the calf took full flight, and he fell into a puddle. He wasn't hurt, except for his ego, and when he got up, covered in mud, he looked to Lana who was creased up laughing and waving. He smiled and waved back, wiping himself down as well as he could then went back to the chase.

Lana walked a little further along the tree line and saw some lovely looking cherries, they were still on the branch but it was within reach if she climbed just a little way. She looked at the tree, assessing its branches and a way to climb for a minute or so and then placed her hands on the trunk.

"Okay, Mr Cherry Tree," she said, "I'm going to just climb a lil way up you if that's okay, and if it's good with you I would really, really like to try that lovely looking group of cherries of yours before they turn...."

With that she started to climb, it wasn't a big climb, one or two branches only, then she reached out and plucked the cherries from their home then clambered slowly and carefully to the floor, careful not to snag her skirts on a twig. She got to the bottom and stood with a smile on her face, proud of her climb and happy at the prize she had won for it.

"Thank you very much, Mr Cherry Tree," she said, and she hugged the tree.

There was a sudden noise behind her, it sounded like a giggle, she turned quickly and fancied she saw a young Dryad through the trees. She only saw it for a second before it hid, but she swore she saw it smiling at her, eye's full of glee and curiosity. Lana started to back up a little, walking away from the tree line and toward the fence at the edge of the pasture. She sat on the fence eating a fresh cherry and thought about the Dryad she had seen. She wondered what it had been doing so close to the forest edge. Hunting for children maybe? Or maybe just curious as to the world outside the woods as Lana was about life outside Butterholt. How long had it been so close? How long had it been watching her and running parallel to her in the woods? She was intrigued by her brief sighting and thought she'd like to meet a Dryad maybe, to talk to one, to spend time with one. But they were elusive and potentially dangerous. They scared her, though she thought their life must be interesting.

2. THE DRYAD

When the hotter days of luchar came Lana was looking forward to spending more time in the pastures with her father, basking in the sun and collecting all the beautiful flowers that bloomed at that time of year. She looked forward to running through the grass and climbing through the leaf laden branches of trees on the edge of the woods. She loved this time of year; it made her buzz with a love of life.

Her heart sank though when the messenger came from the Gesith. Hayal was ordered to make a journey south to a small stead on the border of the hold. He would collect a prize bull from the farm that Gesith Heriloth had acquired and bring it back to the Stead with him. It would take her father seven days, maybe a little longer, to make the journey and Lana would have to spend that time in the milking sheds. It made the whole situation worse though when her father asked Andel to take his place in the pastures. She loved her brother but hated that he got to be out in the open air, in the fields, free and untethered by a list of chores.

Lana's mood grew grey the next morning as she saw her father off, waving him goodbye and wishing she could run after him to share his path south. She dragged her feet as she followed her mother to the milking sheds muttering, under her breath, about the injustice of it all. It just got worse when she got to the sheds, she slammed her little stool down on the floor, kicked up a bit of dirt and straw and sat beside the innocent, unwitting, cow with a grunt. Her milking wasn't done with care or attention that morning and cow after cow let their feelings be known with stamps and snorts of warning.

"Get out Lana! Go home and sulk on your bed. I've had enough of your moaning and you're going to get yourself hurt if you keep at the milking the way you are."

Lana jumped; her mother rarely shouted at her. She looked up at her mother, her face screwed into a tight knot of derision, she grunted and stood up, knocking her stool over, she stamped off.

"Now you just mind young lady! Get out of this mood as fast as you can. You'll be getting no cream until you've come to your senses. And don't be thinking your father will be happy to see you when he gets home. Not after he's heard about your behaviour!"

Lana walked to the path, her arms folded, her brow furrowed. Then, in an act of defiance, she took the path to the pastures instead of the one back home. Walking past the fields she looked through the fence to see where her brother and the herd were. He had followed them off to the east a ways and wouldn't see her if she sneaked in and kept close to the trees. And so, she clambered over the stile and ran to the trees as fast as she could. She hid behind an old oak for a moment to catch her breath and then looked around it to see if she had been spotted. Andel though was too far away and too occupied to have noticed her, so she started to walk a little, looking for fruit and berries as she went. Muttering to herself.

"No cream huh? Pfft well no berries for you then, just see if I care! Not like I want to be milking the cows, is it? I don't even want to be here." She popped a berry in her mouth and fell silent for a moment as she bit into it and sucked out its juice.

She continued to mutter and pop an occasional berry in her mouth as she walked, and then she stopped as something caught her eye. Looking into the woods a little way she spotted a bush filled with plump berries, ready to pick and eat. Getting to the berries would mean going into the woods though. She knew she shouldn't, it was dangerous in the forest. It was one thing to walk the tree line but to dare cross it, that was bad. Once you crossed that line, once you put yourself under the canopy of the trees you were in the Dryad's home. Anything could happen to her, she could be hunted and captured, she could trip over a fallen branch and end up trapped by a sneaky Dryad. She could even be attacked by one of the bigger animals that live in the woods. Even if she got out all right, she'd be in so much trouble if anyone ever found out about it. But those berries looked so good, and she was so angry.

She looked again for her brother, but he was lost among the herd, so she stepped past the trunk of the tree beside her and into the woods.

Nothing happened, no Dryad arrows flew past her head, no sudden fall into darkness. It was just the same here as it was out in the pasture, so she took a few more steps, her courage growing as she went. Having walked a little way she stopped to check that the line of the forest and pasture was still in sight. She looked around her to see that she wasn't being hunted then she walked on, cautiously, toward the bush she had seen. She was deeper in the Heartwood now than anybody she knew had ever been and her own heart was pounding. Her eyes darted from side to side as she walked and every noise made her jump a little. She was shaking now and her anger was lessening a little, replaced by a nervousness that seemed to heighten her senses.

As she walked on, avoiding branches and roots her shoulders dropped into a slump and her stomach tightened a little. She realized, as her rebellious thoughts eased, that she was acting out of childish moodiness. She was almost of age now, a young woman. In a year or so, she would be marrying and settling her own home and yet here she was running off into the Heartwood because she wasn't allowed to go on a trip south. She flopped down to the ground beside an old oak tree and started talking to it as though it was a friend. Working through her mood and her issues. Questioning her behaviour and trying to justify it in some way that she knew was wrong. She sat on a mossy rock a good hour talking to the tree before she fell silent, having run out of ways to justify her behaviour. She sat quietly for a few minutes more and sighed.

"I'm being foolish aren't I, Mr Oak?" She didn't get a response "I should find some nice flowers and take them back to my mam, maybe she'll forgive me. What do you think, Mr Oak? Do you think she'll forgive me?"

Again, no answer came, not that she expected one. She talked to the trees along the forest edge a lot, thanking them for their gifts and letting her climb them, but they never answered.

"You only talk to the Dryads huh?"

She got up and started looking around for some nice flowers. After a short while, she looked at her collection and considered it nice and jolly. She was sure these would help her apology, so she turned around to start her walk back to the pastures and then home.

Lana froze. Standing there, right there, in front of her, close enough to touch. Looking at her, completely still was a Dryad. She was taller than Lana and had pale brown skin, her eyes dark green, it looked as though she was weighing Lana up. Her long brown hair, braided, fell over her shoulders. Her lips were thin and her face stern. She held a bow in her left hand and her right was a balled fist. Lana's stomach instantly knotted, she looked around desperately, her eyes darting in every direction looking for a way past the Dryad, looking to see if others were around her. She tried to move but her feet were heavy and rooted to the floor.

"Please Lady Dryad I'm sorry, I saw the berries and.... I know I shouldn't be here but I just want to go home now, Please... I need to go back to my mam and say sorry... Please?" Tears formed in her eyes as she pleaded.

The Dryad didn't speak. Her eyes never left Lana's; she tilted her head slowly from side to side as if looking at Lana from different angles. Then she looked down and pointed at the flowers in Lana's hand with the tip of her bow. Lana looked at the flowers in her hand and held them out to the Dryad, her eyes wide and pleading.

"I'm sorry, I thought they would be a pretty gift for my mam, I... Well I can't put them back but... if it's wrong to take them then you can have them... I mean, I'll leave them if you want, if I can go."

There was a moment's silence and then slowly the Dryad raised her other hand out toward Lana, in it was a flower, a deep purple flower, Lana could smell its scent, sweet and fresh. She had never seen a flower like this, she didn't know what kind it was, but she thought it must be very special. The Dryad looked at her flower and then up at Lana. She moved her hand toward Lana's and opened it, letting the flower sit in her palm.

"For me? I can take it?"

The Dryad gave what seemed to be a smile. Lana reached out slowly, her hand shaking a little and took the flower from the Dryad, placing it at the centre of her bunch.

"It's beautiful, does it have a name?" The Dryad didn't reply.

"Thank you, Lady Dryad, thank you ever so much. May I leave?" her voice was still quiet, still shaking, unsure.

The Dryad stepped aside and Lana started to walk toward the tree line, not daring to look back, she felt the Dryad's eyes on her the whole way. When she reached the pastures, she turned and looked back into the woods but the Dryad was gone.

"Thank you, Lady Dryad... You are very kind," she called into the woods.

"Well that was something different, wasn't it, Mr Apple Tree?" She looked up at the tree beside her but getting no response she turned and started home.

When Lana got back to the Stead her mother was in the square, talking frantically with some of their neighbours. Her face was red, and she had tears in her eyes. The men of the Stead were organizing themselves into small groups talking about where they would go to begin a search. Lana stopped, for a moment her stomach knotted, and she wanted to turn around, to flee. Run back to the woods and never come back. Her heart was heavy, her face reddened and tears burst from her eyes. She ran.

Not away from the square but towards it, towards her mother.

"I told you to come home, Lana. Where have you been? What have you been doing?"

Lana fought the tears to answer, her throat tight and sore, her body trembling, her face red and wet. She looked down at her feet and wiped her eyes with her sleeve, then she looked up at her mother, eyes wide as they could be. She held out the flowers and through her tears asked for forgiveness.

"I was in the pasture mam. I'm sorry I know it was wrong, I know I've been horrible since dad left. I'm sorry, really I am."

Ellie walked over to her slowly and flung her arms around her holding her tighter than she remembered ever being held.

"I thought something had happened to you Lana, I thought you'd gone. Don't ever do that again okay?"

They stood awhile in their embrace, Lana apologizing through her tears and Ellie telling her just how much she loved her. When they parted Lana handed her mother the flowers and Ellie took them, smiling through her own tears. She held Lana's hand and led her back to their house. She placed the flowers into a small water-filled jar by her bed and lay down with Lana, holding her again.

It was a week later that her father returned home with the new bull. Ellie didn't tell him of Lana's misbehaviour or the frantic hunt she had almost started. The purple flower still bloomed in the corner spreading its sweet scent through their house. It looked as fresh as the day Lana had been given it and the smile it brought to Ellie's face brought back the sensation of being held and the warmth of love she had felt on her return.

Lana never mentioned the Dryad to anyone, she was worried it would bring up the bad feelings of that day. She knew she had caused her mother real pain and that made her feel as bad as she had ever felt before. So much worse than being left behind by her father that day. Besides, she had a secret now and strangely, that made her happy. It was her special moment, her treasure, and she would keep it close to her heart forever.

In the coming months Lana changed, she no longer complained about her chores. She hummed as she milked the cows, and she made the most of her errands around the Stead and up at the manor. She talked to everyone she met, she spent time with Sera and her staff and always had a good word to say. Lana enjoyed the opportunity to talk, almost as much as the treats she would be given, and she got to know her neighbours in the Stead much better than she had before. She found that she also spent a lot more time watching Aeloth sparring with his master or walking the courtyard, so full of confidence, so elegant, so proud.

Lana's thoughts and dreams turned away from distant palaces and oceans and concentrated more on the things she had experienced over the last year. The Dryad intrigued her. She had been in their forest, she had spoken to one, and she had left the forest, alive and with a gift. Why had the Dryad let her go? Why had she given her a flower? Was she still watching from the depths of the woods? Sometimes Lana swore she was being followed as she visited her father in the pastures. Sometimes she swore she heard that same mocking laughter as she spoke to the trees. She never saw the Dryad though, if she was watching, she was hiding from sight.

It was Aeloth though that occupied her mind the most. She often thought of him as she milked the cows, humming quietly to herself; and her dreams often featured him, shirtless, sparring with his tutor in the square. She no longer dreamt of becoming a princess, she dreamt now of marrying her lord and becoming a lady.

3. THE BULLY

A little more than a year passed and Lana, having come of age, took over the milking duties from her mother. In turn Ellie now spent her mornings making the butter and cheeses that used to occupy her afternoons. Andel was beginning to draw attention from some girls in the Stead and Lana imagined he would soon take one for his wife and settle his own home and family. He now worked all day in the pastures as their father had before, allowing Hayal to herd the milking cows in the morning and spend the afternoons with Ellie.

Things in the Stead were going well, everybody was happy and Lana still held tight to her thoughts and dreams, sharing them only with the trees.

It was sultain when news reached the Stead that Aeloth was to marry. His father, Heriloth, had arranged a marriage with the daughter of a neighbouring Gesith and the ceremony was to take place on the first night of samhain. That news wasn't easy for Lana to hear, she knew thoughts of Aeloth were in vain, that she was just a peasant and a Lord would never, could never, want to be with her as she wanted to be with him. But the news destroyed her dreams, it dragged her, kicking and screaming into crushing reality. She really was just a milkmaid and no dreams could save her from that now. Her heart sank in her chest and her afternoons delivering supplies to the Manor became a heavy burden. She started to cut short the time she spent up at the Manor and instead walked the fields beside the milking sheds.

The bull that Hayal had brought from the southern stead had been housed close by, and he had proved to be very mean and grumpy. Lana went into the field one afternoon to greet him and to offer him some food, she was generally good with the animals of the Stead and always wanted to be close to them, but when she approached the bull he stared and snorted at her. She held out the food to him, and he stamped his foot, kicking up dirt.

"Well, you're a grumpy one aren't you, Mr Bull, I've brought you food, don't you want it?"

The bull lowered his head and kicked up more dirt, then started to walk menacingly toward her.

"Well! You just be like that then and ...."

The bull started to speed up so Lana turned and ran. Luckily, she wasn't far from the fence, and she made it back just in time, jumping and clambering over as the bull arrived.

"You really are mean, Mr Bull. I was just trying to be nice." She panted.

Then she turned her back on the snorting animal and started to walk back home when a sound caught her ear. A familiar laughter from the tree line, she turned back quickly, her face tight and red, she was in no mood to be mocked now. A Dryad stood on the edge of the field, leaning against a large birch, her bow stood up on the ground beside her. Lana stood a second or so, giving the Dryad the most intensely evil look, she could muster and then started to march toward her, arms folded over her chest, feet stamping heavily into the grass. This made the Dryad laugh more and Lana's rage grew as her face reddened. As Lana drew closer the Dryad picked up her bow and melted into the trees, disappearing in a moment, only the echoes of her laughter left hanging in the air where she had been. Lana let out a yell of frustration and then ran back to the stead, away from the bull and the laughing Dryad.

4. SAMHAIN

The first night of samhain came quickly and all was set for the wedding. Gesith Heriloth had ordered a great feast on the eve of the ceremony, the visiting Gesith, his daughter and their entourage were housed in the manor and would feast in the main hall along with Heriloth, Aeloth and a few sheriffs. The people of the Stead were to gather in the courtyard where temporary tables had been set up and a meal would be served. The Gesith hoped to prove certain concerns his future family had to be needless by showing his benevolence to the people of his stead.

There were barrels of ale and cider, bread, cheese and a large vat of steaming stew, nothing in comparison to the large feast being served within, but it was a festive occasion nevertheless and the Stead folk were making the most of the unique opportunity to celebrate.

As the night wore on the table at which Lana and her family sat ran low on cheese, Sera, who had no intention of ending her feasting early, told Lana of a cheese wheel she had placed aside in the kitchen. Lana gulped down the last mouthful of cider in her cup and went to collect it. She found herself a little wobbly on her feet and walking into the darker area of the courtyard meant that she stumbled a little on loose stones and in little holes. She stumbled around the side of the kitchen and to the door, which she was surprised to see ajar, then she looked inside and her heart sank.

Lana saw Aeloth pushing a young maid to the kitchen floor. He cursed her name and commanded her to be silent.

"Please my lord, don't..." The maid's face was red and wet

from her tears, her voice uncontrolled and raw.

Aeloth climbed atop the maid, straddling her like he was riding a horse and slapped her face hard.

"I told you to be silent!"

He slapped her again then looked down at her chest, ripping open her blouse and stuffing a torn scrap of it into her mouth.

Lana was in shock, she didn't want to see this, she didn't want it to be true. She wanted to turn away, return to the party and forget this entirely. But she couldn't, she stood in silence, and held her breath, transfixed as the Gesith's son beat and raped the young maid.

Once he had finished, Aeloth stood over the maid, adjusting his clothes and threatened her to silence, to never speak of this to anyone. The maid, crying, in pain whimpered a muffled "yes, my lord" as he took the makeshift gag from her mouth.

Once Aeloth was back inside the manor Lana ran to the maid, still on the floor. Tears, snot and blood were smeared across the maid's face, swollen and already turning blue. Lana sat with her a while, comforting her and trying to put her clothes back together enough to cover her bruised body. Her eye was caught by a sparkle in the dim light. She reached out to see what was there and picked up a brooch, the one given to Aeloth by his wife as a gift on their engagement. Not thinking, she held it tight in her hand. When the maid could stand again Lana helped her back to the courtyard, to her father and the people of the Stead. They would know what to do.

As she neared the courtyard again Ellie, who was impatiently calling for her to hurry back with their cheese, spotted her. On seeing Lana with her arms around the maid, struggling to walk, she ran over to them. Together they helped the maid into the square and to their table where they sat her down and Ellie started to check on her.

"Ara!" The cry came from a table close to them and Lana looked up to see Thenra, one of the manor cooks, and her husband, a blacksmith, running toward them.

"What happened child?" Thenra was shaking, as she reached out to embrace Ara.

"It... it was nothing mam... Nothing... I fell, is all." Ara looked toward Lana, her eyes silently pleading her not to say more.

Lana bit her lip and clasped her hands together, she had heard Aeloth's threat and feared what might happen if she spoke now. She looked down, not daring to catch the eye of the people around her, knowing if they asked, she would have to say something.

"You did more than fall Ara. What happened?" Raan, Ara's father, had a deep voice that seemed to vibrate through Lana's stomach as he talked.

"Honestly, father. Don't fret, I'm fine." Ara's tears and shaking voice belied her words.

"Lana, what did you see?" Hayal's voice was soft and his hand, placed on Lana's shoulder, gentle and reassuring.

"Dad... He said that bad things would happen if anyone found out." Lana couldn't lie to her father, but she had to let him know that if she told him what she had seen it could be dangerous for everyone.

He gently turned Lana around to face him and knelt on the floor in front of her, his hand seeking hers as he spoke.

"A man did this to her?" Lana bit her lip again as she nodded.

"And you saw who it was?" she continued to nod and whispered her answer "yes."

"Who was it, Lana?"

Lana's eyes filled again with tears, and she shook her head as she opened her clenched hand to show the brooch she had picked up. Hayal took the brooch and examined it for a moment before standing again.

"Raan." Lana looked up at her father as he called on the blacksmith, his face was serious and stern now and his voice firm. "We should go back to the Stead. Now."

Raan gave Hayal a questioning look but soon spoke to his

wife. Within a moment the two families were walking back to the stead, the mothers helping Ara to walk and the fathers flanking them, carrying sticks they picked up on the path. As they walked Andel stooped to pick up a sturdy piece of fallen wood and fell in beside Lana.

"I don't know what's going on sis but I'm never letting anything bad happen to you." Lana linked his arm with hers and kissed his cheek.

5. ATTACK THE STEAD

The following day seemed strange to Lana; it wasn't right to be getting up and going to the milking sheds as though nothing had happened. That, though, was how her day started. It wasn't until after the cows had been milked and the urns placed on the handcart that anything different happened. Lana's stomach knotted as she bent to pick up the handcart, and she paused, just a moment. The thought of going up to the manor filled her with dread, it was the worst thing she had ever been asked to do. Ellie placed her hand on Lana's shoulder, turning her gently and wrapped her arms around her.

"Not today Lana, I think it best if you head off home, your Da'll be there and I'd rather you were with him than wandering up to the manor today."

With Ellie's words, Lana felt a crushing weight had been lifted from her chest, and she held her mother tight, thanking her before starting the walk to the crossroads. Hayal was waiting as they arrived at the gate, and they walked together, her father putting his arm around her shoulder and pulling her close. When they arrived at the crossroad Ellie kissed Lana lightly on the cheek and then hugged Hayal before taking the path up to the Manor. They stood a moment as Ellie went on her way and then Hayal turned to Lana and pulled playfully on her pigtail.

"Race me?" He smiled brightly as he spoke and a laugh burst from Lana's mouth. She had spent most of the day holding back tears but the sudden outburst released those too, and she wiped her eyes and cheeks as she laughed.

"You know I'll win!" Lana pulled her sleeve down and wiped her face with it as she taunted her father. Hayal shook his head and smiled.

"I don't know, Lana. I've been running after the herd a lot recently. I reckon am a lot faster now. You ready?" Lana nodded.

"Right then... 3... 2... 1... GO!"

Hayal watched Lana run off down the road a second, her hair flailing behind her, and he smiled to himself before setting off. He had to run quite quickly, he wanted her to win but not by too much.

That evening, when all the families had finished their chores and eaten, they sat around the fire and talked. Hayal told a story about a stead he had visited on his journey south to collect the bull. The story was an amusing one about a dimwitted farmer and a milking stool and Lana found herself giggling along with a big smile on her face, forgetting the events of the night before. A cry came from outside the house as the story drew to a close. Hayal took his walking staff and ran out of the door and Andel followed, grabbing his bow as he went. At times through the year larger animals made their way into the Stead from the woods, looking for food and the Stead folk were always prepared to see them off. Lana ran to the open door, wondering what had caused the commotion this evening. What she saw filled her with dread, it was worse than an animal.

Aeloth and six of the holds sheriffs were dragging Ara and her family from their home and into the centre of the square.

"Listen. All of you! You will remember that this stead, this hold, and everything in it belongs to my father and I. Everything here is our property and that includes all of you! You are here to serve us. If we tell you to do something you will do it or you will no longer be of use to us."

Aeloth nodded to one of the sheriffs who walked to the family's home and set a torch to it. As the flames caught and the house started to burn Aeloth spoke again.

"This family, they dared to bring allegations against me. Against me! To my father. They accuse me of crimes, of being

29

evil and vile. They accuse me of harm, and they demand compensation from us. This is our answer. You will watch, all of you. You will see what happens when you turn against your Gesith, when you speak ill of me."

He drew his knife, and as he did so his Sheriffs drew their swords and circled him. Then, with a look of hatred in his eyes, he turned to the kneeling family, grabbing Raan by the hair he pulled his head up, forcing him to look him in the eyes. He held his knife to Raan's face and spoke in a low growl.

"You made me this knife, blacksmith. You forged its blade. Now you will feel it."

With those words, Aeloth brought the knife around in his hand and cut the blacksmith's throat.

A few of the stead's men moved forward, their makeshift weapons held ready, but they were met by the sheriffs, in their armour, and halted. Raan's body lay at Aeloth's feet, blood spilling onto the dirt of the square.

"Do you see? Do you see what happens now?"

He moved towards Ara and held her face tight, squeezing her cheeks so hard her mouth bled.

"This one talks too much, she tells tales, evil lies, and now she will receive what she deserves."

One of the sheriffs grabbed Ara's hair, pulling her head back and forcing her mouth open. Lana put her face into her mother's body, horrified, as Aeloth cut the maid's tongue out and threw it into the flames of the burning house.

Thenra, no longer caring for her own safety, rushed to her daughter and held her trying to comfort her. Tears streaming from her eyes, her face scarlet as she screamed an unintelligible curse at Aeloth. He looked down at her and threw a single bronze coin at her knees.

"Here is your compensation… There will be no more talk of this. If more is heard the entire stead will suffer."

He walked from the square, mounted his horse and rode back to the manor. The sheriffs stayed in formation, their swords ready to strike at anyone that might make an attempt at retaliation. The stead folk stood their ground, waiting, not giving the sheriffs the excuse to cause more pain. Disappointed they sheathed their swords and followed Aeloth out of the Stead.

Once the sheriffs were gone the women of the Stead ran to Ara and her mother, comforting both and giving aid to their wounds. The men set about putting the fire out and salvaging all they could from the burning house. Little remained however and what did was tarnished, but they took it out into the square so that it could be made right again and used. Once the fire was out and everything that could be rescued was, the adults of the Stead sent their children back into their homes. They, however, remained in the square to discuss what action to take.

When Lana's parents returned home Ara and Thenra accompanied them. The house was larger than some and had a little extra room, they offered to share it while a new home could be made for the family. Beds were quickly made up for them, and they all settled down for what remained of the night. No one truly slept though, and nightmares once again haunted Lana's mind.

When the sun rose the Stead became its usual hive of activity, people going to their various jobs around the farm, but that day they did so in silence. Fear, hatred and anger in their minds and hearts. Ara accompanied Lana to the milking sheds and Lana showed her how to calm the cattle as she milked them. Their mothers stayed home and started gathering the things that were needed to replace those lost in the fire. When the work had been done for the day the men gathered and started to build a new house.

Over the next few months, Lana and Ara became close. It was difficult to communicate at first due to the horrible vengeance Aeloth had taken on her, but they began to create their own way of talking, with gestures and expressions. Lana would take Ara to the pastures once they had finished their work and walk the tree line with her gathering "treats". The girls quickly became like sisters and told each other secrets and gossip.

It was halfway through the second moon after the incident and Yule was close. Thenra and Ara had moved into their own little house again but Lana and Ara continued to work together and spent a lot of time in each other's company. Their trips to the pastures after work became a daily walk and Andel started to join them on their way home. Having Andel walking with them made Lana happy, it was safer in the dark evenings with her brother to protect them, and she suspected that he liked Ara more than he was letting on so it gave her a chance to tease him about it a little. One evening though Ara held Lana's arm as they finished working and asked to go to the fields beside the sheds rather than the pastures. Lana agreed, wondering why her friend might want to change their routine. So they climbed a fence and sat on the cold ground close to the trees. They talked for some time before Lana suggested they make their way home, they were late, and she was concerned that their mothers would be worrying about them.

Sure enough, when they arrived home their parents were worried and quite annoyed at the pair, fearing something had happened to them. Lana waited until their parents had finished expressing their concerns and exchanged a look with Ara.

"Can we go talk outside mam?" She looked over at Hayal and Andel then back to Ellie, sucking on her lips as if to show she had a secret to tell.

Ellie quietly nodded and the four women left the house together and went to Thenra's new home. Once inside Ellie stopped and turned to Lana, a look of concern on her face.

"Well, Lana, what is it?"

"It's Ara." Lana's voice was soft, not much more than a whisper "She's late mam, and she feels sick."

Thenra beckoned Ara over to her and reached out, taking her hand.

"How late are you?" she looked at her daughter, a tear in her eye and Ara held up three fingers to her.

"And you're sick in the mornings?" Ara nodded and Thenra

placed her hand on her daughter's stomach.

"It's his baby, Ara's scared of what he'll do when he finds out." Lana walked over to her friend and gave her a sympathetic smile.

The mother and daughter both burst into tears and held each other, then stood awhile in silence.

"It'll be all right." Ellie placed her hand on Thenra's shoulder as she spoke. "We'll not let anything happen, Ara'll stay away from the manor house, and we'll keep the news to ourselves, much as possible. No one need know the bairns 'is at any rate. Come on, you're eatin' with us tonight."

6. GOSSIP

As earrach drew near, talk of Ara's pregnancy started to fill the Stead and the manor grounds, and rumours began as to who the father might be another farmhand? Lana's brother maybe? Or maybe it was a bad situation with the girl's father that led to her pregnancy and his execution? Lana listened to the whispers each day as she delivered the cream, and she ignored the questions asked of her about the father, saying only how Ara was doing and how far along she was. It angered her that people were talking this way, that blame had been placed upon the family and that Lana's own family were being included in the vicious rumours. Each day brought another element to the stories and each day the accusations against Ara's father or Lana's brother became stronger until there were two camps of thought that argued against one another.

One afternoon, while delivering the cream to the kitchen Lana walked past a group of people arguing over that very issue. The group was split half believing the father had assaulted the girl and half believing that it must be Andel's child as they had taken them in and cared for them. The argument became louder and more heated and when they saw Lana they shouted at her to give an answer. She tried to ignore them, tried to walk past them to the kitchen, but they hounded her and one followed her grabbing her arm. He demanded an answer from her. Lana was angry, her face was red and her brow furrowed. She turned and slapped the man that had grabbed her, shouting at him to let her go. This caused more people to come out into the square to see what was going on. The man, in shock, let go of his grip and let

Lana's arm go. He backed off from her but Lana followed him, shouting.

"You're wrong, you're all wrong... my brother. Her father. They have nothing to do with this, 'cept one's dead now and one helps out... and what do you do? Just sitting all day like useless birds gibbering about it. Why don't you help? Why don't you do something instead?"

Lana was furious now and the more she shouted the more her anger poured from her. A stream of screamed words followed and the people of the square were silent, shocked at such a torrent coming from her.

"You don't have any idea, do you? Any of you... You just sit all day blaming this person and that. But you don't know. We do though, the whole stead knows what happened and who the father is, but we stay still, we say nothing. We care for Ara, look after her and make sure she's well. And when the baby comes we'll do the same... and when the baby is older you'll see... you'll see who the father is... cos that's what happens isn't it... and then you'll shut up. Then you'll not say a word... You won't dare!"

Lana stopped, looked around her and, picking the hand cart up again ran to the kitchen. She dropped off the cream and ran back to the Stead. Lana was still angry and now she was ashamed. She should have ignored them, walked on, said nothing. Her anger turned to fear as she ran. What if Aeloth had heard? What if someone told him about her rant... she hadn't said the baby was his but... her fear grew and when she got home she ran inside and to her bed crying.

Lana's outburst became the talk of the manor. Her flat out denial that neither Raan nor Andel was the babies father led only to more speculation and it wasn't long before Sera visited Ellie in the stead, concerned for Lana as much as by the rumours that were spreading. The two women talked for a while before Sera took her leave and walked the path back up to the manor. Ellie called Lana over and sat her down in front of the fire.

"Sera told me what happened today, are you all right?"

"I lost my temper mam, I'm sorry, I know I shouldn't have said anything, but they were all talking about Andel and Raan and I couldn't bear it any more. The things they were saying were awful."

"It's all right Lana, but I don't think you should be going to the manor anymore. I don't know that it's safe for you up there just now. You'd be best staying near the Stead. I'll take the milk up for now, but you'll need to be heading out and gathering the plants I need in your afternoons."

Lana had been collecting plants for her mother two weeks now, and she began to wander further from the Stead and into fields that were quieter or not being worked at all. She was sure it was safer now as some time had passed without any problems and Aeloth had been seen riding the fields and pathways where Lana had worked without any issues.

No one else was around that afternoon as she searched the field next to the temperamental bull. She had found a patch of plants that could be used to relieve stomach pains and was happily harvesting them, carefully bunching the leaves together and placing them in her sack. Lost in her own mind and humming a little tune to herself, She didn't hear the horse until it was almost upon her. She looked up and saw Aeloth not far from where she sat. He could be at her side in a moment, and she had little time to react, if she were standing she might consider running, but she would hardly have time to stand before he reached her. She decided she should stand, it was proper to greet a Gesith or their family by standing and curtsying, and so she did.

"My Lord." she didn't look up, her eyes focused on her feet.

She hoped he would soon be on his way. He didn't reply, in fact, he didn't make a sound, but he walked toward her. Reaching her he grabbed her arm and placed his other hand on her chin firmly holding her face he forced her head up to look into his. Lana stood a second, in fear and silence looking at Aeloth. This man that she had looked on from a distance and thought handsome. This man who she now knew to be violent and cruel, a man that would take what he wanted, a man that believed that everything and everyone was his own property. She stood and looked at his face, noting the look in his eyes. Anger, arrogance, hunger? She had the sensation that she wasn't a person at this moment, but that she was an animal caught after a long hunt and in the hands of the hunter. She started to shake.

"I have heard of you girl, I have heard that you talked of the whore in the Stead and it's growing condition. I have heard that you shouted and screamed at my courtiers, that you gave them your thoughts." He paused, his grip on Lana's arm and face growing tighter, hurting her.

"Just who do you think you are? Who are you to speak to courtiers without permission? Who are you to take it upon yourself to defend a whore? A whore that I have punished. Did I not warn you all? Did I not show you what happens to whores that talk?"

"My lord, I didn't say... I didn't say what had happened, only that my brother was not the father... Please, my lord, I'm sorry, I meant no harm, I meant no disrespect."

Aeloth moved quickly placing his foot behind her he pushed her to the ground and drawing his knife he straddled her, sitting across her stomach his knees on her arms preventing her from moving or striking. Lana begged, she cried and tears filled her eyes but the Gesith's son did not listen, he did not care. He had waited until he found her alone, waited for weeks, and now he had her he would not let her go so easily. He took his knife to Lana's blouse, cutting it open and free from her body, exposing her breast and her stomach. She struggled, but he was by far the stronger person, and she found she could not move more than her head and her legs. She tried to kick to turn over, but she was overpowered. Lana was caught. Not content with simply cutting Lana's blouse open, Aeloth took his knife to the arms of the garment, cutting it from her body and into rags. And as he did before with Ara he took those rags and stuffed them into Lana's mouth, tying a strand behind her head so that she couldn't spit it out.

"I showed you what I would do, I told you not to talk but you did and now I have you and I will teach you your place."

He slapped Lana hard across her cheek. Lana stopped struggling, she could not move as they were and if she was to be given a chance of escape she would need all her strength and her energy to do so. The look on his face turned from anger to a smile.

"You learn so easily, give in so readily."

He took Lana's belt off, removing her knife and her little purse, he threw those to one side. Then taking his weight from her body he grabbed her arms again and forced her over to lie on her front. His weight was placed on the small of her back when she was face down. He pushed her face into the ground, and his head came closer to hers.

"It's good that you accept there is no escape from your punishment." Taking the pressure off her head he took her arms again, forcing them behind her back where he tried to bind her wrists with her belt.

Lana cried in pain and threw her head back, connecting with Aeloth's nose. His weight shifted and his grip loosened, so she pulled and tore her hands free, then crawled forward.

This was her moment, if she was to escape, she would have to do it now. She wouldn't be given another chance without fighting him and doing that would surely just end in her fate becoming worse. She turned on her side and struggled to her feet. Her body shaking and adrenaline pumping through her she ran, as fast as she could toward the fence of the field beside them. Throwing herself over the fence and landing again in the dirt she struggled to get back to her feet and ran on further. She almost made it to the middle of the field when he reached her again, pushing her violently to the ground.

Her body slammed hard on the dirt, her head bouncing off it before coming to a stop. The fall caused her a lot of pain, she was winded and fighting for breath, her body hurt, her vision was hazy and her head spinning. She was being turned and her skirts were pulled tight, being cut from her body. His hands were on her body. Squeezing, slapping, pushing. Then the point of his knife was in her shoulder and a biting, searing pain filled her mind as he cut his initials into her flesh. Her body and her face now bloodied and bruised, pain stabbing her body and her head and fear disabling her she lay on the clover and dirt, still and silent.

Aeloth stood and removed his hose. She did not fight as he grabbed her legs forcing them open and lay on top of her. She closed her eyes and cried in silence as his hands were upon her again. And then his full weight lay on top of her. But the groping stopped, the taunting stopped. She opened her eyes, her head still spinning. She saw him lying on top of her, his head red with blood, and she saw the bull a meter or so away, staring, head down and stomping his feet.

Aeloth's still body was heavy and Lana was in so much pain she struggled to move to get him off her, but she couldn't. She was stuck. Her mouth gagged, she couldn't scream for help or move. She closed her eyes and drifted into unconsciousness.

7. TIME TO GO

When Lana came round again she was home and in her bed, a blanket covered her Ellie sat beside her, holding her hand. Her head filled with pain, her body stiff and bruised and her shoulder bloody. She looked up at her mother and cried.

"What happened? How did I get home?"

"We went out looking for you, Andel found you in the field and brought you home. What happened to you, Lana?"

She explained to her mother what had happened through her tears and Ellie tried to comfort her as she spoke. A knock came from the door as she finished her story and Sera came rushing in.

"You have to leave, all of you!" Sera's face was red, and she was struggling to breathe as she spoke.

"He died. The Gesith has called for his sheriffs, you need to go. Get away quickly."

Hayal jumped up and started stuffing a few choice things into a sack.

"Get your things together, we'll go by the pastures and get Andel then make our way along the tree line. We should be able to get to Southwood in a few days. With any luck they'll head south along the path before they look that way."

Ellie and Sera helped Lana up and out of her bed and then started to gather together the things they might need. Hayal grabbed his walking staff and headed to the door.

"Grab what you can quickly, We need to go." He headed outside and the door swung closed behind him.

As they finished packing a few things into a sack the door

burst open with a crash, sending splinters into the room as its hinges tore away from the wooden surround. Hayal lay on the floor blood pouring from his nose and four sheriffs ran into the room. They were wearing their full armour and carrying their broadswords.

One of the sheriffs kicked Hayal to his head, sending him into unconsciousness, another two pushed Sera and Ellie aside and the last grabbed Lana by the throat.

"You will be taken to the manor where you will face the Gesith. You will then be taken and hanged for the killing of his son."

"It wasn't her, she didn't do it. It was the bull, it charged them." A sheriff slapped Ellie hard as she pleaded, knocking her to the floor.

"For aiding Aeloth's killer your family will be taken and caged."

The Sheriffs started to bind their prisoners as Andel arrived. He had seen their horses and the cart outside and the state of the door, so he readied his bow. He loosed an arrow as he approached which caught one of the Sheriffs in the back of his knee. The Sheriff turned and made his way out of the house toward Andel. As he left Hayal woke and grabbed the cloak of another pulling him back enough for Ellie to wriggle free. She grabbed the poker from the fire and swung it wildly at the sheriffs head knocking him out. He fell backwards to the floor beside Hayal who struggled to his knees and grabbed the Sheriff's knife from his belt.

"Get your hands off her!" Ellie screamed as she lunged at the sheriff holding Lana, the poker raised above her head. The sheriff turned, pulling his sword from its scabbard as he faced her. His mouth opened in a roar as Hayal slid the blade under his armour and into his side.

Sera was bound and still on the floor now and Ellie grabbed Lana, taking her to the corner of the room to untie her while Hayal wrestled with the remaining sheriff. Outside Andel was struggling and the Sheriff struck him with the hilt of his sword. He laughed as her brother fell then he turned and started back to the house.

Ellie thrust a small sack of food into Lana's hand as she freed her.

"Run... Go now... Quick."

"I can't mam, I can't leave you all here." Ellie kissed her cheek quickly then pushed her away.

"Go. Keep running, do what your Da said to do. We'll come after you. We'll find you. GO!"

And so Lana ran, she ran to the place she felt safest, the pasture. As she left the house she looked back and saw the sheriff that had fought Andel was chasing after her. Weighed down somewhat by his armour and hampered by his injury he couldn't run as fast as he would have normally and Lana was able to put a little distance between them.

Running as fast she could, her heart pounding in her chest and her legs still aching from her fight, she climbed the fence and dropped into the pasture then ran to the tree line. She thought that if she could follow the trees as her father had said she would eventually cross into Southwood where she might be safe. It would take some days but it was her only hope.

She looked back hoping the Sheriff had given up his chase and was terrified when she saw that he had gained ground on her and was closing in. She looked around frantically for some-where to hide, but she knew the only place to do that was the Heartwood. Lana took a deep breath and gathered herself for a second, and then she ran headlong into the woods. No man would dare follow her here, surely?

The tales of Dryads hunting men that strayed into their woods were even more terrifying than those of the children. If the Dryad disliked humans and mistrusted them then they hated the males of the species.

Lana ran a few moments and stopped to look back ex-pecting to find that the sheriff had stayed at the tree line. He hadn't though. He was following, his sword was drawn which slowed him a little more, but he was still running and still close enough to see Lana. So she ran on going deeper and deeper into the woods, stumbling over unseen rocks and fallen branches, her breath burning her lungs. Deeper into the Dryad's homeland she ran, the forest grew darker the deeper as she went, the canopy of the trees high above her blocking the light of the sun.

Listening as well as she could for the pursuit she lost track of how far she had run. Her legs grew weaker with each stride, her bruised body aching more and more and her eyes, heavy and wet, less focused on the woods before her. She stumbled and fell to the ground under a large, old, oak. Sitting a while, scared and shaking, her body exhausted, She stared at the trees through which she had run, expecting that at any moment, the sheriff would bust through and take her. She sat a while before the adrenaline left her body, and she surrendered to sleep. The events of the morning and the previous day catching up to her, her body and mind both exhausted.

PART TWO
The Heartwood

8. PRINCESS

Princess Daowiel had always been more adventurous than her sister. Unburdened by the weight of succession that defined Erinia's life, she had been allowed to join the border patrol and walk the tree line watching the humans. It quickly became clear that she was highly skilled with both the staff and the bow and within a few years she was leading the small group of Dryad laoch that protected the Heartwood.

Often spending three moons patrolling the borders between visits to her home in the ancient palace at the heart of the forest; she had grown as close to her spear sister Lothalilia as she was to her true sister. Between them they had captured or killed a gross of feare in the last year and had gained a reputation as the strongest and most ruthless of laoch since the war.

Daowiel, though, considered her reputation built on a lie; she had let one human go. No one knew of the young nighean she had met on the southern border two years ago. Nobody understood why she insisted now on taking a number of patrols along that tree line. It was bordered with a relatively peaceful stead and few feare from that area ever entered the forest. The eastern borders were the more active and held a higher chance of a hunt. The nighean had captured Daowiel's attention however, its habit of talking to the trees and befriending the animals of the Stead and forest was highly unusual among humans. Oddly, the trees themselves seemed to trust it and even enjoyed its company.

She had considered capturing it when it crossed the borders and entered the forest. She thought the Dryad children would find it amusing and enjoy playing with it, but as it sat talking with the trees and crying, she realised the nighean was different. The trees were reaching out to it, they weren't able to connect or communicate with humans but this one had them trying. Daowiel had never seen that before. And so it was that rather than capture her, Daowiel gifted it a doire flower and let it go. The nighean had been so grateful at the gift and no harm had come from its release. Besides, she found the its clumsy innocence amusing, it would have been a shame to put an end to it.

The human barely noticed it was being followed. Daowiel was sure the only other time she had been seen was when it tried to tame the bull, an event that made her laugh all day. She had watched though as the nighean taught another about the plants and trees along the forests border. Becoming impressed with the maturity it was beginning to show and the sense of community it was developing. She noticed the trees were comfortable when the nighean was near, they cooed at its gentle words and touch. In time murmurs spread from the border trees into the forest and other Dryad started to hear of the human child that talked to trees. The Dryad didn't believe a nighean could cause such a stir amongst the trees and so a tale developed. The tale of a sapling orphan, found and raised by a human family.

Daowiel was called to the palace. Her mother, Queen Olerivia, had heard the talk and the murmurs of the trees and wanted to hear Daowiel's thoughts on the matter. Being the leader of the laoch, she was sure to know about the human.

"You gave the nighean a doireflower?"

"Yes, mother. It seemed afraid and upset, the flowers appeared to give it some comfort. This one is different from other humans, I trust it."

"I hope your instinct proves correct, Daowiel. Allowing a human, any human, to leave the Heartwood places us at risk."

"Have faith in your sister, Erinia. She has watched this one and its family for some time. I am certain she is aware of the threat they pose."

"Of course I have faith. I am simply concerned, some are talking of rescuing the sapling from the humans. Others believe the nighean is destined to take Mortara's throne and lead Dryad and humans together. They are both dangerous thoughts, and we must be wary of them."

"This child milks cows and talks to the trees, Erinia. It befriends the animals. The trees along the border enjoy its company, they trust in it, that is all. I will continue to follow it, but believe me, it poses no threat to us."

"It is fine to watch the nighean, Daowiel. I think it better that you not interact with it again without first discussing it with us. The Gesith of that hold is the worst of feare. We cannot risk one seeing or hearing of you. I trust you will ensure the laoch that speak of the child will stay clear of it as well."

"Is this an order sister?"

The princess Erinia laughed, a wide smile on her face. " A request, sweet sister. There is no better way to ensure you do something than to order you not to!"

Daowiel rolled her eyes and laughed with her sister. "You have my word Erinia. No one will interact with the nighean."

Daowiel was a mile away from Butterholt when the murmur of the trees reached her. A feare had entered the forest, a feare carrying steel. She spun around and placed her hand upon the birch behind her, reaching out through the network of roots to locate the human that dared enter her home. It had barely stepped over the border, raging and thrashing at branches and brambles with its sword. This feare would never see its stead again.

In less than a dozen beats of her heart she stood beside a great oak. Her staff sprung into life as the feare came crashing through the trees behind her.

"I've got you now rabbit, you couldn't run far enough to escape me." The sheriff slowed to a walk, looking down at the base of the oak as Daowiel rounded it and then paused as he saw her.

"Well, lookit that, would you? A dirty tree hag. My lord will be pleased when I take your head to him as well as the rabbits."

Daowiel's eyes narrowed and her lips curled into a menacing grin. She took a moment to look the human up and down and leapt. Her staff struck a heavy blow to the intruder's left arm and it fell back, pulling it tightly to its chest.

"I'll cut you up into firewood for that, hag." It raised its sword and lunged forward, swinging wildly at her head.

She parried the blow deftly and allowed her staff to follow its arc striking again at the injured arm of the feare. It let out a scream and staggered backwards as its forearm shattered. Barely keeping its footing on the forest floor it dropped its sword and grabbed at a branch in an attempt to stay upright. The humans weight and momentum were too much for the branch to hold and it snapped close to the trunk of the young tree.

Daowiel took the opportunity to look back at the oak as the feare staggered, hoping to see the rabbit it had followed into the forest. She saw the nighean lying under the tree, exhausted, bloodied and bruised and a tension built in her body. Her jaw clenched and her hands shook. She turned back to the human, her stare shredding its courage as easily as a knife cuts blossom from a tree.

The human scrambled to its feet. It picked up its sword and took a small step forward, its body hunched and its lip quivering in fear. Daowiel launched her staff, as you might a spear, striking the human square on the forehead, sending it backward again. This time, however, the trunk of the young tree broke the feare's fall. The remnants of the broken branch, pierced the skin at the base of his skull. His body twitched silently for a moment and then fell still. Kept upright, like a resting marionette, by the broken limb that had severed his spine.

With the fight over and the feare dead Daowiel retrieved

her staff and turned her attention to the nighean. The exposed skin on its arms and legs was scratched and bruised and the bandage that covered its shoulder was bloody. It slept deeply, exhausted to the point of unconsciousness, it would, however, recover with sleep and that knowledge pleased Daowiel.

It had always been the princess's hope that she would, one day, travel beyond the borders of the forest. That she would be allowed to explore Mortara, to touch its other trees, to search for Dryad long separated from their home. This nighean gave life to her hopes. If a human could accept its connection to the life surrounding it, if it could learn to work within nature once more rather than force it to their will. Then there was a chance. A chance the Dryad could be accepted once more and walk the land.

She noticed that the nighean had grown since she had last seen it. A sapling still in the Dryad reckoning, but in human terms it would be considered a young woman, old enough to bear a child. She wondered what had caused it to run into the woods, why the feare hunted it and what had caused the wound on its shoulder. Emotion welled within her and her throat became tight, her breathing shallowed, for a moment she considered waking the sapling, treating it and taking it to the safety of the palace. Daowiel began to reach out her hand, but stopped short of touching the nighean.

Remembering the words of her sister she stood and placed her hands upon the oak. Speaking, almost silently, under her breath a serious look on her face. The oak hummed and creaked for a moment and then, with a crack, two small branches formed on either side of the child. Daowiel continued to encourage the tree and the branches grew, forming a circle through the undergrowth around the girl. A clear message to her sisters and the animals of the forest. This child was under her protection.

As the circle closed Daowiel removed her hands and started her walk back to the north.

9. INTO THE HEART

When Lana awoke she was lying under a tall oak, her clothes were covered in dried mud and torn from her flight. Her knees and arms were scraped and her body was bruised. Dried blood caked the bandage on her shoulder, and she was barely able to move her arm without a great deal of pain. Her mind was scattered as she tried, desperately to understand the events of the last two days.

Aeloth's attack had been vicious, that his death had come before he had taken what he wanted was of little comfort. The pain in her body would ease over time but the scar left on her mind would cause anguish as long as she lived. A thought pushed its way into her head, a haunting accusation, 'you should have given him what he wanted, your family would still be safe.' Her stomach tensed as an internal struggle began, memories of the night after the samhain feast, the bloody violence done to an innocent family. The pain it had caused Ara and Thenra. No, her family would still be in danger no matter her actions. The look in his eyes as he grabbed her, the lust she had seen, it was a reaction not to her body but to the violence he would do to her. Had she had given herself willingly he would have sought another way to cause her pain.

What would become of her family now? The sheriffs had said they were to be imprisoned for giving her aid. Would the Gesith be even more enraged at her escape? Would he take out his anger at her on them? He had been miserly and careless in the past but had never shown the kind of violent streak she had seen in his son. She knew there was no way they could have es-

50

caped the Stead. Andel had been injured and her escape had been helped by luck rather than an ability to fight off the trained soldiers. She could only hope they had not been too seriously hurt and the Gesith would not be driven by vengeance.

Lana brought her knees, close to her chest as the muscles in her stomach began to spasm, her mouth filled and her eyes began to sting. She hadn't had a chance to eat before the sheriffs had broken through the door and her retching brought only more liquid. Her throat burned, and she struggled to breathe as the emotion and the thoughts overwhelmed her.

Lana had been lost in her thoughts sometime when she realised she was sitting within a circle of oak branches. She did not remember seeing those when she first sat at the base of the tree and was surprised she had missed them, as large as they were. She saw the shape of a person by a tree at the circle's edge as her eyes gazed around. Lana stood and pressed her back to the tree, picking up a stick from the ground she held it up in the direction of the shape.

"Don't come near!" There was no response and no movement. "Who are you? What are you?" She shouted at the silhouette but again no response came and no movement occurred.

Slowly she bent down, not taking her eyes from the shape and searched the ground with her left hand for a stone. Finding one she stood again and threw it at the shape. It hit its mark, she knew that, but it caused no reaction at all. She walked toward the shape cautiously, slowly, keeping her stick aloft and pointed toward it. Walking closer she saw it was the sheriff that had chased her. He was standing completely still, his body leaning against the trunk of the tree, his eyes wide and unmoving. She kept walking closer, looking for any signs of movement but none came. When she was in reach she struck out with her stick, striking him across his arm. His body fell forward and lay, face down in the undergrowth at her feet. She could see the blood on his neck and his armour and was sure he must be dead, but she poked at his body with the stick to be sure.

Certain he was no longer a threat, she knelt at his side

and began to check for things she might use in her flight. Taking the cloak he wore from his back she wrapped it around her for warmth, then she turned him over and took his belt, there was a knife and a coin purse on it as well as the scabbard for his sword. She removed that from the belt and left it beside him. She tied the belt around her waist, holding the cloak in place and giving her a knife and a little money she could use, if she ever escaped the forest. Lana felt a little remorse at taking the dead man's belongings, but he wouldn't use them again, and they would be useful.

'If I ever escape the forest.' she thought. 'But to where? I can't go back to the Stead. I would be killed for sure. I can't stay in the forest either, the Dryad are sure to find me and take me prisoner, or worse. Neither can I leave my family to the Gesith. I need to find help, somehow. I need to speak to the Tay or the Queen, I need to convince them to pardon my family and set them free. But how?'

Her stomach interrupted her thoughts once more, this time the pangs of hunger reminding her of its emptiness. She searched the area around her for plants and fruits she knew she could eat and took a few moments more in the protection of the oak to silence the grumbling of her belly.

And then, with tears in her eyes, she stood and started walking. She had no idea which was the best way to go but considered that she shouldn't walk South and that if she continued to walk in another direction she would eventually find her way out of the forest; vast though it was it must have its end.

Unwittingly following the Dryad princess, Lana walked deeper into the heart of the forest. As she walked on the woodland thickened, becoming darker. Light from the earrach sun, filtered through the dense green canopy above her, formed puddles on the forest floor. The undergrowth within appeared to glow in the shadows that surrounded her. The heavy scent of wild garlic and the mossy ground added to a building sense of oppression and gloom.

Losing track of time and unaware of the distance she was

covering, she walked to the rhythm of her hunger and need for sleep. The need to concentrate heavily on her footing and the lack of light meant her eyes ached and tired quickly. She began to spend more time sitting in the small pools of light, enjoying the colours and scent of the plants that came to life in the warmth. The dappled light on her skin a growing pleasure, becoming less frequent and more treasured.

Her mood grew as dark as her surroundings. Hope of finding a way through the forest and finding help in the far away city of Southport faded. She was alone, lost and scared. Surviving on leaves and plants, her only company the surrounding trees. Silent, besides the creaks and occasional cracks of their limbs and trunks in the darkness. They listened well but if they responded only the Dryad could hear them.

The Dryad, a threat that kept people away from the forest. Deadly fae that hunted and kidnapped humans at any opportunity. That killed once their games became tiresome. They were here, somewhere. Unseen, unheard but here, behind one tree or another. She was sure they were following her, watching her, tracking her through their home. She waited to be captured, to hear laughter floating on the breeze before being taken and caged. Each moment, each breath in freedom was time stolen from their hunt. Time, she was sure, she would pay for once caught.

In time untracked, as she sat beneath an ancient oak, enjoying a moment of sunlight and a handful of leaves, a sound floated to her ears and gave her hope.

"Is that a stream? Please, Mr Oak, tell me that's a stream." Her voice was quiet, weak and broken.

Her throat tightened and strained as tears filled her eyes. Jumping to her feet she scrambled toward the sound, a gentle gurgling and the faint clack of pebbles turning. She dropped to her knees on the muddy bank and reached into the water with cupped hands. Eagerly drinking the cool fresh water, before splashing it across her mud caked body, her mood lifted. Darkness continued to surround her but in finding a stream she had found direction. All streams went somewhere, and she was eager to see where this one would lead her.

10. THE ELEMENTAL STONE

Lana had been walking through the woods, following the stream for a little over two weeks when she first saw the sunlight streaming through the canopy of leaves ahead. She smiled as she saw it, touching the ground with its gentle glow and immediately started to pick up her pace. There were moments when she had to splash through the shallow banks of the stream and the cool water against her skin, along with the thought that she may have found the edge of the woods, refreshed her and gave her hope.

It wasn't long before the woodland opened up, revealing a large lake, dotted with islands. The calm lake was larger than the Stead in which she lived and seemed to be teeming with life. She could see fish swimming around and insects buzzing over the surface. She saw frogs... or maybe toads and off on one shore a family of deer were calmly drinking from it.

The islands were scattered across the lake, the nearest one not too far from shore, each seemed to have a structure of some kind upon it. Broken walls and ruined buildings stood on some of the islands and on some just standing stones. They looked completely deserted and run down, but they intrigued Lana. She loosened the belt around her waist, letting her cloak bellow out behind her, and she sat on the bank of the lake under the warm light of the sun. Breathing in the sweet scent of the flowers that bloomed around her. She was at peace at that moment. For the first time, in what to Lana seemed an age, she was able to relax. And so she laid back on the warm ground, and she listened to the sounds of the woods. The songs of the birds and an occasional splash as a fish jumped or a bird dived into the lake looking for food. Lana was filled with a sense of relief, this wasn't the edge of the woods she had longed for but it was the next best thing.

The despair that had grown over her in the darkness of the forest depths began to lift in the warm light of the sun. She lay for a while on the bank, her feet cooling in the lake. Lana noticed an abundance of food here, lots of fruit and plants to harvest, if she were lucky, she might even catch a fish or two.

Lana decided she would stay there a while, rest and gather her strength before heading back into the gloom of the sunless forest. She was excited by the idea of exploring the ruins on the islands and swimming a little in the lake. When she was refreshed and strong enough she would head out to the west. Her father had, on occasion, mentioned steads on the western edge of the Heartwood where he had been sent by the Gesith to trade livestock. He had said they were good, honest, people and always gave a good welcome.

Thinking of her father made her heart heavy, she missed her family and was haunted by the fear that she may not be able to help them at all. Certainly she knew returning to the Stead without help from the Tay or the Queen would do nothing other than place her in danger. No, she couldn't think that way. She would find her way to Southport, she would make them help, she had to.

The sun was touching the treetops on the western shore as Lana scrambled up the bank of the nearest island. She wasn't a particularly strong swimmer, there had been little opportunity to practice in the Stead and her arms were aching. The cuts on her shoulder had healed as she made her way through the forest, but she found her movement was still a little limited and stiff. She wiped some water from her body and pulled her hair through her hand, taking a moment to dry herself in the last of the sun's light.

The stone building on the island had collapsed and sections of wall and roof lay in the overgrown grass. Little more than the corner of a room and some low walls remained now, enough to give her shelter for the night and space to lay her clothes out to dry.

The only stone building Lana had seen before was the Gesith's manor, so she thought the people that had lived here must have been fine and rich. She stepped over the low wall and into the building, checking the floor for small stones that might hurt her bare feet. She gathered enough grass to soften the hard stone floor, hung her clothes across the low walls and curled up in the corner to sleep.

The lake was dry, fish lay dead and rotting in the silt and mud. Smoke billowed from the forest, blocking the sun's light. Ash and embers filled the air like fireflies, spreading the blaze on the wind. The sound of horns filled the forest as the human army closed in on the mighty castle.

The noam, giant fae in leathers and furs, were barring the gates of the outer ward. Dryad and sylph archers lined the walls, watching and waiting for the first wave of the human army to appear through the trees. Nymph were erecting marquees in the inner ward, setting up cots to house the injured. But through all the activity and frenzied movement the court was filled with silence. The fae did not speak, they knew what needed to be done, and they did it without words. All ears strained to hear the approaching force through the cracking and splintering of ancient trees afire.

The smoke grew thicker, the ash filled air heavy and difficult to breathe. The oppressive heat of the forest fire began to scold the skin of the fae as they waited. Staring intently through the blood-red clouds for any sign of movement.

A war horn sounded on what had been the eastern shore of the great lake, a response blew in the north. They panicked, had they been fooled by the humans? Were they defending the wrong approach? Sylph warriors, fastest of the fae within, split their forces and ran to cover the eastern and northern walls. The

Dryad remained to the south and readied their bows. The first tongues of flame lit the brush on the tree line. Shadows danced in the smoke.

The Dryad drew the strings of their bows, the noam formed a shield wall behind the heavy oak gates. The silence was broken by the thunderous blow that shook the gates and rattled the bar that held them.

Chaos broke out.

Arrows flew in both directions, both armies firing blind, the humans lit their arrows, seeking to burn as much as pierce the flesh of the fae. Another fearsome crash and the gates moved, testing the strength of the drawbar. Humans and Dryad alike succumbed to the constant waves of arrows that flew unseen in the smoky air. And in time the gates splintered. A raucous cheer came from the southern banks. The human army poured forth in great numbers and fell upon the shield wall of the noam. Spears, axes and swords piercing and slashing, crashing against shield and body. A melee of chaos punctuated by the cries of war and the moans of death.

Lana woke in a sweat, the dream had been so vivid. She swore she could feel the heat of the burning forest on her skin and the vibrations caused by the strength of the attack upon the gates. Holding her knees tight to her chest, she made herself small and hugged the walls as she looked around.

The sun's light sparkled gleefully on the water, the song of the dawn chorus filled her ears. The battle that had been so real only moments ago was forgotten in the beauty of the morning.

A glistening, beneath the dust and stones a few metres away, caught her eye, filling her with a need to investigate. She pushed aside the stones and brushed away the dust to find a brooch. It was, Lana thought, the most beautiful item she had ever seen. A delicate oak leaf made of silver and a pin that resembled a branch. She wrapped it carefully in a dock leaf and put it in her purse. She would use it to hold her cloak when she dressed but today she wanted to swim some more and to explore the building on the next island. That building appeared to be much more intact, whole walls and a section of roof remained and Lana thought it may, perhaps, hold more treasures.

The structure on the next island was in better condition than she thought. Some walls had collapsed and sections of the ceiling were scattered across the ground. One room still stood and appeared quite solid. The door and window were missing and a breeze blew through the space, but a large part of the room was perfectly sheltered. Lana gathered up a pile of grass to make up her bed and spent the rest of the day gathering food, hoping she might find more trinkets.

She was a little disappointed, as she ate, that she had found nothing more than food on the island. Pinning the brooch to her cloak had given her a sense of riches, reminding her of the dreams she had while lying in the pastures as a child. For a moment she had smiled and her troubles had faded.

Her sleep was once again fitful as the ancient battle in the heart of Mortara raged on in her dreams. The human army attacked in huge numbers, wave after wave, clashing with the fae. Noam warriors, valiant and strong, held their line for hours before falling. The Dryad, already suffering as their forest burned, succumbed soon after. The invading force made their way into the inner ward killing the nymph and the injured with ease. Those sylphs, still engaged in the east and the north, took to the air hurling short spears into the forces gathered. Unaware the safety of the castle had already been breached.

The death and destruction, so vivid, upset Lana. Humans and fae screaming in pain before breathing their last and leaving the world. The killing had been senseless, all of that death and agony. What could have caused so much hatred? Would victory on either side be worth the price paid? Thousands of lives cut short, thousands more no doubt destroyed as families died.

Her morning passed curled up in the corner, lost in the emotions of her dream and the events that had led her here. She worried the tears would never end, the pain in her throat and the weight on her heart were unbearable.

Lana stayed on that island while she explored the others, she collected enough food that she could wrap and keep some for her journey. She even found a few stones she thought pretty and kept those in her purse. They made her smile, and that was worth holding on to.

One island remained to be explored. A small island to the east, it didn't have a building on it at all but a large stone, taller than she was and wide. Toward the top of the stone was a hole, about the size of her head, that the sun shone through as it rose in the morning. The light of the sun seemed to split as it passed through the hole, spreading a rainbow of light across the water of the lake. Lana had come to enjoy watching the sun rise behind the stone and it became a ritual for her to sit on the bank of the island with her feet in the cool water and bathe in the light. She had deliberately left exploring that island until last, as she guessed it must have been a special place to the people that lived here.

She had become a better swimmer over the week and reached the island fairly quickly. Once she had dried off a little she started to look around. The large stone was surrounded by a circle of smaller rocks, some rose to the height of her knees, others to her waist. The thick grass and flowers had covered a lot of them and Lana hurried over to the larger stone.

As she approached she noticed the air around the hole shimmered, reminding her of the way a path shimmered like a lake on a hot day. Under the hole, carved deep into the stone was a large rune. Lana couldn't read and didn't understand runes, but she knew they were used by people and fae in the past. She thought that whatever this rune said must have been very important to somebody. Lana drew closer to the stone and reached her hand out to touch it. A sharp pain ran through her body as her fingers touched its surface. There was a blinding light like a thousand suns and a heat like a bale fire inside her. She collapsed to the floor and lay at the foot of the stone, unconscious.

Five figures stood around the stone, their faces hidden by the shadows of the cowls they wore. The sounds of battle drawing closer to the courtyard. They spoke in hushed tones, a language Lana could not understand. But she sensed their tension and their fear.

"We must do this now if there is to be hope."

"But what of our brothers and sister?"

"They have made their choice, they will live and die in this new age."

"What of our people, will they also die?"

"Those that are hidden will survive, they will ensure the future."

"Can we not stay? Can we not join the fight?"

"No, our time is over. We must leave this world to its people."

"If our brother should rise again these people would suffer."

"Then we shall leave some semblance of our selves within this stone. A defence, should that occur."

They each placed their right hands on the stone and their left on the figure to their side. A silence passed over the courtyard and the air began to shimmer.

The figures began to fade to light, becoming ethereal. And as they faded their light began to circle the stone. A rainbow of colour, swirling and mixing, surrounding the stone, filling the courtyard. Faster and faster the light circled and merged. The air became heavy, sparks flew from the smaller stones. The robes that were worn fell to the floor and the light became one. Blinding and white. An explosion of heat and energy sent the stone of the courtyard walls on a flight through the air. And it grew like ripples in a pond destroying walls, sending stone and burning wood across the sky. The invaders and those that defended the castle all died, a death more disturbing than any Lana had seen in her dreams. Their skin melted, their clothes burned. They turned, in an instant to ash and then, in the blast, blew away.

When Lana woke her body tingled and her mind raced. What had happened? How long had she slept? She checked herself over for wounds or pain but there was nothing, just that odd tingling, the kind you have when you sleep on your arm and the blood starts to find its way back again.

The sun was low in the east again, not yet shining its light through the hole of the stone. The grass was bent and broken where she had lain, leaving an outline of her body. She must have been on the island, at least, a day though she could not be sure it hadn't been longer.

Lana stood as the light of the sun shone through the shimmering air around the stone and bathed in its warmth. It felt good on her skin, and she closed her eyes, enjoying the moment and the gentle heat. As the moment faded and the sun rose higher her stomach rumbled with the pangs of hunger and an urgent need to drink, so she looked around the island and gathered some leaves. Then, eating what she had found, walked to the banks and drank from the lake.

Her stomach silent, she swam back to the shelter that had been her home for the last week. The events of her dream playing out in her mind. Who were the figures? What were they saying? What had happened to cause the explosion?

11. THE BRIDGE

L ana had abandoned her shoes on the islands as they were torn up and falling apart, her clothes were ragged and ripped from the brambles and branches, so she kept the cloak wrapped tight around her; held in place by the leaf brooch and the sheriff's belt. The journey though seemed easier this time, maybe it was just that she had a bit more experience of walking in wooded areas now and knew what to look for in order to avoid tripping and stumbling. Maybe it was that she was no longer running from her home but was, instead, now heading towards the help she sought. In either case she thought, by the time the sun had set, she had walked much further that day than in any previous day of her journey. As the light faded and her legs tired, she found a tree with a bit of a clearing around it and sat at its base. A large, old tree, its trunk much wider than her and so tall she imagined it must touch the clouds. She ate a little and wrapped the cloak round her before falling into sleep.

Her dream that night was a strange one. She dreamt she was a Dryad, walking through the forest, talking to the trees. She could sense the life of the surrounding forest, not just that there were plants and insects and animals but that they were all connected, that there was an energy flowing through the forest, an energy the Dryad could tap into and see. Lana thought the trees were sending messages to each other and to the Dryad, that the whole forest knew who and where she was. She came across other Dryad in a circle telling stories and sharing songs, so she sat with them a while. They danced and sang, played music and talked. At the end of the feast the Dryad all went to their trees to join with them, disappearing into them, becoming them. Lana did the same.

It was strange within the tree, warm and comfortable. A gentle pulsing filled her ears, a soothing sound that drew her into sleep. It was, she thought, like being wrapped in a blanket after a bath and having your mother hug you and sing a lullaby. It was a wonderful comfort that she missed.

When Lana awoke she was calm and happy, her muscles didn't ache, they weren't stiff or sore, and she wasn't hungry. She was full of energy, and so she got up and stretched, took a moment to thank the tree and went on her way. As the sun reached its peak and the light broke through the canopy she stopped and looked around. Taking in the sights and sounds of the forest, the plants and the insects, animals in the distance. She stood a while and saw for the first time, not the trees and brambles and branches that were in her way, not the insects that bit or the plants she might pick to aid her. She saw beauty and harmony, she saw the woods as she saw the stead, everything, everyone working together. A community of support. She wondered why she had never seen this before. She stood a few moments, watching and listening, and then she moved on until the light died. When the moon rose in the sky Lana sat at the base of a tree, ate a little and slept.

She was within the tree again, a different tree this time though and this time as that hugging sensation surrounded her she opened herself up to it, accepted it as part of her. As she did so the feeling of peace grew deeper. And now she could feel the tree, not that part that touched her but all of it. The roots, the branches, the leaves. She could sense the gentle breeze blowing around them and the sap flow through the wood in the same way that, on occasion, you feel your blood flow. She sensed the roots reaching down and out for water and nutrients. Lana was whole, she was strong, she was at peace and at one with the surrounding forest.

On waking, she sat a while and looked around as she had the previous day, taking in the sights, the smells, the sounds and the feel of the surrounding forest. Slowly she stood and hugged the tree, thanking it for its shelter, before she walked on.

She walked another seven days through the trees. Each night her dreams became more vivid and each day her memory of the dream and the feelings grew stronger. With each day she saw something new, each day she grew stronger and more comfortable within the forest. Each night the connection with the trees grew easier and stronger. As the nights went by her dreams became deeper, and the connection to the whole forest grew. In her tree she could reach out and feel others now, she could sense the Dryad within their trees, she could hear the trees talk, she could feel them move.

Lana came to a rest that evening under a young rowan tree, she sat at its base and reached out to touch it. Introducing herself to it and explaining she would like to rest beneath it that night. She thought she felt a sense of approval, and so she lay, her back against the tree and closed her eyes.

She was woken by the Dryad, and recognised her as the one she had met that day on the edges of the woods, the one that had laughed at her meeting with the bull. Curious, she looked up at the Dryad, and took a deep breath.

"I'm..." The Dryad placed her hand over Lana's mouth.

"Be quiet, please." Lana nodded and the Dryad removed her hand.

"I am Daowiel, we have met before. I will not hurt you, but you need to come with me. The queen has commanded it."

Lana's jaw tightened and a knot formed in her stomach, but she stood and nodded. Daowiel reached out and took Lana's hand and then, with their hands joined, touched the young rowan. Lana's body started to tingle as it had on the island after touching the stone, but this time her mind was tingling too. It was the strangest sensation she had ever experienced and within a moment she was pulled into her dreams. Daowiel walked forward, her hand and then her arm melting into the tree itself. She continued walking, disappearing slowly into the tree. As the hand Lana was holding started to disappear Lana gave a yelp and tried to pull free but Daowiel held tight and pulled her in.

She was within a tree again, reaching out, sensing the forest; but this time Daowiel was beside her. This time, somehow, it wasn't a dream. It was strange. A little like swimming but not in water, Lana imagined that it is how it would be to swim in honey, much thicker and goopier than water. It was warm, and extremely comfortable. Lana, in spite of her panic, started to feel very safe. And then she felt as though her body and her mind separated, like she was drifting in a dream, her mind flowing through the branches and roots of the Heartwood. It seemed like an age had passed. And then a blinding light struck her, and there was a sharp tug, pulling her forward, pulling her off her feet. She let go of Daowiel's hand and fell to the ground. The wooden ground. She looked at it in puzzlement, it wasn't the dry dirt and grass she had been standing on, it was light wood, smooth and flat. She looked around a little and realised she was in a long, narrow tunnel, surrounded by wood on all sides. Daowiel laughed, and she looked up at the Dryad, unamused.

"You're not very graceful, little one." Lana opened her mouth to protest but Daowiel reached her hand out and cut her off with a word "Come." Her voice was quiet, and she was laughing still but there was no mistake in Lana's mind that it had been a command. She stood again and walked along the wooden path with Daowiel.

"This is the bridge; you have almost reached it yourself once or twice since you left the island. That would have been dangerous for you. This is why the queen has called for you, you are a puzzle to us, a human should not be here."

"What will the queen do to me?" Lana struggled to speak aloud, her voice turning to a whisper.

"I cannot say, Child. Although I believe she means you no harm. You have been allowed to wander freely up to this point after all, most humans aren't given that freedom."

"Why?"

"I have told her of the funny child that tries to talk to trees. When I saw that the feare hunted you, I killed it and left you within a circle of oak for your protection. I had expected you to return to your home in time but watched as you walked deeper into ours."

"Funny child?" Lana's voice was louder, sharper and filled with disgust.

"Be quiet, little one." Daowiel looked upset by the loudness of Lana's exclamation. "Humans cannot talk to trees, for one to try so frequently was amusing as were the names you gave them, 'Mr Apple Tree'." Those last words were laughed as much as said and Lana screwed her face up in response.

"Well... what's so silly about that?"

"You may learn in time. If you listen more than you talk."

With that they reached the end of the bridge and Daowiel took her hand and pressed it to the wall in front of them. Lana felt herself being pulled forward again as her body and mind tingled, this time her grip on Daowiel's hand tightened, and she braced herself for a fall.

12. THE PALACE

They were on a circular wooden disk, so wide you could fit the manor grounds on it and still have space. In front of them, on the far side, was a long walkway stretching outward and upward toward the largest tree Lana had ever seen. Larger than she could ever imagine possible. Hundreds of meters high and wider than the Stead square. She looked up, and up, feeling dizzy and sick as her eyes traced the trunk past vast branches holding other platforms. Up and up and up they went. She stumbled forward again and Daowiel caught her with a giggle.

They walked together, hand in hand toward the great tree and, as they grew closer, Lana could see Dryad moving around it. Lanterns lit the platforms and music floated down from them like autumn leaves.

They entered the tree and Lana was surrounded by that honey wrap feeling again before emerging on a platform high up. There were maybe two dozen Dryad, waiting to see the strange human girl that talked to their trees. They stood in a circle, and all turned to watch her. Daowiel walked her forward and the circle opened allowing them to pass through to its centre. They stood in the space vacated by the Dryad and Daowiel spoke.

"I have brought the child, mother."

Lana looked to the far side of the circle. Sat on a throne made of living branches, curling and winding their way into shape, lit dimly by lanterns and surrounded by flowers was the Dryad queen. Beautiful but serious, her dark eyes gleamed as she looked down at Lana, studying her for a moment.

"Welcome to my home, Ògan. I have heard many stories of you already and you are so young. A sapling still, in Dryad eyes. I am pleased you agreed to join us here."

Lana, remembering her manners curtsied and replied with a 'thank you.'

"How did she handle the journey daughter?"

"She shook like a leaf in a storm, and she fell like a pine cone." Daowiel had the same teasing smirk on her face that Lana had seen when she ran from the bull. Somehow that made her relax, she was still concerned about her immediate future but that smirk made her sure she wasn't in danger.

"Tell me, Ògan. Why did you enter my forest? Why did that feare hunt you?"

Lana noticed the Dryad around the room leaning in slightly, waiting to hear her story. She looked up at the queen and swallowed a mouthful of air. Still shaking a little, she recounted her story. Telling the Dryad queen of the Gesith's son and his attacks on the Stead folk. Explaining that she had been wrongly blamed for his death. Daowiel laughed at the mention of the bull.

"I had considered it a possibility that the foul tempered beast might end your life one day. I had not thought that it might save you from a feare."

"Be still, sister. Let the ògan finish her tale!"

Sat beside the queen was a Dryad with a grim look. Lana saw similarities between her and the queen and thought that, with her long dark hair and golden skin, she would be beautiful too, if only she smiled.

She took a momentary pause and then continued to tell how she had been rescued by her family and ran from the sheriffs to survive. She explained that she knew the sheriff would catch her if she stayed in the pasture, and so she took a chance and ran into the forest. That she had thought no man would dare follow her and that it was her only chance of escape. As she finished, she worried the queen might send her back to the Stead to face punishment for her behaviour. Or maybe she would simply put her in a cage with a collar and a bell around her neck and let her people hunt her. She looked up at the queen, eyes wide and sorrowful, biting her lip, waiting for a response to her story. The queen was silent and still for a moment, a moment that seemed like an entire morning. When she finally spoke her voice was calm and soothing.

"You are safe here, Ògan, no harm will come to you in my halls. It seems you have faced a trial no nighean should face. You will rest here awhile as my guest and tonight you will eat with us." With that the queen stood, not waiting for a response, and ordered her Dryad to prepare a feast.

It was a meal like none Lana had ever had, made entirely of plants, nuts, berries and fruit. It was lovely, sweet, filling and intoxicating. A thick mead was served alongside the food that made Lana feel as though she were free from the world and free from her body. She felt strong and carefree, that her mind had been released from the constraints of her body and flew through the branches above her. When the meal was over she was shown to a room, small but comfortable. A bed stood in the corner, covered in a blanket made of leaves. A wash bowl on a stand occupied another corner. She curled up under the leaves, surprised at the warmth and comfort they gave, and she fell into sleep.

Lana woke, unsure how long she had slept, unsure as to where she really was. But she was comfortable and warm. She sat up when Daowiel spoke.

"Good morning, Ògan. My mother wishes to speak with you in her chambers."

In a light daze she jumped up, grabbing her clothes and pulling them on, she followed Daowiel out of the room and to the queen's chambers. They were announced and left alone with the queen and Daowiel's sister. This meeting was very much more relaxed than the formality of the night before. They sat close as they talked, often with smiles and laughter at some of Lana's stories.

"Tell me, Ògan. Why is it that you speak to the trees? Were

you taught to do so?"

"Well, it just seems polite to thank a tree if it lets you eat its fruit or climb up into its branches. Your majesty. It just feels right. And if you're thanking trees it makes sense that you can talk to them as well. Be no point thanking them if they didn't understand."

In the Dryad's laughter Lana was able to see their family resemblance. Their eyes lit up and their smiles gave comfort. It seemed to Lana the seriousness of the day before was not normal for this family. That they were used to laughter and enjoyment of life, that the formality of bringing a human into their hall had been as alien to them as it was to her.

They talked at length about Lana's time on the islands and the things she found, the queen was very interested in knowing what had happened by the stone and asked Lana for more and more detail of her journey from that point on. As the day drew on into evening and Lana grew tired of talking, she took advantage of a rare moment of silence and asked a question of the queen.

"May I ask, Your Majesty, why am I here?" The queen's look changed again, her smile fading, her brow furrowed.

"Maybe it's time, mother? Maybe she's ready to learn?" Daowiel looked serious and a knot started to form in Lana's stomach.

"I will give you a gift, Lana, and a promise. One day you will come back here, to me, and I will tell you why we have brought you here. You will have many more questions at that time and I will answer as I can, though some may be beyond me. For now, however, you are not quite ready."

The queen produced a pendant of wood on a delicate rope, she handed it to Lana who was delighted to see the image of the grand tree palace delicately carved into the surface.

"You are welcome in my woods, Lana, and will never face harm within; so long as you continue as you are now. This pendant is a symbol of my trust and my faith in you. It is my seal and will be recognised and give you protection should you encounter Dryad outside of my forest. Your lore keepers will, no doubt, recognise it also and will know you are a friend of the Dryad Queen."

Lana thanked the queen, a tear of happiness in her eye. She reached into the purse on her belt and pulled out a stone she had found, a pretty gem of blue and green that reminded her of the sky through the leafy canopy of the lakeside trees. It shone in the lantern light and the queen's face showed her delight at it.

"You will eat with us again tonight and rest, in the morning Daowiel will take you to the edge of our forest, there you will find your path."

"Thank you, Your Majesty." The queen smiled and shooed them out of the room.

The morning came all too quickly for Lana, she had been nervous when she first arrived in the queen's home but quickly found herself enjoying the company of the Dryads. She missed being amongst people, amongst friends. When Daowiel came to wake her she took her time, slowly pulling on her ragged clothes wrapping herself in her cloak. She knew she had to go to Southport, and she wanted desperately to find the help she needed. She longed to go back home to her family, but the thought of being on the road again, alone, made her sad.

"I have something for you Ògan. If I were able, I would accompany you on your journey. It has long been my dream to see the land outside of our home and I wish you to be safe. I must, however, remain here and continue to protect the forest. Take this in my place. It may not be a raging bull, but it will serve as protection in need." Daowiel opened her hand and presented a short stick to Lana. It was a perfect fit for her hand and easy to hold comfortably though only ten centimetres long, perfectly straight and round. Made from dark wood and polished to shine, it was decorated with intricate and beautiful carvings along its length. Leaves, vines and runes intertwined with an occasional flower inlaid in white. It felt light in Lana's hand as she took it and was warm.

The gesture brought a tear to Lana's eye, and she instinctively hugged the Dryad. "Thank you, Princess."

"I am named Daowiel, Ògan. We have known of each other for many years now, in some ways we have grown together. You can consider me a friend first, a princess second."

As they walked across the bridge once more Lana reached out for Daowiel's hand, the Dryad princess smiled as they connected, and they walked closer to one another. Once they reached the far side they placed their hands on the wall in front of them and Daowiel turned to Lana.

"Tell me, Ògan. Where would you go from here?"

"I need to go south eventually, but I can't go near the Stead. I should go west again, I think. Then I can head south once I'm out of the woods."

"Close your eyes, allow yourself to feel the tree and the forest, as you felt them in your dreams."

Lana closed her eyes and sank into the soft, honey like comfort as they stepped into the tree. She allowed herself to open her mind and join the forest. In a moment she knew they were moving, flowing through the pathways of roots and branches that connected the trees. And then, the familiar pull as they emerged. She didn't stumble this time and the look Daowiel gave her was one of respect, there was no laughter.

"You are not far from our western border, beyond the tree line is a human stead, not very different from your own. Those that live within do not know us, we watch them but do not reveal ourselves. It would be better for you not to mention your journey through our forest, those that believed you would not, I think, be kind. I wish you good fortune on your journey, Ògan, and look forward to your return."

With that Daowiel let go of her hand, smiled warmly and turned back to the tree from which they had emerged.

"Wait... I..." Lana sighed as Daowiel disappeared. "Thank you, thank you for everything."

PART THREE
The Road South

13. FREYBRIDGE

After two weeks of following the road south, Lana stood at the gates to Freybridge. She had passed through a number of steads and hamlets on the journey, trading chores for food and shelter. She had made some repairs to her clothes and had been given some old shoes, they were mismatched and a little too big for her, but they made the walk more comfortable so she was pleased to have them.

A sheriff stood at either side of the gate, their faces showing the boredom of a quiet day. Workers were laying stones over the dirt path; creating a wider, more permanent and smoother road for the growing town.

The stone road cut a straight line through the town beyond the gates, on either side were stalls in front of low buildings, some with two floors, but most had only one. Men and women stood at their stalls calling to the people passing by, trying to entice them with offers on their wares. She walked past stalls selling fresh meat, skins, dried meat, fish and vegetables. She looked at the clothes that were being sold, thinking the styles strange and the colours garish. Her own clothes were simple in design, straight and colourless. They were a flecked mix of grey, cream, brown and black not pretty or stylish but warm. Part of her wanted to wear clothes like those on the stall, a part of her wanted to be pretty and have people exclaim as she passed. A dress caught her eye, blue like the sky on a clear, sunny day. The skirt was flared, the bodice was laced with fine green ribbon and the sleeves were made to be close in their fit. When she thought of what the clothes might cost and how impractical they were for work she shook her head as if to shake the thought of them from her mind.

"Oy! Clear out you, you're driving me customers away."
Lana looked around to see who the stall holder was shouting at.
"Sorry, I don't... What do you..." Shocked, barely able to get her
words out, she stuttered until she was cut off.

"Go on! Get out of it! You'll not get no coins 'ere. There's no
use in you begging along this street. Go and bother them up by
the gates." The woman was red in the face and clearly working
herself up into a frenzy of anger.

"But. I'm not begging, I'm just looking at the..." Lana tried
to explain again but the woman started yelling.

"Sheriff! Sheriff!" The stall owner wasn't prepared to listen to her and Lana didn't want to be around the sheriffs she was
shouting for, so she walked away, quickly heading deeper into
the town.

'Well she was unfriendly. What kind of person shouts at
people just for looking at the things they're trading? She can't be
very popular, going on like that.'

In the centre of the town the street opened up into a
square. The buildings surrounding it were larger than those
along the road, some even had a third floor and their own
stables. Wooden signs hung above the doors, a couple had paint-
ings of animals on them and others had the faces of people. She
had been told, by an oddly dressed man on the road, that she
could use the coins she had to sleep in a bed and buy food at the
'Stag Inn' so she walked over to the building that had a sign with
a stag on it.

Lana followed a small group into the hall of the inn and
waited as they spoke to the landlord.

"I'll need two rooms." The man speaking was old and
frail looking. His hair and beard were white his too thin frame
covered in an oversized blue tunic. "One for the women, three
cots if it's not too much but two will do if that's cheaper. I'll
need a room for myself and my apprentice too."

The landlord looked the group over, his face screwed up

as he saw the sylph. A young fae, the point of ears peeking through her shoulder-length blonde hair. "That one'll not be stayin' in me rooms. It can stop in the stables with the horses. The scruffy one an'all, I won't be havin' the likes of those in me inn. We're a reputable establishment we are."

The old man looked back in Lana's direction and stared right at her, his nose turned up. "I am a lore seeker. I do not keep company with beggars and brigands. That... waif is not in my party."

"I am NOT a beggar!" Lana protested loudly but no one took notice of her.

"Right then I'll have your rooms prepared, you can have that table for your meal." The landlord pointed over to a trestle table by the fire and the group made their way over to it.

"You two... OUT!" He swung his arm up and pointed to the door. "You're lucky I'll 'ave you in me stables!"

"I'm not a beggar!!" Lana tried again, louder this time.

"Yeah? And me nose ain't red. OUT!"

"But... Your nose is r..." The sylph placed her hand on Lana's shoulder.

"Do not bother. I have food we can share." She turned Lana away from the room and gently pushed her forward out of the door.

Once they were back outside Lana turned to the sylph, her cheeks red and her lips screwed up. "Why did you push me out? His nose is red and I'm not a beggar, I'm a milkmaid AND I've got some of that money. See?" She took a few coins from her purse to prove her point to the sylph.

"Put that away. It would matter not if you were the Tay's only daughter and had enough money to buy his inn. Your clothes mark you as a beggar and his kind have no interest in those that do not look the part."

"Are the Freybridge people a different kind?" Lana asked.

The sylph's name was Selene and Lana was pleased to have met her. They sat together in a corner of the stables and shared their stories as they shared their food. Lana was guarded over what she shared of her journey, but she gave enough information to explain her need to leave the Stead and head south. The sylph though was open and seemed pleased to have the opportunity to share.

Selene was a couple of years older than Lana, which in fae terms made her a minor. She had been sent to Southport three years ago to take an apprenticeship within the great library. She was put under the tutelage of the old man, Wendannor. Wendannor, it seems, didn't much care for people in general but had a particular dislike for fae and women. That put Selene in a difficult position. She enjoyed the access the old man gave her to his library, but she was little more than an unpaid scribe for the most part of her days. She was treated with disdain while the boy, Coryn, was praised for any work he completed. Wendannor had gone so far as to recommend Coryn for a formal position within the library, despite Selene doing the majority of the work and the research.

At the turn of the year Selene had discovered evidence that a missing scroll was located at Norhill. A fortress nestled in the lower peaks of the Sgàil Mountains. Rumoured to be the final teachings of the Goddess Chaint the scroll was considered to be almost mythical and the finder would take their place in history. They would also win a financial reward that would see them, more than, comfortable for life.

Within the week Wendannor, Coryn, Selene and Kaorella, the old man's maid, were heading north to make his fortune. The travel itself had not been too bad according to Selene but the old man's behaviour had been so bad that the men hired to guard them had deserted them once they reached Norhill. Taking their pay as if they had completed the journey. This made the old man even more difficult and Selene was pleased he never enjoyed her company, so she was able to avoid him.

Selene's investigation led them to the catacombs under the fortress. Long sealed and abandoned, the catacombs had been forgotten by most in the city and it took some weeks to find an entrance. Having gained access the question of who would explore them was asked. The old man had no intention of doing any of the work involved in retrieving the scroll, the maid was needed to keep him pampered and fed. With the warriors gone that left only Selene and Coryn to enter the darkness.

Chaint was the Goddess of the night and the catacombs reflected that. The darkness was absolute, there was no natural light at all, no sconces for torches or braziers for flame. So pervasive was the darkness that the torch Selene carried lit no more than a hands' width around it. Coryn whined as the darkness surrounded him. He was used to being coddled by the lore keeper and the shock of being ordered to hunt for some scroll he'd never be able to read in the depths of the dark goddess's ancient lair was too much for him.

"I ain't going no further. It's your fault we had to come here. I'm supposed to join the library not wander around some ancient cesspit with a bleeding sky fairy. You can lose yourself in the dark for all I care. I ain't following you."

Selene turned to reply to the boy but his torch was extinguished or gone, and she had no idea where he might now be. Turning again and reaching out her right hand she groped her way along the wall, hoping it would lead her to the goddess's temple and the manuscript.

Coryn was sitting with Wendannor when Selene returned with the scroll. He had complained to the lore keeper that he had been abandoned in the depths when his torch had gone out and Wendannor was furious. He took the scroll from Selene and ordered her out of their lodgings, she was told to stay at the stables until their departure.

Word of the old man's petulance had spread throughout Norhill, and he struggled to find people to guard him and his precious cargo on the road back to Southport. In fact, only two people came forward in answer to his call. A red-headed tuath warrior and a dark haired deasin hunter. Both young, both female, both cost more than he wanted to pay. Neither made him happy, but he was desperate, rumours of their find were spreading, and he feared the road home was becoming more dangerous with each day he waited.

The journey back had taken two weeks so far and had passed without major incident. The guards had needed to draw their weapons in threat a few times but nothing had escalated beyond that. Selene found the tuath warrior, Brighid, to be friendly but intimidating. Tinnion, the deasin hunter, was more reserved and intense, they barely spoke to one another though Selene didn't sense in her the hate that some in the southern taydom often held toward fae.

Hearing about the bias Selene experienced against her surprised Lana. Her family and her friends feared the Dryad, they were prepared to defend themselves if the Dryad attacked or tried to sneak into the Stead and kidnap their children. They didn't do that because they hated the Dryad though. Did they? Lana certainly didn't hate the Dryad, or any other fae. The war had been fought hundreds of years ago. Humans had been free since then; they were even in charge of the country and nobody from those times was still alive now. It didn't make any sense to hate people when they hadn't done anything wrong.

Selene smiled as Lana explained her thoughts. "I hope everyone thinks as you do, one day."

"Selene? If that man was like that because he doesn't like fae, why did he make me leave?"

"Sometimes people have so much hate in them they have to share it around. Your clothes are ragged, your hair is unkempt and you're a little muddy. You look to him like a beggar, a person that has no money and a lot of people in towns do not like people with no money."

"We don't use money in the Stead. We share what we have or we work for it. I found these coins, but I don't know what they're worth or how to use them properly."

"Let me see, I can show you."

Lana emptied the purse she carried on the stable floor between them and separated the coins and the stones she had collected on the islands. She looked up at Selene in anticipation as the sylph sorted the coins.

"There are seven types of coins in all, the lowest value are the rural coppers, that is what these are." Selene gestured to a pile of around ten coins. "One of these will buy you a jug of drink or some food at an inn. You'd get two or three of these if you worked a day in the kitchen."

The sylph went on to explain the value of the coins, giving Lana an idea of what she might buy with each. She then counted up the value of the coins Lana had, and they discussed what she might do with them.

"With what you have here you could buy yourself some new clothes and shoes, pay for your stay in an inn for a night or two on the road to Southport and rent a room for a week once you get there. It's far from a fortune but it will help you to survive while you petition an administrator for help with your family."

"You mean the Queen? I'm going to tell her what happened. Or the Tay if the Queen's too busy when I get there."

"You won't see the Queen, Lana. I am sorry. She does not live in Southport and only nobles are allowed to attend her court. The Tay lives in Southport but again he only sees nobles. It will be an administrator you see to plead for help. He will decide what course to take. There are a few in Southport, if we arrive together I will direct you to one."

Lana was happy that Selene was willing to give advice but the news made her sad. She had always thought the Queen was a woman that was close to her people and gave help where it was needed. To hear she wouldn't even see her was a blow that destroyed her childhood dreams and her hopes of finding help.

Seeing the despair on Lana's face Selene spoke again. "There are thousands of people in Southport. That is many, many times more than the number of people in this small town. It would be impossible for the Tay to see them all. The Queen must look after all the people of the country. That is too many people to be counted."

The conversation turned to more pleasant things and Lana learned about the library and the Tay's palace before drifting off into sleep.

She dreamt of sun filled days in the pastures and stories with her family that night. A dream she didn't want to leave.

So, when she woke in the morning and saw her new friend was gone, she sat up against the stable wall and pulled her knees up tight. Thinking, in silence, of the things she had lost she began to cry. It was an hour, or more later when she decided she could move on, and, swearing she would never allow herself to be banished to the stables again, she strolled down to the riverside. She bathed and untangled her hair before going back to the main street and buying the dress she had admired the day before. With a new pair of leather shoes and a dress the colour of the sky she felt like the princess she had dreamed of in the pastures. She fastened her cloak around her with the silver leaf brooch and made her way to the southern gate.

She walked throughout the rest of the day, stopping only briefly to eat some bread and cheese she had bought. Her shoes were incredibly comfortable and made the walk much easier on her feet. The sun turned the western skies orange as it grew closer to the horizon, a beautiful sight that brought good omens for the morning's weather. The skies along the road to the south however, were filled with smoke.

14. CAMP FIRE

Fire burned brightly around the base of the tree sending thick, black smoke into the air. Two robed men were talking loudly over the sound of the cracking wood.

"You sure this will kill the hag?"

"Of course, the book tells us so. Have faith and we will prevail."

"It... it won't come out, will it?"

"It is in flame, it is dying, it can no longer hurt us."

Lana felt the scream as much as she heard it, the high-pitched screech sending shivers through her body. She ran toward the tree, shouting for the men to put the fire out.

"We shall not! A tree hag burns here, evil, dangerous, faithless fae. It will die in the flames of the circle and the woods here will be cleansed."

Picking up a stick from the ground Lana approached the men at a run.

"Put it out!"

"Go away child. Or you will get hurt."

She lunged at the men, swinging her stick wildly and making contact a couple of times, but her shouting was more worrying to them than her physical attack. The younger of the two men, who had questioned the elder, grabbed Lana wrapping his arm around her neck and holding her arm behind her. She cried out in pain, kicking out and scratching at the man with her other hand.

"Why do you interfere, child?" The older man stood before her, a serious and stern look on his face.

"You're killing the Dryad and the tree! That's evil. You

have to stop the fire."

"The tree hag is evil. Godless and violent. It hurts and curses the loggers making their living from these trees. It must die, the copse must be cleansed of its blight."

"The trees are her home and you're cutting them down, killing them and hurting her. And now you're killing her. You're the evil ones."

"You call us evil? We, who follow the book. We, who are the circle. You have been possessed, child, and you must be cleansed too. Put her to the flame."

The man holding her turned, dragging her with him to face the burning tree. The heat of the flames pricked her skin, growing increasingly uncomfortable but not yet painful. She stamped down as hard as she could on the man's ankle, causing him to grunt in pain and loosen his grip a little. Grabbing his arm, she pulled it forwards enough to move her head and bit deep into his flesh. He yelled and cursed as she wriggled free, punching and kicking him before moving out of reach.

She saw the anger in his eyes as he turned, his face red, his jaws clenched, he shouted a curse before lunging at her. His bright red face coming within inches of her own as he fell at her feet, an arrow in his back.

The older man stood a moment in shock before he turned to find the shooter. Lana picked up the stick again and ran at him bringing it down on the back of his head. He stumbled forward, and she struck again, this time across his back. Beating the man to the floor she yelled at him to stay on the floor before she stopped. Removing her cloak, she turned to the tree and started whipping with it at the fire.

The dark haired hunter that she had seen with Selene walked from the trees and helped her to extinguish the flames.

"You'd risk your own life to save a Dryad tree?" The hunter's voice was soft, her tone level though questioning.

"They shouldn't kill a person for protecting their home. That's not right. They said she's evil, but they were the ones doing evil things."

"What are you going to do with the one you beat down? He'll not stay there long."

"I... I think he should run away and never come back. I didn't want to hurt him but I had to make him stop. I think, if there is a Dryad here, she won't let him come back again."

The huntress struck the man's side with her bow. "You heard the child. Go. And consider yourself fortunate that she allowed you to continue your life."

They watched as the man scrambled to his feet and ran from the copse tripping and stumbling on his robe as he went. The sun was gone now and the sky was dark. The huntress turned back to Lana "Stay away from trouble child. You aren't built for it. And if I were you, I wouldn't stay in a grove with a Dryad either. If it is there, it will be dangerous."

With that the woman slipped into the darkness and disappeared.

Lana turned to the tree and placed her hand upon it.

"If you can hear me, I hope you're okay. I'm sorry your tree is all burned." She turned to go but her hand was caught. She spun to see the Dryad, burned and scarred, her body only just showing through the flesh of the tree. Lana placed her fingers on the necklace the Dryad queen had given her and stepped back.

The Dryad fell to the floor and held out her hand to Lana. In her palm was a seed. Lana knelt in front of the Dryad, her heart heavy and tears welled in her eyes. "I'm sorry, I was too late, wasn't I? I tried... I'm so sorry."

The Dryad placed the seed in Lana's lap and collapsed, her eyes closed, her body motionless.

Crying, Lana placed the Dryad around the base of her tree and covered her with fallen leaves. She wished the Dryad peace in the after and sat a while in silence, mourning the death and regretting her inability to save her.

It occurred to Lana, in the morning, that if the huntress was close enough to have helped her then Selene and the others must be camped close by. She checked that the seed was safely in her purse and walked hastily back to the road, determined to find her sylph friend.

As the sun reached its height Lana walked into the temporary, roadside camp of Selene and her companions.

"Well, if it isn't the child that fought the circle to save a tree." The huntress slapped the arm of the red-headed warrior and gestured to Lana with a nod.

"That wee bairn? Are you sure? It was dark after all... could there have been a dozen of them and you just didn't see?"

"No, just her. And a twig. Mind she looked to have quite a bite on her too, so I wouldn't get too close to her mouth, she'll take your arm off!"

The two women were trying, but failing, to hold back their laughter as they talked. Selene approached her friend and placed her hand on Lana's arm.

"Come and sit with us, Lana. We have a little spare food and water."

Lana followed her friend and sat with her amongst the women.

"Lana, this is Brighid." Selene gestured to the tall warrior. "Kaorella." The maid sat to Brighid's left "And I believe you have already met Tinnion." Lana smiled at the huntress. "Lana was the 'beggar' in Freybridge, though as you can see now, she is no beggar. Simply a traveller from a stead with little knowledge of towns."

"Hmm. Simple, she most certainly isn't. And not the child I thought she was either. Forgive me Lana, I thought by your height that you were younger. I see now a young woman rather than a child."

"That's fine. I'm pleased to meet you again, it's nicer this way. Thank you for your help last night."

"You're welcome, Lana. Giving a lesson to the Circles priests has become an interesting hobby on this trip." Tinnion smirked. "Though I think you should stay away from them, or get a bigger stick."

"Who is that? What is she doing here?" The boy was younger than Lana but taller. He was stomping over to them, a knife in his hand. "Who told you you could join us?"

"Be quiet, laddy, and put that knife away before I decide to take it frae you." Selene's description of Brighid proved accurate. The warrior seemed friendly, she smiled and laughed with her friends but when she decided to be stern, she was incredibly intimidating. Lana was certain she would rather be Brighid's friend than her enemy.

The boy, Coryn, stuttered an indecipherable reply and stomped away toward the old man muttering to himself.

"That one is growing way too much like the old man. He'll gain hisell a spanking before we get tae Southport. Mark my word on it."

The companions took to the road again and Brighid invited Lana to join them. Wendannor, the old lore keeper, was annoyed and refused her space on the cart's benches so Brighid had her sit behind her on her horse. Tinnion drove the cart, her bow on the bench beside her. Kaorella, Coryn and Wendannor sat on the benches in the back with the supplies and a locked chest containing the scroll.

Wendannor refused to allow Selene to ride with them, so she ran along beside them. Lana was disgusted at this and opened her mouth to berate the old man but Selene stopped her.

"It is not a problem, Lana. Walking the road is no hardship for me, and if the circle were to attempt to stop us again it would prove better that I am on my feet rather than on my rear." The pair shared a smile and they all set off.

Lana got to know her new companions a little better as they travelled. The evenings in front of the campfire were ideal for stories and though they always drew disapproving stares from Wendannor and Coryn they would often stay up late laughing with each other. While the women grew closer to one another the old man and his apprentice became more removed and irritated by their growing friendships. Lana couldn't understand why they reacted the way they did and tried to engage with them a number of times without success.

The travelling arrangements meant Lana spent a lot of time with Brighid. She enjoyed the tuath's sense of humour and happy demeanour, finding her laughter infectious.

Brighid was the daughter of Cohade MacFaern, clan chief and Gesith of Lochmead. She was only nineteen years old but already had a reputation as a skilled warrior, winning many tournaments across the northern taydom with her athletic abilities and precision strikes. She had been in Norhill to collect her new swords, Tatha — the silent one and Athfhinn — the very shiny one. Brighid had commissioned the blades from Hjalmarr, the legendary blade-smith, and they had been forged from the highest quality steel. The blades were incredibly strong and had more flex to them than a normal sword, making them almost indestructible. Talking about them made Brighid's eyes shine with delight. She was incredibly proud to have them and Lana soon learned that if Brighid was being quiet, asking about her swords was a sure way to get her talking again.

She had heard news of the company travelling south not long after collecting the blades. Rumours that they carried something legendary and were prepared to pay well for protection caught her imagination. As she was travelling to Southport anyway, she thought joining them would be a good way to earn some coins and, perhaps, bolster her growing reputation. When Lana asked her why she was heading to Southport she grew quiet and whispered.

"The Feannag Trials"

15. REST STOP

Along the major roads, at the edge of each hold, were rest points. Designed primarily as a place to house patrolling sheriffs, they often grew into small villages. Each rest point housed a barracks for the sheriffs and an inn for travellers of the road. There would often be merchants selling their products on stalls and, on occasion, a healer or physician. On the larger, more popular, routes you might find small houses where merchants took the chance to settle more permanently.

The company stopped at the first rest point south of Freybridge. An opportunity, after three nights of camping by the roadside, to sleep in a bed and rest with a jug, or two, of ale beside a fire. Selene had helped Lana organise her money so that she could take advantage of the rest points, making sure she didn't spend too much on the road. The company made their way into the inn, with Wendannor preparing his purse for the night's lodgings. As they were approached by the innkeeper the old man demanded a room and a meal for the boy and himself. Then he turned to the women, a smirk on his face and spoke.

"The five of you seem so cosy by a campfire. I would hate to separate your group. Do enjoy the stars this evening."

"But sir, when you asked me to travel with you, you promised me food and lodgings." Kaorella was shaking a little as she spoke. It was unusual for her to question her employer and it made her nervous to do so.

"It is unfortunate then, that you have given so much attention to these women. I am sure their company will provide you comfort enough."

"Hey now. Our agreement was that you'd be paying for beds on the journey as well as the coin once the job wis done." Unlike the maid, Brighid didn't shake as she spoke. Her voice was strong and her demeanour suggested it would be better not to argue.

"Our agreement was that you be paid to protect me, not to keep me awake at night with the pointless chatter of your gaggle."

"You're currently breathing, old man. That implies our job has been done. Put your hand back in your purse, and we'll let your forgetfulness go without further comment." Tinnion had placed herself between Brighid and Wendannor. Cutting off the tuath's path to the old man and giving her a moment to breathe before acting.

"Very well, I shall honour our agreement and purchase you two a room."

"You have to take one for Kaorella and Selene too." Lana spoke up. Her voice and her presence not as intimidating as Tinnion or Brighid's but just as sure.

"This is of no concern to you, beggar." The smirk returned to the old man's face as he turned his attention toward Lana.

"My mam says you shouldn't make promises you've no intention of keeping and you made a promise to them too." In an attempt to look more ferocious Lana furrowed her brow and stuck out her chin after she spoke.

"You are profiting from the protection I have purchased. If you are concerned about the lodgings of the women you are welcome to dip into your own purse."

"Right then, I will. And when I get to Southport, I'll tell everyone I meet about the lore keeper that can't keep his own word." Lana turned her face away from the old man and smiled at the inn keeper. "Could I have three meals please and a room with three beds?"

"Of course. I'll have them prepared for you, dear." The inn-keeper gave her a smile and then furrowed his brow and gave the lore keeper a look of contempt before walking away.

The sun was still an hour or so away from setting as they finished eating and Lana excused herself and left the table. Their food had been enjoyable but was sitting heavily in her stomach making her bloated, she thought taking a walk would help her ease that.

There were trees at the back of the inn and Lana wandered over to them thinking she might find some small items of food to pack away for the journey. As she foraged through the undergrowth an arrow whistled passed a foot away from her head and buried itself in the trunk of a tree. She threw herself to the ground and crawled to cover behind an oak. She peeked around the trunk but saw no one. Then she felt something on her shoulder, something solid and weighty. She yelped and flung herself to the floor again.

"It's just me, Lana. I was hoping we could talk." Lana turned to see Tinnion with a smile on her face that made her relax.

"You scared me!" Lana laughed, rather nervously as she spoke.

"I'm sorry, I didn't mean to make you jumpy. Can we talk?"

"Of course. Just err, can we do it without the arrow?" Lana pointed to the arrow Tinnion was playing with.

"Oh, yes, sorry." Tinnion shook her head as she spoke as if to shake herself awake. "We haven't known each other very long and I've seen you rush headlong into things you should have avoided. I really like that you have principles and that you stand up for people, that's a good thing. But you're putting yourself into difficult and dangerous situations."

She reached out to take Lana's hand as she spoke. "Southport is going to be very different to the life you're used to and I'm a little worried you might find it a difficult place to be. You can't trust everyone you meet. You will meet a lot of people that don't share your principles, and some are dangerous. Some are very dangerous."

"But if they are dangerous why don't people stand up to them and stop them?"

"Because sometimes that isn't an easy thing to do. And, for a lot of people, it isn't the right thing to do. You can't help people if you're dead Lana and sometimes doing the right thing at the wrong time can kill you."

"Are you saying that I shouldn't try to help?" Lana was a little disappointed in her friend and her voice became sharp as she asked her question.

"No, no... I'm saying that it's often better to take some time to consider the best way to help. It isn't always as simple as rushing in with a twig."

Tinnion went on to explain that her family, hunters in the town of Coldford, had built up a large debt to the taydom. Failure to pay the debt by samhain would result in her father being jailed. The price owed had grown beyond the ability to manage and it was clear they needed a way to meet the deadline without drastic action. One option had been to marry Tinnion to the hold's Gesith, a proposal had been made and the lord had offered to pay the debt in return for her hand. Being the wife of the Gesith would require Tinnion to give up the freedom she had as a hunter and provide an heir. The Gesith was older than her father and had led a life of comfort which had resulted in him developing a rather rotund physique that Tinnion found far from appealing.

The pressure to accept the proposal built as the year went on and samhain grew closer, the family hunted more, selling the skins and meat of their prey but were still a long way from paying off the debt.

Hunting deer, bear and big cats brought a steady living, enough to keep the family comfortable but Tinnion knew the only way to avoid marriage was to hunt something extraordinary, something so rare it would bring a great price in the markets of Southport.

It was said that frost trolls roamed the ranges of the Sgàil Mountains, rare and dangerous, the beasts were talked of as le-

gendary creatures and few in the south believed in their continued existence. There was no denying though that the miners
working in the Sgàil mountains believed in them. A troll hide,
being extremely difficult to get, would be guaranteed to bring
enough gold to pay off the debt.

Tinnion now had two.

Certainly, she would now be able to raise enough coin to
avoid a wedding as well as securing her own future. Tinnion was
excited to be heading south. Thinking beyond what had seemed
the clear path of action had resulted in the miners of Norhill becoming safer and Tinnion making new friends.

When she finished telling Lana her story she held out her
other hand, revealing a few coins.

"I spoke to the old man; he soon realised the right thing to
do." Tinnion placed the coins into Lana's hand and smiled at her.

"Thank you, Tinnion!" Lana held onto Tinnion's hand a
moment before letting go.

Tinnion was right; she had put herself in danger with the
priest. Paying for the room and meals of her friends had left
her short of the money she would need in Southport. She had
been prepared to make that sacrifice for her friends but was relieved she now had the money back. She didn't want to ask what
Tinnion had said to get it.

The company was approached by three men as they prepared to leave in the morning. Each wore light leather armour,
swords hung from their belts, and they had round shields on
their backs. They led a horse which carried provisions for their
journey, the size of the packs suggested they were very well-
prepared.

The eldest of the three informed the group that they
were soldiers returning to Southport, he invited the company
to travel the road and camp together. The old man was thrilled
to have more masculine company, he was not enjoying the
company of the women at all. It was a bonus that they would

provide extra protection he would not have to pay for. The soldiers, on the other hand, seemed more interested in spending time with Brighid and Tinnion than Wendannor and Coryn.

It didn't take long for Wendannor to see how the addition of the three men would affect the group. The eldest, a captain named Laywyn, was barely able to draw his gaze away from Brighid. In turn the tuath warrior savoured the attention and teased the man relentlessly. He looked to be around ten years older than Brighid, he was friendly and seemed to be an honest man. His obvious infatuation with Brighid appeared to fluster him and his face was often as red as her hair.

The youngest of the men, Allric, was closer in age to Tinnion and Brighid and spent his time trying to get the huntress's attention. Unlike Brighid, Tinnion didn't seem to be so interested in her suitor and watching him struggle to engage her was, at times, uncomfortable.

Leuthere, a large man with a great ginger beard, walked alongside the wagon. He had a deep, booming laugh and a habit of pointing out the flirtations of his colleagues with jokes. Lana sat beside Tinnion on the driver's bench watching her companions interact. She found Leuthere's laughter infectious and often had to bite her lip to avoid the glares Tinnion gave her when she joined in.

The lore keeper and his apprentice insisted their shelter be built away from the women and invited the soldiers to join them. The soldiers however decided an evening spent passing a flagon of wine and sharing stories with the women would be a lot more entertaining. It certainly was for Lana whose jaws soon ached from laughing.

The following day was spent between chatting, yawning and nodding off as the wagon trundled along the road. Brighid had taken over the driving that day as Tinnion, in an effort to avoid Allric's flirtations, took their horse and went on ahead with the promise of catching some meat for their supper.

The light-hearted conversation and playful teasing ended quickly that afternoon. Tinnion hadn't returned for their mid

day stop but that hadn't really caused concern. Hunting something large enough to feed a group of this size would often take
a while so, aside from a few jibes at Allric, nothing was said of
her absence. They walked the road for another two hours in the
afternoon when their horse, wild eyed and frenzied, came gal-
loping along the road toward them. Tinnion was nowhere to be
seen.

16. HUNTED

T he wagon came to sudden halt. Brighid leapt from the bench and started a run down the road, Laywyn and All- ric followed. Lana wasn't as quick to react but jumped down and ran after them anyway.

"I'll be staying here to guard you lot then." Leuthere said with a smile. "I'm not built for all that running anyway to be honest, I'm more a stand yer ground type."

The three warriors spread out across the road ahead of Lana, Brighid and Laywyn to either side, looking for signs of their missing companion. Allric ran up the centre of the road, ready to help whoever found her first. Up ahead the fields gave way to hilly woodlands, the perfect place for Tinnion to have hunted. The warriors slowed their pace, looking more closely at their surroundings for Tinnion's tracks, not wanting to miss a sign through haste. As they walked on the trees to the side of the road grew taller, the woodland beyond them became denser and the shadows from the canopy above grew from puddles on the ground to a lake. The warriors continued their search and started calling out to their friend, hoping for a response to give them direction.

Lana stopped, something caught her eye, she wasn't sure what, but something in the trees wasn't quite right. She walked over to the side of the road, looking at the ground for tracks but finding none. The grass around the trees seemed undisturbed, but something was definitely odd, she could see that, she just couldn't see what it was.

Slowly she walked deeper into the woods, following that

feeling while looking for signs Tinnion had passed that way. The light faded as she walked under the thickening canopy and it became harder to see the ground, the undergrowth becoming denser and tangled. A young tree just ahead of her was scarred, the bark of its trunk split and torn away. There were claw marks at the level of her eyes and teeth marks a little higher up. She examined the bite marks, and found they were fresh, wet with a mix of spittle and sap.

A void formed in her stomach, creating a sense of emptiness through her body, the sound of her breath filled her ears. She walked on, trying to control her body's reactions. The ground became uneven forcing Lana to reach out to a nearby tree to steady herself. Sticky and wet, she thought she must have found another chewed upon trunk but, as she looked, she saw the tree intact and the liquid covering her palm was a deep red, thick and warm.

A few steps further and another tree was smeared with blood, there was a trail now. Something she could follow. She wasn't sure she wanted to see what waited on the other end of it however. Wishing she had called on Brighid before entering the woods she took a gulp of air and called out. Her voice breaking, the sound caught in the dryness of her throat. The squeaking of a mouse more than a shout.

The woodland grew much denser, the darkness closer, the musty air heavy as it filled her lungs. Lana stepped carefully, painfully slowly as she followed the blood trail. Expecting with every footfall to feel the claws that had torn the bark from the trees tearing at her skin.

An arrow jutted out from the tree she rounded; a small patch of dark fur embedded with the tip. Tinnion had been here, she was close even now, and she had marked an animal. But was she the hunter or the hunted? Was the blood from the beast or from her?

A few more steps, a few more trees behind her and another arrow, protruding from the undergrowth like a bramble, entangled in the fern. A misstep in the dark, a slickness under foot, Lana slid and fell. Under her a puddle of the blood that marked the trees. Her stomach wretched, the muscles pulling tight her throat tensed but her mouth stayed dry. She scrambled to her knees, one hand on a tree at her side the other on her stomach, and she emptied her stomach on the ground.

Her body shaking, her knife drawn, she stumbled on. Every moment felt like an hour every small sound from her steps like a crack of thunder filling the woods. The smell of death hung on the air, and a little ahead of her the body of a deer lay hidden in the trees. An arrow had found the vein in its neck and Lana's body relaxed a little. It was the deer's blood she had found, not the blood of her friend. But where was Tinnion if her prey was here? A closer look at the fallen animal revealed a tear in its side, the same kind of mark she had seen on the tree.

It didn't take much longer for Lana to find her friend but it didn't give her any relief. Tinnion was lying still, her eyes closed, blood covered her. At least, blood covered the parts of her Lana could see. Lying across her friend, claws bloodied, teeth bared, was a large, black bear.

Arrows bit deep into its flesh, its fur was ruddy with blood but it still moved, twitched and groaned as it struggled for air. It was so much larger than her friend and looked to be crushing her body under its weight.

She squeezed her eyes closed and shook her head. But her mind took her back in time. She was in the bull enclosure, on her back. Her clothes torn from her body, her head spinning. He was on top of her, his strength holding her, his weight pinning her to the ground. The heat of his body oozed across her skin as he kicked her feet apart and pushed himself between her knees. Her eyes closed for a moment, and she heard her heart beating, pounding, no. Not her heart, the rushing of the bull, its hooves striking the ground as it ran toward them. The warm spray on her face as the blood speckled her skin.

Lana opened her eyes and held up her knife, looking in shock at the blood covering her hands. Her dress and her face had become speckled, sticky and red. She struck again and again at the flank of the beast. Her breath deserted her, and she fell to her knees, exhausted. The bear was still, no longer groaning, no longer twitching, no longer fighting for breath.

Lana put her shoulder to the great beasts' side and pushed as hard as she could. It took time and every ounce of strength Lana had left within her body but the bear rolled over. More arrows peppered its front, their broken shafts snapped close to its flesh. In its chest a long bladed knife, Tinnion's knife. Exhausted, Lana collapsed, trying to catch her breath, as the bear had been, she lay close to Tinnion.

17. DOING IT FOR HERSELF

L ying beside her friend, her body and her heart heavy. She didn't dare look at Tinnion's still form, why had she arrived so late? What help would she have been if she had arrived earlier? One strike from the bear's claw-tipped paws would have finished any assistance she could have provided. But still, she thought she should have been with her friend giving whatever help she could. Catching her breath and fighting back the tears that had been running down her cheeks she pulled herself up to her knees and checked her companion over. Her body was covered in blood but Lana saw no evidence that the beast had managed to claw her. She had scratches on her hands and face but nothing too deep. Perhaps the blood was only the bears? Wiping the blood from the hunters face she gently called to her. Hoping, beyond reason to get a response.

She detected the slightest hint of warm air from Tinnion's lips as her fingers passed over her mouth. Lana placed her head to her companion's chest and listened. It took a while to pick the sound out but it was there, a heartbeat, faint and slow but real. The silent sobbing she was fighting back turned to laughter, and she let it out into the world.

"Wha...what's...so ...funny?"

"You... You're alive. I thought the bear had... I'm just so happy."

Standing, her legs still shaking, she took Tinnion's hands and pulled her up to a sitting position. Her friend groaned and gripped her hands tight. Looking to the body of the great bear beside her she spoke again, her voice barely more than a whisper.

"This damned bear nearly did for me Lana. I was sure it was still alive when I blacked out."

"It was, it wasn't moving when I got here but it was trying to, I think your knife must have punctured its lung 'cos it was struggling to breathe. I. I ended it and pushed it off you. What happened?"

"I was following a deer; I'd hit it but it ran on through the trees. I caught up to it and was about to start binding its legs, so I could drag it out of the woods when that beast came crashing through the trees. Damn thing wouldn't stop, no matter how many arrows I put into it. I emptied my quiver but it kept coming, so I pulled my knife. It crashed into me, knocking the air out of me and sending me to the ground. I felt the knife sink into it, but I was already seeing stars."

Lana smiled and wiped her face with her cloak. "How are you feeling? We should get out of here, the others are looking for you and… Well, all this blood; if there's anything else in the woods we won't be alone long."

"You're right I just. I don't know if I can walk yet, Lana."

"I'll help. If we can stand you up? You can just lean on me as we go."

They made their way to the road together and Tinnion sat on the ground while Lana shouted out for their friends. In a few moments the three warriors came running back to them. Brighid helped Tinnion to her feet and the huntress ordered the soldiers to head into the woods and retrieve the deer.

"I didn't fight that damned bear to end up eating nuts and dried bread again tonight!"

By the time they got back to the wagon their companions had set up camp for the night at the edge of the field. A fire was burning, and shelters had been put up around it. Wendannor and Coryn, as was now habit, had insisted their shelter be a little removed from the others. When Lana and Brighid arrived with

Tinnion held up between them Kaorella started barking orders at them and Selene.

"Go, heat some water on the fire. Use the big pot mind... No. The big one... with the handles..." "Get me some rags." "Bring me the herbs from my bag." "Go get me some leaves, big ones mind, dark green an all."

She lay Tinnion down and fussed over her while the three women ran about gathering and fetching the things she demanded. After a while Tinnion, confused, looked up at the maid. "What do you need the red berries for?"

The old maid smiled and winked at her patient. "I'm feeling peckish, aint I..."

When the men returned Laywyn carried the deer across his shoulders and Allric had the hide from the bear. They placed the spoils of Tinnion's hunt beside the fire and Allric wandered over to the shelter.

"I brought you these. Thought you might want them as a souvenir, maybe you can make a necklace from one?" The young soldier handed Tinnion a few teeth he had taken from the bear's mouth. He had cleaned them up, but they looked just as dangerous as they had covered in saliva and blood.

They ate well that night and Tinnion showed signs of gaining her strength back. She discovered the joys of having Allric fussing over her and encouraged him with smiles and light touches of her hand. Lana poked her gently on the arm as she sent the young man to fetch her some fresh water.

"I didn't think you were so keen on him, Tin?"

"Well, he's persistent and what's the harm in giving him a bit of a smile from time to time?"

"You're going to have him wrapped around your finger by the time we get to Southport, he won't know what to do when he's back on duty!"

"Me? Now what makes you say that? I'm just being friendly." Tinnion laughed.

They slept early and long, hoping to put the day and a

good distance of road behind them the following morning.

After two more days of travelling, they stopped to make camp by the side of the road. The woods still stretched quite some distance here and Lana thought they had a similar feel to the Heartwood. The company were well practised at setting up camp now and Lana moved around the clearing gathering fallen wood for the fire. A little into the woods on the western edge of the clearing stood an old oak tree, its branches reached out in a wide circle, its trunk was thick and tall and the dark green leaves formed a canopy above her. She reached out and placed her hands on the tree, saying hello and introducing herself to it, thanking it for its shelter and the fallen wood it had provided.

"Are you sure you've no got pointy ears?" Lana turned to see Brighid walking towards her, a big smile on her face. "You've been ages, we thought you'd wandered off and been gobbled up by a wee Dryad. Instead, I find ye here talking to the trees like yer one of 'em."

"Now you know my secret. Shh!" Lana laughed and walked back to the camp with her friend.

She had grown to really enjoy Brighid's company, the tall tuath seemed to always have a smile on her face, and she often told jokes that would make you laugh or blush. Her conversations with Laywyn were like a funny sparring contest and it was clear Brighid was winning. Watching the back and forth between the two had kept Lana amused over the last two days. That it clearly annoyed Wendannor was a bonus in Lana's mind. The old lore keeper had made it clear during their journey he had no time for any of the women. They existed to guard and serve him, in his mind, nothing more.

The combination of later sunsets and having the three soldiers in their company meant the evenings had become longer and more boisterous than before. Leuthere and Brighid, so similar in their personalities, told stories and jokes that made Lana's cheeks redden, laughing long and loud with their friends. Allric sung songs, most of them with his eyes firmly on Tinnion and professing feelings of love. Liquor was passed around that made her tongue burn, she had tasted it the night they ate deer but had found the taste hard to like and the burning sensation worse, so she stuck to drinking cider and water while her friends grew steadily less sober. The old Lore Keeper had insisted his shelter be made in an area between trees further away from the group than normal and could be heard tutting and moaning about the revelry of the camp. Lana sat, drinking her cider and listening to the tall tales and soppy songs until she was too tired to stay awake. Then she said goodnight and curled up under a tree, wrapping herself in her cloak She fell asleep to the sounds of laughter and chatter, a smile fixed on her face.

It must have been a few hours later when Lana woke with a start. Her companions were asleep and a fair few were snoring. She sat up against the trunk of the tree and looked about, searching in the dark for whatever had roused her from sleep. A knot formed in her stomach and a strange sense of danger filled her, and then she heard the snap of a twig somewhere close by.

Time slowed to a near stop.

The sense of danger grew, she saw Tinnion wake and start to move, rolling over and reaching for her bow. The now familiar, pulling sensation and warmth of the tree filled her. Her mind started to reach out into the woodland around her, and she wondered if she was still asleep and dreaming. She saw, or sensed, men in the woods moving toward them, armed and dangerous men. Men with sharp axes and cruel faces, men that cut the wood and gave no thanks. The warmth at her back started to spread, and she realised she was sinking into the tree. Tinnion had her bow now and was rolling into a kneeling position, her mouth was open to shout and her hand was on an arrow. Lana let out a cry as the tree enveloped her, hoping to rouse the others and alert them to the danger.

As the tree closed around her, her sight shifted, and she could see everything that was happening from different angles and places, she could see each man attacking and each member of her party, everything happened so slowly, and she was able to change her focus to see it all simultaneously. An arrow came from the trees to the west. Brighid and Laywyn woke as Tinnion's shout merged with Lana's and echoed around the clearing. Tinnion loosed her first arrow and reached to her side for another. The sky became heavy, there was a feeling of pressure on the branches, the leaves started to move in a breeze that hadn't existed a moment ago.

The arrow shot from the trees struck Laywyn's thigh just as Tinnion's arrow struck the opposing archer through his eye. Laywyn swiped at the arrow shaft with his blade, cutting it down near to his flesh, as the archer crumpled to the floor. The other soldiers started to react, reaching for their blades as they scrambled to their feet. Brighid now stood beside Tinnion, a blade in each hand, ready to meet whatever would come from the tree line. Selene stood, a knife in her hand, not as sure as her companions but ready to defend them if needed, Kaorella was curled up beside the sylph trying to hide. Away from them and closer to the tree line the old man stirred, his mouth open to scold those making a noise as he tried to sleep. His young apprentice woke and reached for the knife on his belt.

A cry came from the trees and the men rushed forward. Poorly dressed, poorly armed, they carried axes and old blades, some with pitchforks. All except one, a man in a robe with a staff of wood and steel. She counted close to thirty of them in all, a whole stead full of men charging out of the woods to attack her friends.

It started to rain, heavy drops landing on leaves, bending them with their weight. The wind picked up, bending branches and catching cloaks.

Tinnion loosed another arrow. Laywyn and his men moved forward to meet the enemy and Brighid started a run, her blades already moving. Another archer amongst the men fired an arrow. Lana felt helpless and scared, not for her own safety but for her friends. She was sure she couldn't be harmed, not here in the tree.

Coryn made it to his feet, his knife glistened dark orange from the light of the fire, he started to shout and raised his blade to attack as the pitchfork pierced his skin, pushed deep into the soft flesh of his stomach. The face of his killer turned to a smile as he struck. A man at his side carrying a club, struck the lore keeper square on the back of his head as he sat up to protest.

Brighid cut the arrow from the air as she neared the attackers and started a leap. The soldiers clashed with the forward group of men, their swords striking and parrying. Tinnion's arrow found its mark, taking the second archer through his heart.

The rain reached the woodland floor and the skies opened. A bolt of lightning flashed across the sky.

Lana couldn't help but notice in the stark light of the storm that the soft, friendly face of Brighid was now stern, grim and determined. It struck Lana, though, that her eyes were filled with pity rather than hate. Unlike their attackers her friends showed no signs of enjoying this fight or wanting to kill their assailants.

As Brighid came down from her leap the blade in her right hand slashed the face of the man in front her, opening his flesh from the ridge of his forehead to his chin in a fissure of blood. Her left side blade dug deep into the neck of the man beside him. Tinnion loosed another arrow.

The woods echoed in thunder.

Laywyn pushed his sword through the chest of an assailant as Allric parried the axe strike of another. Leuthere crashed into his target with his shield, sending him backwards into the crowd with a roar.

Coryn fell to his knees, holding tight to the shaft of the pitchfork. His hands stained with his own blood, his eyes were half-closed, his face a mask of pain and despair. He toppled over onto his side as his killer picked up his knife to replace his own weapon. Wendannor was lying nearby, blood on his tunic and in his matted hair, unmoving, silent, still.

Lana's body began to tingle once more, like a million pins

stabbing at once. Stinging. She was sure she was awake now, aware, hyper-aware, of the events surrounding her. She pulled her consciousness back into her body and turned, leaving the tree and standing on the bridge she had first seen with Daowiel. Lana ran toward the far side picturing the oak she had introduced herself to earlier. She placed her hand upon the wall and pushed herself through. The warmth and comfort of the tree was fleeting, she was aware of the oak surrounding her only briefly, and she stepped out. Emerging behind their attackers, she stumbled over the body of a fallen archer.

Brighid and the soldiers continued to cut their way through the front line of men that attacked. Brighid was fluid in her motion, like water finding its way around rocks. Laywyn and the others, in contrast, pushed, parried and struck with force. Tinnion was a deadly frenzy of arrows, never missing. The speed of her hand and deadliness of her aim seemed to contradict the absolute calm on her face.

Their assailants, full of momentum pushed on, confident in their number. A tall man, bigger than the rest lifted a large hammer and struck the chest of Allric, sending him crashing to the ground. He left the young soldier on the ruddy ground and turned his attention toward Leuthere as another man struck the young man, splitting his skull with an axe and ending his breathless struggle and his lovelorn life.

Laywyn drew his sword across the stomach of a man and turned toward the hammer carrying giant. Brighid, dancing and spinning cut down another two assailants and kicked a third to the floor. Selene comforted Kaorella, holding her, promising she wouldn't allow anyone to harm her.

Lana knelt, picking up the archers bow and grabbing an arrow from the row he had placed in the ground. She pulled back on the heavy string and sent the arrow flying into the back of the staff-wielding man. She felt the heaviness of the air and the charge flowing around her as a bolt of lightning struck the centre of the crowd sending two men to their knees and killing a third. The smell of burning flesh filled the air.

The fight went on. Leuthere, big as he was, was pushed aside by a blow from the giant's hammer just as another assailant fell to Laywyn's blade. The giant man roared and stared at Laywyn beckoning him forward, a look of hate in his eyes. Laywyn held his sword high and started a run toward him. Tinnion shot another man, her arrow landing deep within his chest and Brighid took the hand from an axeman as he swung at her.

Lana sent another arrow into the crowd hitting a man in the back of his knee and sending him toppling forward. The lightning struck again and the injured man flailed on the ground before settling into a contorted, smoking, heap.

Laywyn and the giant man met, the hammer swung, the captain ducked, his blade thrust up and forward. Brighid parried a blow and pushed a blade up through the soft skin beneath a man's chin. Tinnion stood, striking a man with the tip of her bow and forcing an arrow through his neck with her hand. Leuthere, struggling on the floor, parried a blow from a club. Lana dropped the bow and ran forward drawing her knife from its sheath.

The skies erupted with a crash of thunder so loud and forceful that it shook the trees and the people in the clearing. The rain fell in sheets killing the fire and muddying the ground.

Laywyn's blade struck its target and the heavy form of the giant man collapsed upon him, forcing him to the muddied ground. Tinnion drew a short blade from her belt as she used her bow to strike out at the man in front of her. In a moment her blade pierced their skin. Brighid stood, bloodied blades in each hand, daring the wary men around her to attack, they started to back away from her reach. One cried as Lana's blade slid into his side and the others fled.

The thunder shook the trees, the lightning struck, touching more men with its deadly energy, burning their skin and sending them to the ground in great cries of agony. Some laid still but breathing, others were dead, their hands curled into rigid claws, their mouths open and their legs buckled. The remaining men started to run, their faces full of fear and defeat.

They weren't followed, they were free to go with no attempt made to capture or kill them.

The storm stopped as suddenly as it had arrived, the woods fell silent, Lana and her companions let their arms drop to their sides, taking a moment, breathing. Laywyn pushed the hulking body of the giant off him and struggled to his feet, his leg bleeding badly from the arrow embedded within. Brighid went over to help him, placing his arm around her shoulder and taking him to their shelter. Tinnion moved around the clearing checking those that had fallen for signs of life.

Lana walked through the carnage back toward the shelter and her companions, as she reached the centre of the clearing and the washed-out fire pit she collapsed. Exhausted, her body shaking, her eyes closed, her mind blank she fell into a deep dream-filled sleep.

18. A CLEAR ROAD

Lana woke lying beside Wendannor in the back of the waggon. Brighid and Tinnion were up front driving, Laywyn was sat to her right, his thigh bandaged but bleeding. Leuthere sat beside him with a bloody bandage around his head, he was pale and leaning heavily against the side of the waggon. Selene sat on the other side beside Kaorella who was fussing over the old man's wounds. Lana sat up and leaned back against the bags of scrolls and books they were transporting.

"What happened?" her voice was weak and her throat sore, she covered her mouth and coughed a couple of times.

"You collapsed when the battle was done, you don't appear to be injured. I believe the experience was overwhelming for you." Selene spoke softly, her hand laid gently on Lana's arm. Her sympathy for Lana was clear in her manner despite her analytical words.

Lana pulled her legs up to her chest and sat quietly without speaking, she didn't lift her head or look at her companions. Her eyes grew heavy and wet, and she wept silently as they trundled along the road.

When they came to a stop to rest the horses she scrambled out of the waggon and ran into the field beside the road, leaving a path of flattened wheat behind her. Lana found she was still a little unsure on her feet and soon fell to the ground where she sat and cried. She started to remember the battle, the smell of burning flesh as the lightning struck, the blood soaked ground and the sensation of her knife digging into the flesh of the man she killed. She saw the bodies of those that had died, some bleeding out, some missing parts of their bodies, some were burnt and mangled. Lana threw up as the images flashed through her mind. Her throat was a hot ball of pain, making it hard to swallow, her face red and stained with tears.

She cried herself out and sat quietly, her stomach convulsing as she sniffled and struggled to breathe through her pain. She didn't hear Tinnion as she approached and jumped a little as she felt her hand upon her shoulder. The huntress knelt behind Lana and gently pulled her back, holding and comforting her. When she spoke, her voice was soft and filled with emotion.

"They killed Allric and Coryn, Wendannor's head is broken, I don't know that he'll survive and Leuthere is close to death. Laywyn won't ever walk properly again. Fighting, killing, it's never easy, it's never good, but had we not fought, had you not fought, we might all be dead. Or worse. It will haunt you for a while, their bodies, the smell, the blood. You'll hear their shouts and their cries in the dark. In time, though, you'll find peace again. These things are normal, if you didn't feel this way, if you didn't cry, that would be wrong."

"Something happened to me, Tinnion. Something. I don't know how, I don't... I didn't do it; I don't think I did... I don't know..."

"What is it? Are you hurt?"

"No. Not that, I. I didn't tell you everything back in Frey-bridge, I didn't tell you where I'd been. I was in the Heartwood before I met you, in the forest with... with the Dryad... they helped me... they took me in the trees and helped me... and, and I did it... when they came for us... I did it... I was in the tree and on the bridge and then I was behind them and I found the man you shot and took his bow and... I don't know how I did it... I'm not one of them... I'm not..." Lana was shaking, her words tripped from her, trying to explain something she couldn't understand.

Tinnion wrapped her arms around her and held her close.

"There are people in the North, warriors, a bit like

Brighid. Sometimes in battle they change, they go berserk, they do things they shouldn't be able to, find strength they shouldn't have. They fight in a frenzy, but they never remember, they don't know what happened. Only that it did. Some believe they are possessed by old gods when they fight. Sometimes battle just does that to people. Don't worry, I'm sure there's an explanation. It was the first time you've been involved in anything like that. It's normal you don't remember everything."

Lana knew Tinnion was trying to comfort her, she knew she was speaking out of kindness, she knew though, that Tinnion was wrong. She had been inside the trees, just as she had in the Heartwood with Daowiel, she had been on the bridge, she had travelled from her sleeping place to the other side of the clearing, and she had done it the way a Dryad would. She didn't know how, she didn't think she could ever do it again, but it had happened and it worried her.

They sat a moment or two longer, until Lana stopped shaking and her breathing calmed, then they made their way back to the waggon and their companions. Tinnion took Brighid to one side as Lana helped settle Leuthere onto the floor of the waggon where she had lain before, he was slipping in and out of consciousness now and Lana knew Tinnion was right. He was dying and might not even make it to the next rest house. Lana had grown close to the soldier. He was strong and tough in appearance but soft and gentle in personality. He had, more than once, covered Lana with his blanket as she slept and Lana had seen him helping Tinnion onto the waggon when she was struggling with her injury. Once he was settled Lana sat next to Laywyn and lay her head on his arm.

Laywyn placed his arm around her and drew her head to his chest. "He's a good man, I always knew we'd win a fight with him at my side. He had taken Allric under his wing, tried to teach the kid how to stay safe in a battle." He fell quiet.

They drove on long after sundown, hoping to beat death's horse and get to a rest point as quickly as possible.

They were on the road another few hours before they

reached one, when they did arrive Laywyn spoke to the soldiers waiting to inspect passers-by, and they were waved through without checks. Between them they carried Leuthere and Wendannor into the barracks and to the healer's room. Brighid placed her hand on Lana's shoulder as they got the two men settled.

"Come wi me, hen. This isn't the place for ye."

They walked back outside and sat on a bench in front of the building.

"How are ye feeling?"

Lana nodded "I'll be fine, I was just scared, I think." Brighid smiled at her warmly.

"Show me your knife. I hadn't noticed it before but it looks a little dull."

She took the knife from its sheath on her belt and handed it over. Brighid held it a moment testing its weight and its edge, then she set it in motion, blurring from one hand to the other, changing position and twirling around her fingers.

"Aye, that's no a bad knife you've got. Remind me later and I'll show ye how tae keep it sharp and look after it." She handed the knife back to Lana who put it away, safe. "I think mebbe it would be good if I showed ye how to use it too. What do you think?"

"Would you?"

"Aye, of course! It's better for me if ye know how tae stop a person yourself." She grabbed Lana's shoulder and pulled her toward her, hugging her and laughing. "Ye did well you know. I'm proud o' ye."

Lana smiled, these two women, these two strong warriors, had seen that she was struggling with her emotions after the battle, and they had both reached out and given her comfort. She knew she was with friends again, people that cared for her, and that eased her mind a little.

It wasn't long before the others came out of the barracks, and they walked together to the inn. They found a table, ordered food and drink and arranged a room for the night.

Kaorella had Wendannor's purse and had paid the bill from it. Brighid encouraged Lana to take ale instead of the soft cider she had been drinking and it wasn't long before she was a little light-headed. Laywyn joined them again after they had eaten and told them he had been given extended leave until his wound healed, he didn't seem fully present, as though his mind were still back on the battlefield but after a cup of ale and a few comments from Brighid he started to cheer up and the evening became quite merry. They sat in the hall late into the night and Brighid had to carry Lana up to the room when they finally retired. She lay on her cot, slurred a "goodnight everyone" and closed her eyes. Tinnion laughed.

"She's going to have quite a head on her tomorrow."

"Aye, but she felt a wee bit better there tonight."

19. THE OLD MAN GOETH.

L ana woke with a shock as the cold water struck her face, she opened her eyes to see Brighid and Tinnion standing over her with buckets laughing gently.

"Hey! Wha…"

"Come on sleepy, it's breakfast time, and we have things to do. Bring that knife of yours down with you too, and we'll get it sharp."

Lana sat up slowly and groaned, holding her head in her hands.

"Do we have to go now? Can we not stay a while?"

"We're gonna be here a few days actually, but that doesnae mean ye can laze around snoring all day, you've stuff to learn afore we move on."

So, she dragged herself out of her bed and clomped her way down the stairs behind them to the inn's hall. Kaorella and Selene were already sitting at a table and had ordered breakfast for them, a plate of sausages, bacon and bread. Lana didn't think she could stomach food, but she forced some bacon in nevertheless.

"You said something about us staying here?" She looked up at Brighid, her eyes still half closed.

"Aye, the old man's no fit tae travel, so we'll be here another three days, or, so they reckon."

"What about Leuthere?"

Brighid shook her head, clenching her jaw and Lana cried.

They finished eating and left the inn. Selene and Kaorella

went to the healer's quarters to check up on the lore keeper, Brighid and Tinnion took Lana to an open area behind the inn. They sat on the grass in the sun, and talked a little. They discussed the battle they had been in and how Lana was feeling, both Brighid and Tinnion told her about their first experiences fighting and killing and how it had affected them. Listening to their stories assured her, these women were the strongest people she had ever met, and they had each been through what she was going through now. She wasn't alone, and that gave her strength. Lana asked if they would have the chance to say goodbye to those they had lost, and they assured her they would do that before they left. Lana was relieved she wasn't alone in her feelings.

"I suppose at least they can rest with peace, knowing those men won't hurt other people now their leader's dead."

"Aye, and Laywyn being the one tae end him was justice, I suppose." Brighid lowered her head.

"No, not that one with the hammer, the priest."

"Wait, Lana. What priest? I didn't see any priests." Tinnion placed her hand on Lana's arm as she questioned her.

"I shot him, before he got to the clearing. He had a long white robe and a staff that had a steel tip on it. He was wearing the same necklace as the man that was burning the Dryad tree. You remember it?"

"I do. Another priest of the circle. Brighid, this can't be coincidence. We've been running into circle priests since we left Norhill. What is the old man having us guard exactly? Did they tell you?"

"No, they didnae, I assumed it wes just a few o' them books they seem to be keen on doon here."

"I think it's time we found out. The Circle are like rats, Where there's one there's a dozen. If we're going to be running into them every other day between here and Southport I want to know about it."

"Aye ye could be right at that. We're no in a hurry though, we can ask Selene when we stop fer lunch."

"Oh, I can tell you that! It's a manuscript that Chaint wrote. Selene said it's really important but no one believed it really existed 'cept she found it. Now they're taking it to a... Lie... Libey?"

"The Great Library?"

"Yeah, that's it. They're taking it to the Great Lie-Brare-ee, so they can get lots of gold or something for Wendannor."

"Well that explains it. The Circle hate the old gods, they'd destroy every trace of the fae and their gods if they could."

They talked a little more before Brighid picked up a stick and started to show Lana how and where to strike an opponent. She pointed to areas of her body explaining how she might stop an attacker without serious injury and how she might strike if she needed to kill.

Then she stood Lana up and, using sticks, showed her how to best stand and move when dealing with an attacker. They practised a while and Lana's muscles began to ache as Selene and Kaorella came around the corner and called them back to the inn for lunch.

In the afternoon it was Tinnion's turn to teach Lana. They took the bow Lana had picked up and a few arrows and Tinnion showed her how to shoot. It was difficult for Lana, she had never been good with a bow and the one she had found was difficult to draw, it took a lot of effort and strength just to send an arrow a few feet, shooting a target was something Lana thought she might take a while to work up to. Tinnion and Brighid were very supportive and encouraging, but they also pushed her beyond her comfort level and her whole body ached by the time they were finished and returned to the inn for the evening. Laywyn met them at their table and the evening grew rowdy again, though Lana decided she would go back to drinking cider again. She didn't want to repeat the headache she had suffered that morning.

The next two days went the same way, though Laywyn joined them in the mornings and commented as Brighid trained

Lana. Sometimes he would make suggestions of his own and Brighid would tease him.

"She's not a great lump of a man like you, she cannae just be pushing people around. She needs to know how te move and use their own attacks against them, not punch her way out of a melee."

Though Brighid was always teasing Laywyn he seemed to want to spend as much time with her as possible, and he'd ask to walk with her alone a few times over the day. She teased him about that too but always went with him.

It was lunchtime on the fourth day, Lana was lying across a bench at their table in the inn, waiting for Kaorella and Selene to return from the barracks. Tinnion sat opposite her, laughing as she moaned about never being able to move again.

Brighid and Laywyn had gone on one of their walks. They'd been gone since breakfast and Tinnion confided in Lana that she thought Laywyn might ask Brighid to marry him. Lana knew Laywyn liked Brighid but didn't think they'd get married. Brighid had a plan for her time in Southport, something to do with her whispered secret.

When Selene and Kaorella came in the maid was clearly upset. Wendannor had died and, though he wasn't a pleasant person to work for or be around, his death meant Kaorella and Selene's life would have to change dramatically on their return to Southport. It also meant that responsibility of the scrolls and manuscripts they were transporting as well as the Lore keepers' purse were now Selene's. It was up to her to ensure they arrived in Southport safely. More used to giving advice than making decisions, the responsibility didn't seem to sit well with the Sylph, and she hesitated to take the purse from Kaorella.

That afternoon was spent discussing the rest of the journey. Brighid and Tinnion suggested selling the waggon and buying horses for the last leg. It would be quicker and the circle priests wouldn't be looking for five women and a soldier on horseback. The company agreed, though Kaorella had protested, she didn't like horses and was a little worried about the idea of riding one.

The conversation turned to their plans once they reached the city. Lana had explained her reasons to travel to the women of the group but went over them once more for Laywyn.

Tinnion explained that she planned to sell her troll hides and return to Coldford to arrange the release of her father.

Selene hoped that returning to the library with the manuscript she had discovered would earn her a place within its walls at last. If she was refused a place she would return to western isles and her family. Her dream had always been to serve as a lore keeper however, and she would take any opportunity that presented itself in order to achieve that dream.

Kaorella wasn't sure where her future lay. She had family in the city and would stay with them while she looked for new employment. She had built a reputation over the years as a good and patient cook and believed she wouldn't have to wait too long for a new opportunity to arise. The question for her was more likely to be who she would choose to work for.

Brighid explained she had been invited to Southport in order to take part in the Feannag trials. She had used the word before, when telling her story to Lana but Lana had no idea of its meaning. The others in the group, though, were clearly impressed.

"Brighid?"

"Yes, Lana?"

"What are the Feannag trials?"

Laywyn interrupted before Brighid could reply. "They're held at random by the queen's command. Only the best warriors in Mortara are invited. Thirteen in all. There are various tests and, in the end, a tournament in which they all fight. The winner is given a title and a purse. The last one was held around six years ago. They say the winner of that one is richer than any Gesith now. You won't be wanting an old soldier holding you back." Laywyn looked upset and Lana remembered what Tinnion had said. If he had hoped to marry Brighid he clearly worried the fame and fortune she might win would end his chances.

Brighid laughed "who knows what might happen? I might even lose." Lana knew Brighid was kidding, that her confident statement was mostly bravado. Brighid was a great warrior and always seemed so sure but Lana had spent enough time with her to know she would never assume victory and would never abandon her friends so easily.

Lana excused herself early that evening, her muscles were sore from the training she was doing, and she found it hard to hide her growing sadness from her friends. She had grown close to each of the company on their journey, they had helped her through her problems and listened to her patiently. She felt they had become almost like a family during their travels. They helped each other, held each other, given comfort and advice to one another. They had laughed and cried and fought together. They had lost friends and companions; their lives had been changed. And they had done it all together. The thought of them drifting apart when they reached the city made Lana's heart heavy. An emptiness crept through her body and her mind.

Her dreams that night played out her fears. Each of her friends faded away to nothing, and she was left alone. Alone in a city she did not know, lost and afraid.

They woke early the following morning, packed their belongings and made their way down stairs for breakfast. Ordering a larger meal than normal they sat and ate for the most part in silence.

"I wish we could stay together." They all looked over at Lana, and her cheeks grew warm.

"You know that we cannot, Lana. We each have a need for employment or commitments to fulfil."

"I know, I just... Does it have to mean we can't at least see each other though?" She was fighting back tears as she remembered her dreams and her voice was cracked as she spoke.

"Ah'll be in Southport at least as long as you are Lana, I'll mek sure we see each other whenever we've a chance." Brighid gave a warm smile, lifting her shoulders and closing her eyes as if her whole body was behind it.

"I shall also remain in Southport should things go the way I hope, I see no reason we cannot meet each other in the evenings. I too would miss you all were we to part and would prefer to continue our friendship." Lana linked her arm with the sylph's as she spoke holding herself close to her friend.

"I'll be honest, I was starting to think I might retire from this soldiering lark and settle down with a private employer. Find a wife, start a family, that kind of thing. I'm not entirely sure where my future lies, but if you're wanting the company of an old man I imagine I'll be about for a while." Lana sensed a sadness in Laywyn's voice as he spoke, he didn't look at Brighid but Lana was sure he had been thinking about her friend.

"You aren't that old Laywyn! I'm sure you'll find a good wife, you're a sweet man, really. You're bound to have opportunities." Lana wasn't so subtle and threw Brighid a glance with a wide grin as she spoke.

"Aye Laywyn, plenty o' lassies in Southport I reckon. Yer bound tae find one tae take ye."

Tinnion addressed the group next. "I have things I have to take care of as you know. I have to admit it would have been nice to have company while I do that too. Who knows after that though? There are animals in the woods outside Southport too."

Kaorella jumped in before anyone else could speak, still looking worried about the thought of riding the rest of the way. "I was born in Southport an' I'm sure I'll die in the city, in one kitchen or another. But. From what I can tell you'll be the one that does the leaving Lana. You're looking for help to go home and be with your family. Once you have that you'll be making your way back to Butterholt in a hurry, I reckon. I know you'd like for us to stay friends and spend our days together and I'm not saying leaving will be easy for you, but when you've a chance to get back you'll be wanting to take it."

"I... You're right, it's true. I have to make sure my family is safe, it's why I'm going to Southport, but... I feel like you're all my family too, now. I wish we could all go together. I don't want to miss any of you the way I miss my family."

"When I was younger, I knew my life would be spent away from my family. My father had been a soldier, and I was sure to go in that direction. I knew people in my stead that were sons of blacksmiths and carpenters, shepherds and loggers. They all knew their futures too. They'd stay in the stead; they'd marry a girl from the Stead and their families would build their homes in the Stead. They all grew close to one another, relied on one another, where I always considered myself outside of that. I was friends with them of course. I liked them, but I knew my life would be spent away from them."

As Laywyn spoke he reminded Lana of her father, a man she knew she could trust, a man that had the wisdom of experience and would help her to stay safe.

"When you know that your life involves travel, when you know you aren't going to be in one place forever the relationships you form are a little different. You aren't someone that was meant to travel. You put all of yourself into the people you love. That is a wonderful thing, Lana. But it hurts you when the time comes to pack up your things and move on. When the time comes for you to move on, I will miss you. But I will remember some moments we have had and I will smile. Hold on to the moments, enjoy the time we get to share and when you miss us don't be sad, be happy that you had that time."

Lana moved from her seat, walked over to the soldier and hugged him.

"I'll always remember this moment."

PART FOUR

Southport

20. WELCOME
TO THE CITY

They trotted along the cobbled road, passing market stalls and wooden buildings with the odd signs that Lana had seen in Freybridge and at weigh points. She knew now that most of them were inns and had pictures that represented their names. People were selling farm produce and clothing, a few stalls sold old metal ware and one was selling hunting equipment. The people were dressed as they had been in Freybridge. Some had wooden buildings behind their stalls, others had tents and wagons. There were no stone buildings though and Lana was a little disappointed by that.

"It's a big place, I thought it would be... more... special though." Lana kept her voice low but couldn't hide the disappointment in it.

"What's that then, dear?" Kaorella clung to her horse nervously, it had been a little over a week, but she still hadn't come to terms with riding.

"Well, Southport. I thought that it would be, I dunno, grander? Like, really big, stone houses and people wearing lovely, flowing clothes and such... It feels a bit... dusty, I really can't imagine the queen walking around here, she'd get her dresses all dirty!" Kaorella snorted as she laughed, a funny sound that made her laugh even more and brought a large grin to Selene's face.

"Forgive me, Lana I shouldn't laugh." Kaorella managed to get her laughter under control enough to explain. "This isn't

Southport my dear, this is Shorebridge. A little town what grew up on this side of the bridge for them that wanted to sell their goods but couldn't afford a shop in the city. These people're from the farms and steads around the area. They makes a little more money if they sell their things here, so they travels a bit every month or so to come over. "

"So, we're not in Southport?"

"No dear, that'd be Southport over the bridge." Kaorella pointed through the crowds to the east and Lana's mouth fell open as she saw the city in the distance.

Near the bridge on this side of the valley was a large wooden building the soldiers used as they checked the wagons and carts going to and from the city. The bridge itself was wider than the road that led to it, wide enough for two wagons to pass each other with space. There was also room enough for people to walk along its sides. Walls ran along its edges to prevent falls and, at intervals, the walls became small turrets that held lanterns. On the far side of the bridge, atop a sheer cliff, stood the city's walls. Gleaming white, like fresh snow in the sun, they grew from the cliff and stretched thirty foot or more into the sky.

"Oh." Was all Lana managed to say.

They rode on toward the bridge where they were stopped and their belongings checked. Selene was coming into her own now, sounding more confident and full of authority, She explained who they were, what they were carrying and the importance of their journey. They crossed the bridge and rode under the arch that gave them entrance to the city. The sylph let out a long held breath as they rode on and Lana gave her a smile. "You did really well." She whispered to her friend.

Every building here was at least two storeys and as grand as the Gesith's manor in Butterholt. Alleys and streets led off in all directions with people bustling along them, busy with their lives. There were no market stalls here, no people shouting adverts for their goods. Shops lined the streets, each with a hanging sign depicting their wares above their doors. It was quieter and yet noisier than Shorebridge at the same time. The noise was different though, talking, walking, bells ringing in doorways, horses' hooves on the stone road.

"This is the outer part of the city, Lana, the trading area. Most of these buildings are commercial properties, shops or inns. There are very few large homes in this circle, though it is the busiest area of the city." Lana listened carefully as Selene explained the layout of the city.

"We will be riding straight through this area and into the central circle, that is where most of the cities residents live and where we will find the library and the administrative buildings."

Lana was struck by the city's size as they rode into its central circle. They rode past parks with trees and large grassy areas larger than the Stead she had grown up in. Statues and fountains dotted the wide, paved, streets that they circled around breaking up the pathways and providing places to meet. Far fewer people wandered around here and the streets were quieter than the outer circle. Every house was larger than the Gesith's manor and sat in its own grounds. And then they came upon the library. Built with the same white stone as the city walls, and larger than any building Lana had seen, it was a spectacle in itself. Surrounded by statues of kings and queens. It had large stained-glass windows and a domed roof that made it the most elaborate building in the circuit and the grandest thing Lana had ever seen.

At this point the companions split, Kaorella left them to go to the lore keepers house, she would tell the staff of the events on their journey and the old lore keepers' fate. A messenger would be sent to an administrator, and they would then put the house in order to be returned to the crown as the law of the city demanded.

Brighid and Laywyn rode to the administrator's office where Brighid announced her arrival for the trials. She was given the rest of the week to train and ordered to report for the first trial seven days hence.

Once registered the warriors lead their horses back to the outer circle where they had agreed to meet their friends and take lodgings at an inn.

The others took the bags of manuscripts and scrolls into the library. Selene informed a Lore Keeper of the death of Wendannor and his apprentice. She handed over the documents, explaining their origins and how they came to find them. The keeper was astounded at the collection Selene had retrieved and instantly called for the Lore Master.

"We must have these examined, if this one proves to be what it appears then... Well, then it would be the greatest find in centuries. And you, you would be... I think, I imagine you would be rewarded greatly."

"All I have ever desired is a chance to show my worth as a Keeper of Lore."

"We shall see what the Master thinks of the matter, child, though I would support such a thing if asked."

"Thank you, Keeper." Selene nodded with a smile.

The Master of Lore was astonished at the claims made over the manuscripts. Calling for a magnifying glass and a guarded light, he opened the scroll said to have been written by the goddess, Chaint.

"This... My word this is remarkable! The form, the strokes, such artistry! And the message, oh my. A meeting of the gods, the war close to won, a chance of escape. This is, well, this changes it all. It really does. Who would have thought it at all possible?"

"Master?"

"Yes, yes... Have this taken to my private study. Ensure no one else reads it. In fact, take it yourself, lock up the door yourself. Make sure to bring the key straight back to me." The Master of Lore handed a large iron key to the keeper and turned to Selene.

"Now tell me, child. Why have you neglected your studies here? I was told that you had fled back to the isles. Clearly that is not the case."

"No, Master, I had not fled. I was unaware of studies, master, aside from those given by Keeper Wendannor, rest his soul."

"Then I fear the Keeper had been keeping you far too much to his own needs. You shall move your belongings from the man's house and into our residence. You will be tested at the turn of the moon in order to be named Keeper. Your discovery has proven you too worthy to be a seeker."

Selene was speechless but had a smile on her face and the beginnings of a tear, forming in her eye.

"I am sure you have much to prepare, we will see you by the week's end."

"Yes, Master." The young sylph nodded.

As they left the room Lana put her arm around her friend's shoulder and congratulated her on her success.

"You must be very pleased, Selene. I'm so happy for you and proud to know you! You'll be a Keeper by next moon!"

"It is all so sudden, Lana. I had thought the Master would be weeks pouring over the manuscripts. I hadn't expected such a quick response. I am happy of course, just surprised. I will not neglect my promise to help you though, Lana."

It was getting late when they left the library, and they hadn't stopped for food that day, so they rode back to the outer circuit and found the inn in which they had planned to eat and stay the night. The 'Old Lords Inn' was a lot cleaner and better presented than any they had stayed in so far. The food was hot, the bread was fresh and the cider Lana drank was chilled. Their rooms were large, the beds were soft and in the corner they had the traditional stand with water. Lana's even had a mirror above it. Laywyn had a room of his own, Brighid and Tinnion shared a room and Lana shared with Selene. Staying here, in a room so grand, was like Lana's princess dream, A palatial room for a royal child. The company all slept well that night, the ordeals of the road behind them. The memories of the battle growing weaker with distance and time.

In the morning Lana dressed in her travelling clothes and walked with Selene to the judicial offices in the central circle. Lana tried her best to lay out her story for the duty judge, she stammered and floated around the details as her nerves took hold of her. Eventually, having listened to Lana describe how grumpy the bull was for the second time, the judge stopped her.

"You're here to report the Gesith or his son?"

"Well, your honour, Aeloth. The son I mean, he's. Well the bull killed him you see, so he's dead but the Gesith sent his sheriffs to kill me, and they hurt my family, and he didn't help when Ara's dad told him what happened to her, or when they burnt down their house and killed him. I think the Gesith should be brought to justice for that, your honour."

"Bringing a case against a Gesith is a serious affair, one which I am not in a position to judge. Only the Tay, perhaps even the Queen alone, can pass judgement on a Gesith."

Lana sighed but nodded her head. "I understand, how do I get to the Tay's court?"

The judge laughed. "Oh! Oh dear, the thought… No girl, you do not take the case to the Tay. Only a noble may attend the highest courts."

"Forgive me, your honour," Selene spoke up before Lana could reply. "That being the case, could you advise me as to how my companion might have her case adjudicated?"

"Well… She is a serf; I doubt that she would gain the ear of most nobility. Though she is not unattractive, it may be the case that she could find an old lord to take pity on her and take her in. Were that to happen she might be able to persuade him to take her case to the Tay."

"Your advice is to…"

"Wait! What do you mean 'not unattractive'? What are you trying to sugg—"

"Lana. Calm." Selene stood in front Lana and placed her hands firmly on her shoulders.

"You cannot let this man anger you. We will find a way

into the Tay's court; I will help you find a noble to sponsor you."

Lana's face was screwed up into a ball of rage, her eyes narrow and her lips tight. "Fine. But we should go before he gives any more advice. I don't think that I could take another suggestion from him."

"Of course, we should go back to the inn and meet with the others. They may be able to suggest another way forward."

Selene turned back to the judge. "Thank you for your kind advice, your honour. We shall give it due consideration."

With that the friends left the courtroom, Selene holding Lana's arm and leading her away, just in case the judge's words still echoed in her mind.

Having eaten, the friends ordered ale and wine and shared the stories of their day.

Brighid and Laywyn had spent the day training, getting Brighid ready for her trials. Laywyn had tried to convince her to use a longer sword and defend herself with a shield but, though she was skilled in doing so, she preferred to fight with two blades. Laywyn was a fighter that used his strength and experience to win a melee, Brighid used her athleticism and her speed. To watch Brighid fight was to watch a dancer at work, blades whirling, feet shifting. It wasn't that she did not have the strength to bully her way through a fight as Laywyn did, but her skill meant she had no need to rely on it.

Kaorella was preparing herself to start a new job. The inn keeper had known her previous employer had expired, and he immediately took advantage of her staying in his inn. He offered her a position before anyone else could. She would be the head housekeeper, managing the maids and ensuring the guests were well cared for. The offer meant that she would begin her new job in the morning, taking a room in the basement as her own. The inn, though not the best in the city, was pleasant enough and the innkeeper had ensured her he had plans to improve its reputation. He had also been keen to ensure she would accept and the wage he had offered was plentiful.

Tinnion had spent the day arranging a buyer for her skins, she had returned to the inn with a little over double the price she needed to pay her family's debt. She was preparing herself to start the journey home to Coldford though she didn't seem so keen to depart.

"I feel a lot closer to you than ever today Lana. We both have family in trouble and journeys to make, yet we've been through so much as a group. I'm finding it difficult to imagine the journey without you all to talk to."

"Ye'll sharp get used tae it again Tin, and ye'll find it a heck of a lot easier hunting meat for only one. Nae more need tae go fighting bears tae feed a whole company of hungry mouths."

"Well there is that." Tinnion laughed. "How did your day go Lana? Are you getting ready to leave us all too?"

"No, the judge made it clear he couldn't help and the advice he offered wasn't much use either."

"Oh? What did he say?"

"He said that I'd have to see the Tay and possibly the Queen to get help but that neither would see me without a noble as a sponsor. Then he said I should find an old lord and... "

"She nearly went after him like a cat does a mouse. I wasn't sure if we would leave the court without chains!" Selene laughed as she spoke, it was unusual to hear the sylph laugh at something she said and Lana creased up. In a moment the whole group was laughing.

"I'll do it Lana, ye've no worries with that. But I'll no' be able tae until my trial's finished. You understand."

"Do what Brighid, sort our rude judge out?"

"No, silly! I'll sponsor yer place in the Tay's court. Have you forgotten I'm a Gesith's bairn?"

"Oh Brighid! I hadn't realised. The two things didn't connect in my mind. Are you sure you can do that?"

"There's got tae be some benefit o' having that title." Lana jumped up and flung her arms around Brighid, squeezing her tight.

"You're the best, Brighid! Thank you!"

"Your trial won't be ending for another five weeks will it Brighid?" Tinnion interjected, raising an eyebrow inquisitively.

"Aye that's right. Starts next week and goes on fae four."

"And then you have a tournament?"

"Aye."

"It would be wrong for me not to be at the stadium to support a friend. I can pay my families debt here in the city and I'd still have enough money to pay for my stay here. I have no need to go rushing back to Coldford."

"Really? You'll stay?" Lana's grin was infectious and the whole group was aware that a celebration was growing.

They drank a little more than their fair share of ale and wine that evening and Lana was unsteady on her feet as she climbed the stairs to their rooms. She fell on her bed and hoped her head would be clear in the morning. She didn't relish the thought of passing another day with a pounding head.

21. JEWELL

Lana's hopes came to nought and, though she was awake early in the morning her head hurt and her mouth was dry. She felt as though she might sleep an entire day and still be tired. Selene was still sleeping, snoring and too heavily to be roused. So, she washed and then made her way downstairs for breakfast. Tinnion and Brighid were already seated and had ordered up a large platter of food for the group. Lana greeted them and slid along the bench by the wall to her usual place. She was halfway through a sausage as Selene and Laywyn descended the stairs. A few 'mornings' and hangover grunts followed, and they all sat down to eat. The platter was gone in no time and Brighid shouted for Kaorella to have someone bring more.

"We're warriors and travellers, you ken! We cannot be satisfied wi this wee plate o' sausages."

It was Kaorella herself that brought through the second platter, full of sausages and bacon with fresh baked rolls of bread around its edges.

"You ever done any serving Lana? One of my girls has come down sick and I'm going to be short for a couple of weeks. The last thing I need, starting a new job. You'd get free room n food and a few coins for yourself as well."

"I haven't Kaorella, I'm sure I could learn though. I guess it's mostly fetching and I've done enough of that."

"Have your breakfast then and then come through to the kitchen. I'll sort an apron for you and you can start."

"Okay." Lana knew she only had enough money to last her in the inn a week, she knew she would need to find a way to stay in the city another moon at least after that. Being handed the chance of some work so quickly was a blessing and would save her some coin as well as earning her some.

When their bellies were full Laywyn and Brighid made their way to the inn's courtyard. They carried wooden practice weapons. they chatted and laughed as they walked together, little space between them.

"Well, I should be taking my belongings to the library. My room will be ready now and I should start preparing for my exam. Will you still be wanting to meet again this weekend?"

"Yes, of course. I was hoping you could show me around a bit. I used to dream about exploring a city but when I look out of the window I think I'd get lost if I did it alone. You wouldn't see me for a moon!"

"What will you do this week, Tinnion?"

"Well, I thought I might have a wander out of the gate and around the island. See what there is to hunt, keep myself in practice while I'm here."

That week and the next passed quickly. Tinnion turned hunting into a success in the woods around the city. Lana worked as many hours as she could, saving her coin and keeping busy in order to pass the moon quickly. Brighid had departed at the start of the week, her trials were underway. She returned to the inn in the evenings telling the story of her day before retiring early. Laywyn moped for a day, lost for something to do, and then went out searching for work. He hadn't announced his retirement yet but his leg was no better, and he thought it would be worth looking for work that would be easier than soldiering with a similar pay.

Selene had promised to show Lana and Tinnion around the outer circle that weekend. They had arranged a day when they could be without work at the same time and met in the square outside the inn.

The Main Street of the city was lined with fine shops, Selene was fascinated by those selling books and concentrated her tour around those. Tinnion, on the other hand, pulled the group toward fletchers and those shops selling furs. Between them Lana wandered around in awe, watching as her friends checked item after item. Tinnion haggled over a quiver of arrows, stubbornly refusing to move from her named price and assuring the fletcher that given time and patients she could make a product of similar quality herself at a fraction of the cost.

Lana's eye was caught by a fine looking cloak, her dress was holding up well and still, in her eyes at least, looked fine. The cloak she had taken from the sheriff, however, was ragged and torn, the dirt of their journey so ingrained that it would never be removed. The beautiful leaf brooch she wore looked out of place on a cloak so worn. Checking the price, she counted out the coins in her purse, they fell short of the coin the seller was asking and Lana wasn't keen on spending all she'd saved. So, spurred by the bartering of Tinnion she thought she would try to haggle herself.

"I can give you five country bronze for it." She placed the coins on the counter.

"I'm afraid the lowest I could go is twice that." The shopkeeper was rather dismissive at the sum and it knocked Lana's confidence.

"I... I can give you one more but not any more than that. I've already got a cloak, see?" Lana placed her last coin on the counter and pulled her cloak around her to push home her point.

The seller laughed "That old rag is set to fall apart, I wouldn't warm my dog with it."

Lana pouted and lowered her head, she reached out to pick up her coins and then stopped. She put her fingers into her purse and slowly drew out a green stone she had found on the islands.

"What about if I paid with this?" She opened her hand and showed the stone. The shopkeep moved to take it but Selene's hand darted forward clasping over Lana's.

"Pick up your coins, Lana. There is somewhere else we should go before you spend your money." The shopkeeper's face dropped as she realised she had missed her chance.

Selene asked to look at the stone when they were back on the street. The sylph examined the stone for a few minutes, turning it and holding it up to the light.

"It's pretty, isn't it? I saw it when I was on the island and kept it. I like the way the light changes the colour in the middle. I'd be sad to let it go but it's only a stone and that cloak looked so warm. I have a blue and a red one too, so I wouldn't miss out too much on the prettiness."

"It is very pretty Lana, but that is not all that it is. If you're intent on selling it to pay your way we should take it to an appraiser. I know a trustworthy one in the central district not far from the library."

On the trio's return to the inn they found Brighid and Laywyn already sat in the dining hall halfway through a jug of ale. Laywyn had a bruise up his left arm but it didn't seem to be bothering him too much, Lana noticed how quickly he removed his hand from Brighid's knee as they walked through the door anyway.

"The three of you look as tired as I feel." Laywyn quipped to hide his hasty movement.

"Well these two dragged me all over the city, I'm sure we visited the same book shop a half dozen times and Tinnion was as bad looking at arrows of all things! I mean I spent half the day looking at them and I still wouldn't know why one is better for killing a rabbit than another."

"Oh, shush now, sit down and get a drink. It was you that had us marching to the central district." Tinnion prodded Lana playfully with the butt of her quiver as she spoke.

"Oh, very fancy! What was it ye were all doing up in the posh part o' town? Wis Selene showing' off her new room?"

"No. Our young friend here seems to have been carrying around a purse full of gems this whole time. We went to have them appraised."

"A purse full of gems, is it? So, whit was the result?"

"They didn't have an answer for us straight away, they've

given a receipt and Lana's due to return next week. They'll tell her then. The old man had a smile on his face as he first looked at them though. That gave hope."

22. TRIALS

Sir Reynard had done this before, he had seen warriors come and go and had pushed them until they broke. The trials always started with thirteen warriors, by the end there would be one. They came from all over Mortara—human and fae, male and female, their background didn't matter.

For the first four weeks the warriors would be put through set trials. Kept secret so that no warrior could prepare, the trials would test their physical, mental and emotional strength. When the four-week trial was over the remaining warriors would compete in a tournament. The trials would be private, known only to Sir Reynard and the warriors being tested. The tournament would be held in the city arena in front of crowds with the public cheering or booing their favourite warrior. The last fighter on their feet would be named champion of Mortara.

Sir Reynard showed each of the warriors through into the courtyard and then, without saying a word, left and lowered the heavy iron gates sealing them in. He climbed the stairs to the viewing gallery, sat on the ornate chair there and watched in silence.

In the centre of the yard was the freshly killed carcass of a cow and a pile of wood. Nothing else was provided and there were no instructions as to what the trial was. Brighid looked around at her competition, two sylphs, a female carrying a Bo staff and a male, who like Brighid, carried two blades. Two noam stood against the wall furthest from her, watching the rest and talking with each other. They were large men, similar in appearance, each carrying a battle axe that looked to weigh as much as Brighid did. The rest were human, five males and three females, each carried a different weapon, blades, spears and axes. A larger man carried a war hammer.

Brighid smiled as the others started to circle one another, hands on their weapon hilts and wary looks in their eyes. One of the giant noam coughed and dropped his war axe to the stone under his feet. The clatter startled a spear holding man, and he spun, hurling his weapon at the source of the noise. The second noam, seeing his fellow fae attacked started forward, axe raised. Though not quick the sight of his power and fearsome look overwhelmed the spearman, freezing him in place. The axe came down with terrifying force, aimed directly at his skull. Brighid's blade intercepted the blow directing it to one side. The spearman lost his ear to the attack but kept his head.

"Put yer weapons aside!" Brighid raised her voice. Everyone stopped. "Do ye really think the man would be bringing us here to watch us slaughter each other on day one? There's a four-week trial wi a tournament tae come, if you lot 'ave gone and lobbed each other's heads off by the end of the day there'd be little point o' that!"

The weapons that had been half drawn were put away those that had no home were put down.

"The tuath is right. We are here to show our abilities. Not to fill graves." The female sylph laid her staff against the yard wall and walked toward Brighid. "I am Wren, from the Breeze-hills."

"Brighid MacFaern frae Lochmead." Brighid offered her hand and the sylph took it without hesitation. "It's good tae meet ye, Wren."

"Now, is anyone feeling hungry?"

The second day started in the same way as the first. The trialists were locked in the courtyard, though in place of the cow and the firewood there were thirteen chains each attached to a plate set firm in the ground. On each end not attached was an open cuff.

"The last one free gets to go to their bed, the twelve in chains will paint the courtyard through the night." Sir Reynard outlined the point of the trial with a rare smile before making his way to his seat. By the time he sat down Wren had chained one of the noam by the ankle.

Brighid was finding the trial rather easy, a warrior renowned for her athleticism. She danced and dodged as the others tried to chain her. In a move that surprised her fellow competitors she dodged an attempt by the male sylph, Yorane, spinning out of his way and taking his chain as her own, her spin turned into a leap as she cartwheeled over a dark haired human woman by the name of Hauk. Her trailing hand clasped a cuff to the warrior's ankle as her forward arm touched the sand of the ground. From the cartwheel she turned to a roll stopping at Yorane's feet, reaching up she caught the astonished sylph with his own chain. She came to her feet just in time to avoid an attempt by Saevel, a human from Eastwood with a penchant for shouting war cries as he attacked. Chainless, she used his momentum to hurl him to the ground where Wren ended his chances.

Back on her feet and looking around, Brighid realised that only she and sylph remained, so she picked up the chain Saevel had dropped and readied herself for a dance. Sylphs are faster and lighter on their feet than humans, their ability to leap far outdoing any other race. It was no surprise that Wren would be the last one she faced, though it was a concern to her. Of them all Wren was the only one she thought could defeat her, she was also the one Brighid had grown closest to the previous day.

The dance lasted much longer than Brighid had imagined, the end perhaps the fairest though most surprising possible. After both had tried, and failed, to trap the other Wren approached Brighid slowly. She offered her hand as Brighid had the day before and looked down at the cuff of her chain with a smile. Nodding, Brighid took the sylphs hand and together they ended the trial.

Both were allowed to leave for the evening, the rest

stayed behind to paint.

On the last day of the trials first week the warriors were faced with a simple task. They must rate their competition giving reason behind each choice. Each trialist was given the chance to line up their opponents in order of their skill and each one in turn chose the same top six, though ordered differently the names were the same.

Wren, Yorane, Brighid and the noams, Ethrok and Matuk. When one of those five were asked to select the name that replaced theirs was Bernulf, a young man from the Southport city guard.

One warrior stood out as being placed bottom by each of the other trialists. Tarron's head was bandaged and bloody, he had earned the name 'Tarron One Ear' after the scuffle of the first day. His week had been marred by his nervous reaction, and he had managed nothing to reduce the memory of it. His failure to excel at any of the tasks earned him a weekend locked in a small cell, to be released when the others returned for their second week.

Batul, a young female warrior from Mountain View Meadows in the east of Mortara, raised a concern that the order appeared to be an unwarranted and harsh punishment. Sir Reynard explained that it was intended to be. The trials were designed to find a warrior that would excel in the most difficult of environments. If a weekend in a cell proved too much for a warrior that was struggling, they would be free to leave the trial. As would anyone who thought it too harsh.

The second week of the trials were entirely different. Each of the warriors was given a long rope and a large hook.

"Somewhere in the caves around the cliff faces of the island there is a chest. Within it are seven tokens. Retrieve a token and return here with it before the end of next week to secure your place in the tournament. Of those six who fail, three will secure their place by winning battles, the losers will leave."

"What if all the tokens are not returned?" It was Tarron that asked and the look he was given by the group spoke of disappointment at his word.

"Then the tournament will be over quicker."

"It seems like the pointy ears have the advantage with this. It's hardly a fair trial."

"An interesting way to announce your retirement, Tyik." Yorane scowled at the man.

Tyik lifted his hammer. "How bout I retire you now, fairy?

"

"Feel free to try." The sylph drew his blades and stood with them relaxed at his sides.

"Stop!" Sir Reynard interrupted. "If you're planning on staying to watch these two pummel each other, give them room."

The group spread out, forming a large circle around the two warriors and waited to see what would happen.

Tyik looked surprised by the decision to let them fight but that only lasted a second. He took his hammer in both hands and charged forward. Yorane stepped aside as the warrior drew close, letting him pass before turning and slapping his behind with the flat of a blade. Tyik spun, his hammer aimed at the sylph's head, finding nothing; the momentum of the heavy weapon staggered him and Yorane helped him to the floor with a kick of his foot. A laugh rang through the courtyard, a laugh that filled Tyik with rage. It was one thing losing a brawl, quite another being humiliated. He rolled and came to his feet. His face bright red he steadied himself and took a breath before rushing at Yorane, lowering his head and taking the sylph around the waist, tumbling to the ground. Then, rising to his knees he struck Yorane square on the jaw. Trapped under the larger warrior Yorane had no way to avoid the man's blows and his face was soon bloody. Tyik leant to one side to pick up his hammer from the floor and gave Yorane a little space. The sylph brought his knee up sharply sending Tyik tumbling from his position.

The sylph rolled away, coming to his feet far enough away to be out of reach. Left without his blades, blood dripping from his nose and mouth, he wiped his face and took a deep breath. Tyik had his hammer in hand again and stepped forward, swinging it toward his foe. Yorane ducked and punched the man hard in his gut. As he stood straight Tyik doubled over. Yorane took Tyik's blade from his belt and buried it into the flesh of his thigh.

As Tyik dropped to the floor Yorane struck his face with a kick, breaking his nose with a crack. Tyik lay on the ground, breathing with a whistle, but still. Yorane wiped himself down and strode over to his blades, he picked them up and retrieved his rope and hook before slowly walking toward the gate. The others followed him, leaving Tyik on his own in the dirt.

23. A GAME OF CHANCE?

Brighid was away on the second week of the trials, Tinnion was out of the city hunting again, Selene was well settled in at the library and Kaorella was working into the evening. Lana had just finished eating her dinner in the kitchen, she didn't want to pass the evening in the small room she had been given. It was nice to have a room to call her own, but it was small and dark and Lana liked to sit in the inns hall and observe the customers with a glass of cider.

Laywyn was at their usual table moping over Brighid's absence. He was due to start working in the morning, an old lord in the central district had employed him to train his son in defence. He was happy to be employed, happy that it would be easier on his leg than remaining in the army whilst allowing him to use his skills.

Lana sat with him and chatted while watching a game of dice in progress on the next table. Four men were sitting drinking heavily and gambling bronze coins over the game. A young girl, around the same age as Lana, stood watching on the far side of the table. Lana had seen her in the hall a few times before, but she never remembered serving her. The girl held a tankard and a roll of bread and cheered on a bearded man as he played.

"Why don't you join the game Laywyn? I think you could use a bit of fun and you might even win a few coins in the bargain."

"I don't know that I'm in the mood Lana, and that lot are halfway drunk already. I'd have a lot of catching up to do."

"I'm sure you'd manage. I've seen you in worse states than that!" Lana laughed and nudged her friend.

"Aye there is that, but I'm training the young lord in the morning. It wouldn't be good if I turned up with a bad head and the smell of ale on my clothes. Maybe I'll go for a walk instead. Get a bit of fresh air."

"Would you like me to come?"

"No, no. Stay and rest, you've to work in the morning too and it's been a long day. I'll be back before you head down to your room, I'm sure." Laywyn stood and pushed his chair under the table before heading out of the hall.

Lana got herself another cider and watched the dice game some more.

One of the men at the far end of the table was on a good winning streak and ordered more ale. His winnings were piling up beside him near the table's edge. With each win he drained his cup and was becoming drunker with each roll of the dice. As Lana sat, she noticed that, though he continued to win, the pile of coins beside him didn't seem to have grown for around half an hour. She thought some coins might have fallen off the edge of the table and was about to say something when she saw something strange. The girl that was watching put her tankard down on top of a couple of stray coins, when she picked it up again they were gone. She bent down, looking under the table and along the floor to see if the girl had knocked them off, but she saw no sign of them. As she sat back up she saw the girl was looking at her, so she smiled and wiggled back on the bench to get comfortable against the wall. The girl walked away.

Lana sat quietly with another jug of soft cider as the four men became drunker and the game wound down. The man at the far side didn't notice the missing coin, though Lana thought his attention was fully occupied on trying not to fall to the ground. When they were all gone, she checked under their chairs to see if she could see any money, there was nothing. Laywyn had not returned, so she headed down the stairs to the cellar and her room.

Laywyn found himself wandering through the narrow streets off the main road through the city. He was ashamed at leaving Lana all alone in the inn's hall but his mood was sour. He had hoped he would find more opportunities in Southport for him and earn more money in private employment. Brighid's absence was making things worse. He had hoped to speak with her about their futures before her trials began, but he never found himself alone with her without a sword in their hands.

A drunken man stumbled out of a door ahead of him, almost hitting the wall of the building opposite. The street was narrow and his staggering form blocked the walk, Laywyn tried to squeeze his way past him when the man spun suddenly bringing his great fist down on Laywyn's chin. Laywyn's legs buckled under the blow, he reached out and steadied himself against the wall but the bulk of his assailant was on top of him before he could ready himself. The man pulled a small wooden cudgel from his coat and laid about Laywyn, covering him in bruises and splitting his lip. The flesh above his eye swelled and split, his eyes clouded over, and he blacked out.

It was mid-morning when Laywyn staggered through the kitchen door of the inn, his face was swollen and bloodied, his clothes rags and his belt missing. His blades and his purse were stolen.

"What happened to you? I can't believe your student could be that rough?"

Laywyn simply grunted in reply

"Come on in and sit, we'll patch you up." Kaorella pulled a chair from the kitchen table and helped him into it.

When Lana arrived in the kitchen he was bandaged and cleaned up. His left eye was swollen shut and his lip was fat. The bruising to his face was dark and ugly and his nose crooked. She ran over to him and held his hand. He explained what had happened the evening before and Lana felt a flame of anger grow in her. He wasn't able to describe the man that had ambushed him, he wasn't even sure which street he had been walking along but Lana swore a silent oath that when the group were together again they would find him.

24. CAVES

The island on which Southport was built rose out of the ocean four hundred feet or so. Grey and imposing. A winding staircase was cut into the rock under the great bridge, a winding path down to the harbour that had given the city its name. The rest of the island was sheer cliff face, interrupted at times with caverns. It was said that pirates had used those caves closer to the waves and those nearer the top contained ancient monuments to the gods.

Yorane and Wren were the first to leave the city, Brighid and Bernulf close behind. The Noam came next, confident they would soon find the cave. Tarron gathered the others as they left the city and spoke to them to them quietly.

As they left the city Brighid, Bernulf and the sylph all headed to the south. When the others were out of earshot Brighid called to the sylph who stopped and waited for her to catch them up. The tuath smiled as they gathered.

"'There're seven tokens,' she said. There's nae need for us four tae be in competition, if we're together we've more chance of getting what we need and bein' back first."

"What are you thinking, Brighid?" Wren looked intrigued.

"We take advantage of oor strengths. The two of you are a lot lighter than either of us, you're better wi' heights and in being off the ground than us too. We're stronger and have more stamina than you. We can split intae couples. Bernulf and Yorane, Wren and I. We'll work close, but far enough apart tae ensure we're no' going over the same ground. Bernulf and I will anchor the ropes and the two of you check out the fissures and caverns on the face."

The sylph exchanged looks before Wren spoke. "That seems like a good idea, whichever of us finds the right place can call on the others. I agree to work with you Brighid, you've shown yourself to have honour. What about the two of you?"

"I agree. We have a better chance together. What say you, Bernulf?" Yorane was in.

"Aye, seems good to me. Where'll we start?"

The plan was working well. Wren was so light Brighid hardly felt any strain on the rope as she held it. They worked out a series of cues in order for Brighid to know what was happening below and soon grew into a rhythm of working. Bernulf and Yorane worked twenty feet away and seemed, from where Brighid stood, to be doing quite well. Once a section was explored the four would gather and discuss what was found.

Four days passed and the sylph had crawled through so many caverns and fissures they had lost count but nothing of importance had been found. A few coins in the lower caverns, a find that hinted at the tales of pirates being true, but nothing more than a spur for the imagination. The evening was drawing in and Brighid was pulling Wren up for the final time of the day when she felt two tugs on the rope. Their signal for her to hold.

It had been some time and the sun was set when she felt the tug to bring Wren back up the cliff, and she hauled quickly but with care. By the time the sylph was back at the top the men came over, and they sat down to eat. As they settled in for the night Wren spoke.

"I found something down there, though I can't say it's what we're looking for, not for sure. There's a fissure in the face I almost missed. I squeezed my way through and found myself in a cavern. I couldn't see very well, it was too dark, and I didn't notice anything in there at first. Then I felt air coming from the back, there was a passage, low and narrow, but big enough for someone to crawl down. I think we should check it out in the morning."

The four warriors stood together in the cavern, they were

scraped and bruised from their crawl along through the passage but content they had found something of significance. Whether it would turn out to be the chest of tokens they hoped for they weren't sure. But something important was here.

Ahead of them was a wall, easily eight feet in height, built up from stone that had been shaped into blocks. To the extreme left and right there were arches each leading deeper into the chamber through a labyrinth of walkways. They decided to split up with Brighid and Wren going left. They'd use the ropes to keep track of their paths.

As they entered the labyrinth Bernulf fell, he staggered back to his feet and a loud crack was heard. A plumb of smoke and dust blew from the crawlway they had entered through as the ceiling above it collapsed, blocking their exit.

"We'd better hope there's another way out now. I dinnae reckon we'll be goin' that way again."

Some walls in the labyrinth were made of cut stone, some of wooden planks, rotting and crumbling, others were carved from the cavern rock itself. All of them towered above its occupants, leading them deeper into its heart, their torches threw flickering shadows around them.

When the first rope came to an end, Brighid tied the second to it and the women walked on. They managed three more steps before the floor fell away, stone crumbling beneath their feet. Wren almost fell with it. When the sylph was back on solid ground, Brighid brought her torch lower to examine the path, there were holes along the corridor, some large, some small. Each of them revealed a drop through to a cavern below, a drop that would badly injure a person, if they survived at all.

"Well this ain't goin' tae be easy. What do you reckon?"

"The ground is solid enough here. If you anchor the rope with your hook I can run over with the end, once I find solid ground again I'll anchor it with my hook and, well, You seem to have good balance. You'll manage." The sylph smirked.

25. SHOPPING

Laywyn's body ached from head to toe, he was stiff and grumpy. He had lost his job and there was no news of Brighid. Lana had tried to keep his spirits up when she wasn't working. Tinnion was still out in the forest, she was making a lot of money with her hunting. He rarely saw Kaorella now, her work keeping her in the kitchens from dawn til dusk more often than not. Selene had stopped by the previous night and arranged to meet Lana today, they were going into the central district to get the appraiser's opinion of Lana's gems.

Laywyn struggled from his bed and dressed, after what had happened to him he didn't want the young women to be wandering the streets of the city alone with a purse full of coins.

He picked up his training sword, it was blunt iron but the hilt looked real enough and would be enough to put off chancers. Anyone serious enough would need him to fight and though there was no edge to the blade it could break a bone if swung with enough force. The swelling of his face had gone down enough that he could see again, and he felt a desire to show he was still a man of courage and ability after his beating. He took himself down stairs and sat at a table with Lana.

"Let me get you some breakfast, Laywyn. What would you like?"

"You should save your money, Lana. You've paid my way all week and nursed me too. You'll run out of coins fast and I'll owe you more than I'll ever afford if we keep this up."

"Don't be silly! What's the point of having money if you can't help your friends a bit? Besides, I don't have to pay for my own room no more and I'm able to get a bit to eat from Kaorella when I need."

"Well, thank you, Lana. I really will find a way to pay you back."

They ordered breakfast and ate together as they waited for Selene.

The appraiser bought the green stone from Lana, a big smile on his face. As they left the shop she asked Selene if she might have enough to get her cloak and help Laywyn buy a new sword and clothes.

"How much did he give you Lana?"

"He gave me two gold coins. How much is a sword?"

Laywyn's mouth fell open in shock.

"Two country gold? That makes you the richest person I personally know, Lana. You've got more than enough to buy a full wardrobe of clothes and blades as good as Brighid's!"

"Oh, no, not country gold he said it was day tea gold or something."

This time it was Selene's face that showed shock.

"Wait, Lana. Was it Deity Gold he said?"

"Yes! That's it. I imagine it's not as good as the other, but will it be enough to help?"

"Lana. Deity gold is named for the gods, it is the purest coin and the most valuable. Two pieces will be more than enough to buy a new wardrobe of clothes and arms for us all. It will see you comfortably through your time here in Southport and get you through most of your life at home too. "

"But it was only a stone Selene, how could it be worth so much?"

"Beautiful objects have value, Lana. Here in the city beautiful stones are prized for the coin they bring as much as for the joy."

"Can we go to the shops then? We can get Laywyn his sword and my cloak and... Well if I've that much we can buy you a book too Selene!"

Their first stop was to buy Laywyn a new sword, he tried

a few out before settling on one that suited him best. A long sword with a brass pommel and a leather strapped hilt. The blade itself was plain steel and it wasn't the most expensive blade in the shop but having it by his side brought a smile to Laywyn's face, and he stood tall again. The next stop along the road took them to the seller that Lana had tried to haggle with, she bought herself the cloak and Laywyn some basic clothing to replace his tattered garb. In the corner of the shop was a mirror, Lana stood in front of it and pulled the cloak round her. She fastened it with her leaf brooch and admired her new look.

"You look like a lady, Lana. With your dress, your cloak and your brooch."

"I feel like one Selene! It's ever so pretty and warm."

Once Laywyn was changed and his old ragged clothes in a sack with Lana's old cloak they made their way down to the manuscript shop, a place that Lana knew Selene could spend the whole day exploring.

After watching their friend thumb her way through a display case full of books Lana and Laywyn stepped outside to get some air. Across the Main Street and at the mouth of a narrow alley a large man was arguing with a girl half his size. The large man held the girl firmly by the arm, his red face close to hers, close enough that his natty beard and the flame from his rage touched her face as he shouted at her. They looked like father and daughter and their argument was the kind you only see between relatives. Heated and full of claims of betrayal. The man was shaking the girl, and she started to scream back at him demanding he let her go. He raised his hand to strike her but the girl struck first, she slammed down her foot against his ankle and punched at the arm holding her. His grip loosened for a moment, and she ran, heading down the alley like a rabbit down its burrow.

The man straightened, revealing his true height and looked around. In a moment Laywyn stepped forward and shouted. "Hey! Hold there!" He started to run toward the large man but his warning had sent the man fleeing, down the same alley. By the time Laywyn got there the large man was gone. Lana had run after him, and they met again halfway into the street.

"That was him, the bastard that jumped me. I wish I'd seen it sooner I'd have gotten there before the girl fled."

"It's funny you say that, I think I know her. She was in the hall the night you went out. I've seen her a few times over the weeks we've been here, hanging around, watching dice and card games. I'm sure she'll be round again."

"If she does, point her out. I'd like to have a word with her myself."

26. PIT FALL

T here were a number of hunters in the forest outside the city, each one had an area allocated to them. Should they wander away from their own territory they would be run out of the forest by the others. It had taken Tinnion a couple of weeks, but she had finally managed to secure an area to hunt in. She had had to show her skill and prove her worth working with others before they would allow her to set out on her own. Now that she was alone she was determined to make the most of it.

There were deer, foxes and birds that could bring her some money in the city for their skins or meat and plenty of rabbits and smaller animals for her to eat. There was nothing dangerous in this part of the forest, though on occasion a lost boar might wander through, they never stayed.

Tinnion had set up a shelter and built a fire pit, her tradable goods were starting to build up, and she knew she would need to head back into the city for the weekend. She would sell her goods and visit her friends before coming back out and hunting more. Brighid had kept their room on in the inn, and they were splitting the cost so there would always be a place for them to go in these early days.

She was stalking a deer as it walked off the trail, looking for leaves to eat. Close now, it was only a matter of setting herself into a position to loose an arrow or two when the deer suddenly stumbled and fell. Thinking another hunter had wandered into her area she stood and called out. There was no reply. She waited a moment and called again, when no response came she moved with caution to where the deer had fallen. As she walked through the long grass and undergrowth she was surprised to see the deer gone. On further inspection she saw there was a hole on the path the deer had been taking, well hidden by the undergrowth. She knelt at the edge and flattened the grass out to find its borders. The deer lay still four feet below having broken its neck in the fall. This wasn't a natural hole but it didn't resemble a hunter's trap either. Tinnion marked the ground and started back to her camp to get rope. She would lower herself, tie off the deer and haul it back out with her.

As she dropped to the ground she saw beyond the body of the deer, just below where she had knelt earlier there were wooden beams rising a foot from the floor. They looked like the frame of a door or heavy window, buried in dirt from an apparent cave in. She scraped away at the soil, exposing more wood, it certainly went deeper than the eye could see. Kneeling, she saw that a room opened up beyond the frame and curiosity caught her. Though she could have easily scrambled through the hole now she would prefer to seek help. Maybe Laywyn would come if he hadn't yet found work? They could dig it out together and see what lay beyond.

She tied the legs of the deer and, using the rope, scrambled back up and out of the pit.

The hall of the inn was busy, smoke and the smell of stale ale filled the air. Tinnion wandered over to the table where Lana, Laywyn and Selene sat; happy to see her friends. She ordered up food and a jug of ale before nodding at Laywyn.

"Too much ale and a kiss of the flagstones?"

"Something like that. Yes. How's the hunting?"

"It's going well, I made myself a pretty penny there this week. Enough to share a jug or two with friends anyhow."

"Very kind, I'm starting to feel like a kept man these days. I'll be gaining a stomach and growing soft before long."

"No luck finding an employer then?"

"I was lucky enough to find one, but not so lucky as to keep him."

Tinnion laughed. "Any news of Brighid?"

"We've heard nothing at all this week, not of any of them. To be honest I'm starting to worry a bit. I was thinking about heading over to the arena tomorrow."

"He's been brooding all week, Tinnion. He says he's worried about growing softer but if he did he'd be blubbering at the mention of her name." Lana giggled as she teased her friend.

"Well, I have to confess I'm quite pleased you're at a loose end Laywyn, I was hoping for some help in the woods."

"Oh! Could I come too?" Lana interrupted, excited at the thought of exploring the forest.

"Don't you have work?" Tinnion looked concerned. "Or were you so careless you lost your employer too?"

"Oh, no. Her Ladyship quit her post, took her room back and lives the best life." Laywyn mimicked the accent of the poshest Southport residents.

"It appears I've missed a fair bit this week then."

The friends told each other their stories, Lana filling Tinnion in on her good luck with the gem and Laywyn's bad luck in the alley. Tinnion described what she had found. They drank and ate and talked late into the evening, their happiness filling the hall.

They rose late the next morning and took breakfast quite slow before taking a walk to the arena to see if there was news. Laywyn spoke to a guard there and learnt the trial was in progress and none had yet returned. A promise was made to pass a message along when Brighid and the others came back. So, the friends took the Main Street to the shopping district where they bought spades, buckets, picks and more rope. Then they left the city and made their way out to the forest.

The afternoon was drawing on by the time they arrived in Tinnion's camp. So they set up more shelter and started the fire. There was rabbit to eat and Lana had brought bread from the city and a flagon of wine. They didn't stay up too late that night as they were excited to see what Tinnion had found and wanted to make an early start.

Tinnion dug out the dirt around the frame, Lana packed the buckets and Laywyn hauled them up on the rope, emptied them and let them down again while keeping watch for other hunters that might stray from their patch. They had created a few steps down to the base of the frame by the time the sun was on the horizon. It had been a door, there was no doubt, and the earth that had fallen in was soon cleared, but the space beyond was dark, and they thought it better to return in the morning. Laywyn helped them climb from the pit, and they headed back to the camp for the night.

27. A CASKET

Wren found the solid ground after lightly skipping her way across some twelve feet of crumbling stone. She anchored the rope with her hook at waist height and called on Brighid. Taking each step slowly, clinging on to the rope and testing each footfall before laying down her weight, it took Brighid what seemed like an age to cross. She let out a sigh of relief as she reached the safety of the solid ground. Muscles she didn't realise she had strained soon relaxed and she reached out to the wall, leaning against it as she caught her breath.

"Ah've tae be honest, Wren. I'm no a big fan o' heights."

The sylph warrior laughed. "I can see that, Brighid. Hopefully this will be the last time you need to face them in this trial."

They continued their strategy of taking the left path at each junction, hoping that by following that rule would make the centre and the exit easier to find. There were places where a gap had formed between ceiling and wall and in those instances Wren, with Brighid's aid, climbed the wall to see what could be seen.

It was on one of those climbs that she saw the stone. Six feet in height with the likeness of a crow carved into its face, at its base lay a chest, a lock in its clasp.

"There's a chest here, Brighid." She dropped to the ground as she spoke. "There's not enough room to squeeze through the gap, I'll take the rope and run on ahead, if I can find the entrance I'll call on you to follow, if not I'll make my way back, and we'll try to break through."

"Aye, that seems a good plan. I'll see if I can make a dint in this stone while yer gone."

They removed the hook from the rope and Wren took off at a run into the maze. Brighid started scraping the wall between two stones with the point of the iron hook. It'd take time, but she was sure she could free up the stone and break through if it came to it.

Tinnion built a small fire at the bottom of the pit and lit three torches from its flames. Laywyn volunteered to go into the darkness first, Tinnion followed, mumbling something about gallantry and being safe without men. Lana brought up the rear but stayed close, ensuring she stayed within the circle of light cast by her friends' torches.

They were in, what appeared to be, an entrance hall. It wasn't very large and at the far side was a heavy iron and wood door, partly rotted, partly rusted, but still recognisable and still hung in its frame. They pushed the door open and entered a hall. Ancient sconces hung on the wall, some contained the dried shafts of torches so Tinnion wrapped them with cloth and set them alight.

Shadows danced across the floor as the flames flickered. The light oozed into the room, exorcizing a thousand years of darkness. In the centre of the back wall there stood an altar and behind it a statue of the goddess Qura and Zeor god of the skies. Deities of the sylph. On the altar a casket, the lid strapped with brass, the lock tightly sealed.

Lana's body began to vibrate, sweat broke out on her brow, her eyes rolled back in her head. The vibrations became stronger, shaking her. She collapsed to the floor convulsing, struggling for breath. Then it stopped. She lay still, breathing peacefully, eyes closed.

The hall was lit with a thousand candles and torches. Silks hung from the walls, their bright colours contrasting the dark grey walls. Cushioned benches formed a circle in front of the altar and a carpet of flowers covered the floor.

"Our sister sends a message. We are to meet in Mortara's heart." Zeor was dressed in blue robes, his face framed by his cropped white hair and beard. No lines of age nor blemishes marked his deep ochre skin. His voice and manner were calm but Qura could see the concern in his eyes.

"Is the end upon us already, brother?" The goddess was the twin of her brother, her curled white hair like clouds resting upon her shoulder.

"It seems so, dear Qura. The humans are using our children's weaknesses to win this war. It is their time, but our sister Ophine has a plan."

"Then we should prepare, Zeor. I shall leave a gift for our children to come. A treasure to guide them through the darkest of times."

Lana rose from the floor and walked to the altar, her head high and still, her eyes open but unseeing. Her jaw dropped, lips apart, her arms loose at her sides. A marionette, moving without thought or life.

"Lana. Are you okay?" Tinnion's voice was soft and shaking. She got no response. "Lana!" She shouted. Lana walked on without a glance.

Reaching the altar, Lana laid her hand upon the cask and spoke.

"Thoir tiodhlac ghorm, Deòir màthar ghlan, m'ulaidh gu bràth."

Thunder clapped, filling the hall with its powerful sound. The air pulsed, the walls shook. Tinnion and Laywyn dropped to their knees, covering their ears with their hands, their cries of pain unheard in the sudden storm.

Lana stood, unmoved and untouched by the force that had struck down her friends.

She opened the casket, the lock now in two, and took out a circlet, placing it on her head. The milky blue stone at her brow shone, like a full moon on a clear summer night.

And then, like the marionette with strings cut, she fell once more to the floor.

Brighid pulled the heavy stone from its place in the wall, there had been no word from Wren as yet but the rope was moving to and fro. With one stone now removed it would be easier to work on the rest, she would only need to remove two more to enable her, and Wren, to squeeze through. So she continued to scrape and chip away.

It was as she removed the third stone that Wren re-appeared. She had found a way through the labyrinth just in time to help Brighid climb through the hole. A moment of laughter at the timing passed before they examined the chest.

"Well, we don't have a key so do we break through the lock or the lid?" Wren ran her fingers over the curved top of the chest as she asked her question.

"The lock is steel, new and firm. Ah reckon the lid'd be reinforced too though. Let's see what damage one o' the stones does."

Brighid walked back to the hole she created and picked up one of the stones she had dropped. Carrying it to the chest she raised it above her head and threw it down on the lid. There was a loud crack as the stone hit the wood, then it fell to the floor. She had managed to make a hole in the chest, but a small one.

"A few more like that aught tae do it. Go grab yersel' a rock and get throwin'."

It didn't take them long to break through the lid and retrieve their tokens. Gold coins with the same crow motif as the stone. Taking two more they squeezed through the hole and followed their rope back to the labyrinths start. Once there, they were able to track Yorane and Bernulf and hand them their tokens.

"So, all that remains now is to clear out that passage before we starve to death, and we've won, right?" Bernulf had a wide smile on his face but his lacklustre voice gave away his despair.

"I have another idea, though it might not work out." Wren grinned. "As we passed through the labyrinth we came across a patch of ground that had collapsed into a cavern below. It was a long fall but if we join the ropes we should make it. There's a good chance the cavern joins an opening I saw in the cliff face."

"That seems more plausible than clearing the passage, where is this?"

There was nothing below Brighid but twenty feet of dangling rope and the jagged cavern floor. They had tied knots along the length of the rope to make the descent a bit easier, but they didn't give her comfort. Her body shook and her mind was filled with slipping. With each move her hands became slicker, and her grip became harder to compensate. Her palms blistered as she slowly lowered herself but the closer she got to the floor the tighter she held to the rope.

There was a short drop at the bottom and when her feet touched the floor she dropped to her knees. Shuffling to one side she lay down to catch her breath and calm her shaking nerves.

Bernulf came down the rope next. The young Southport warrior didn't suffer with the nerves that Brighid had and came down the rope at speed. He wasn't so far from the ground when his hand slipped, and he fell. His leg caught in the rope, and he swung back and forth. The rope, snaked around his calf, he began to slide, and he panicked. He strained his stomach to lift himself up and grab the rope again before it let him go, but with each stretch he swung more and the rope evaded his grip. He dropped further; the rope loose. He was only able to grab the rope again when his head was two foot from the floor. The young warrior flipped, his arms strained and his back struck the floor with a crack.

28. CATCH UP

Lana woke in her bed at the inn, her head felt heavy, her memory was hazy. She remembered entering the hall and watching Tinnion light the torches, but at that point things became shrouded in mist.

"Welcome back to the world, Lana. How do you feel?"

Lana looked over at Tinnion and felt a weight lift from her chest. "I think I'm okay. What happened?"

"You... Well, you went a little strange on us. You said something strange and the world went to hell. Then you opened the casket on the altar and took out that circlet you're wearing. None of us have managed to take that thing off you, whenever anyone touches it there's a spark, and we're sent across the room with an arm we can't move."

"But you're not hurt? You and Laywyn? You didn't get burned or break anything did you?"

"I feel like I have the 'morning after head' of a three-week party. Other than that, I'm fine. Laywyn is about the same, he's down stairs drinking his way to a genuine hangover."

"Wren, Yorane, Brighid, Ethrok, Matuk and Batul. You six returned with tokens. You will go forward to the tournament. Tyik, Onas, Saevel, Tarron, Hauk and Tola. You six failed this task and will compete to see who will stay." There were solemn nods as the names were announced, Sir Reynard was as serious as they had ever seen him.

"I am afraid that I have received bad news. Bernulf will be unable to continue, the injury he sustained in his fall was serious."

"Can they heal him?" Brighid had insisted that Bernulf be treated by their best medic on their return. She was concerned he would pass away during the night, the sound made as he hit the floor had haunted her dreams.

"He'll survive, but he has lost the use of his legs." Brighid bowed her head at the news, hiding the pain on her face.

"What does that mean for the tournament?" Tyik's tone annoyed Brighid, there was no grief in his voice, no concern for his fellow competitor.

"You will compete in duels. The three losers will then compete in a melee, the last one standing will join the winners in the tournament."

"What weapons will we be given?"

"You won't be given practice weapons, you'll be using your own. This is where it gets real for you."

Lana found that taking the circlet off left a feeling of absence in her mind, that she was the only one able to touch it made her wonder what it meant to her life. Strange things had happened to her since she entered the Heartwood, things she wanted to understand, things she felt she never would.

She looked around the table at her friends. It was the first they had all been together since their arrival in the city, and she was happy to have them all there. They spent the evening sharing jugs of wine and ale, platters of food and stories from the last two weeks of their lives. A lot had happened since their arrival in Southport and Lana found their tales interesting.

She felt a sense of pride as Selene told them of her growing status at the Great Library. The Lore Master himself had requested her to assist him in translating the text of the document she had found and many at the library held the opinion that he would soon make her his aide. A sign of respect and trust that would give her authority beyond her current role.

Brighid told them all of her adventures in the trials and the friends she was making as they progressed. They were saddened to hear that the mini tournament to secure the final places at the public event were held in private with only Sir Reynard and those competing present. Brighid was as excited as everyone else there to see who would be joining her at the grand tournament the following week. Lana linked her arm with Brighid's and cuddled into her to give comfort as she told of the escape from the labyrinth and the terrible price paid.

It was the evening before the Tay's court so it was no surprise when Lana announced that she felt the need to retire, as sad as that made her. She gave a kiss to each of her friends and trudged her way up to her room. Brighid had already informed the administrator that she would be sponsoring her cause, and she spent the day putting together a statement that would explain her plight quickly but with the gravity she felt it needed.

29. THE TAY

The finery on show at the Tay's court made Lana feel lowly. The dress she had thought so fine and been so proud to wear since Freybridge looked like an unshapely sack in comparison to the vibrant colours and tailored cuts of the clothing worn by the lords and ladies there. She sat next to Brighid on a velvet cushioned seat at the edge of the hall and watched as lords argued over gambling debts and trees that hung over into the boundaries of their neighbours' land. The women of the court addressed the needs of their children to marry and the difficulties in finding the finest silks to make their dresses. She thought these people lived in a world that was separate from the world in which she lived. They seemed to share the space but their experiences and priorities were so different that Lana could not understand the importance being placed on them.

In time Brighid was called upon to stand, she introduced Lana who was asked to present her story to the court. There were gasps and open mouths as Lana recounted the events of Samhain and the grisly revenge Aeloth had taken on Ara and her family for speaking against him. When she told of his attack on her the Tay questioned her further.

"These events are deeply troubling, Lana Ni Hayal. They speak of behaviour unbecoming of a Gesith's son, a man who represents our queen in his hold. But I am forced to ask, what evidence can you provide that I can take your word and find fault with a man unable to defend himself."

"My Lord I... He... " Lana struggled to speak, tears welled in her eyes, and she felt the burning heat of shame in her face. Her stomach convulsed as the memories of that day were brought back to her mind. The sharp pain as his blade cut her skin. She reached up to her shoulder, feeling the ghost of his knife in her flesh. "My Lord, he marked me with his initials."

The gasps around the room were audible. There was muttering behind hands and words passed between lords and ladies not intended to be heard by her.

"He branded you?"

"Not a brand my Lord, he used a knife."

"Lord Tay. Are we to believe the son of a queen's Gesith carved his name into this cottar like some barbarian? I simply cannot accept that the word of milking wench could carry such weight in this court."

Brighid spun to face the man that had spoken, an older lord whose comfortable lifestyle showed on his waist and his ruddy red nose.

"Will ye be questioning MY honour sir? I stand by the words of my companion and it is ME that will face any challenge." The old lord fell back in his seat, muttering meaningless words to himself.

"Is this mark you speak of in a place that may be shown within the realms of decency Lana?"

"It is on my shoulder, my Lord."

"Then come forward and show me."

Lana approached the Tay's chair and pulled aside the shoulder of her dress to reveal the scar. The Tay looked to a lady at his side who stood and examined the cuts more closely, touching the scar lightly and pressing the surrounding skin.

"It is true my husband, the cut was deep and will never truly heal. This poor child has suffered greatly." The Tay's wife pulled Lana's dress back into place and then took a silk from her sleeve and wiped the tears from Lana's cheek. "I believe the child, Gathwyn, no one would ever go so far to lay a false claim."

Tay Gathwyn nodded to his wife, a solemn look upon his face.

I am truly sorry for what has been done to you, Lana.

Though I don't know what I can do against the queen's man in his hold. I would need to consider this further."

"My lord. I beg you to help my family. They did what they did to keep me from death, they don't deserve to be locked away."

"Come back to me in three days, Lana. I will take some time to think. I know that you must want quick action and I will do what I can."

"Thank you, my lord."

Lana was standing outside the inn's main door taking in the smokeless air. The act of smoking a pipe seemed strange to Lana, none of her family had ever done it and of her friends only Laywyn indulged himself on occasion. While she admitted the smell of the tobacco was sometimes sweet the smoke it produced was anything but pleasant, the thought of deliberately breathing it in was odd to her. As she stood, contemplating the smaller things in life she noticed a figure on the corner opposite. It was the girl she had been watching the dice game, the one that argued with Laywyn's attacker.

She sauntered across the road, moving casually so as not to alert the girl, and dallied outside the shop on the corner. It was a trinket shop, selling brooches, lockets, and other intricate works of metal.

"Oh, this is beautiful." Lana spoke out loud to no one in particular, then turned to the girl. "What do you think of it? Do you think a piece like this would suit me?" She pointed to a golden locket with a deep green stone at its centre. The girl came over, curious.

"A dunno really, I mean it's nice an all but it's a bit fine aint it? For a scullery maid I mean."

"Oh, I'm not really a maid, I was just helping out a friend is all. My name's Lana... I saw you a few times over there. You must enjoy the cider!"

"Yeah it's all right. So, what is it you do now then? If you don't mind me askin'."

"I... well, I don't really do anything. I'm here to petition the Tay for his help with a problem back home. I just help out my friends from time to time as I wait."

"What kinda problems you got then? Havin' to marry the wrong fella or somethin'?"

Lana lowered her voice so that only the girl could hear. "No, the Gesith's son, he... well he beat me and cut me."

"Bastard! They're all alike, these toffs and their sons. Take whatever they want, no mind for us what's got to live with it after." Lana nodded silently.

"I saw you arguing the other day with a man. Was he...? Does he hurt you?"

"What? Oh! Right, yeah, that. He would I s'pose if 'e could catch me. But nah, he... well he runs a house, see, and there's a few of us live there. He tells us what to do and gives us hassle if we don't do it, or, if we do anything else 'e don't like."

"Do you not want to leave then? Go live somewhere else?"

"Heh A would all right, if I could. It's not so easy though, is it? When ye've got nothin' and yer owin' whatever you get to him."

"Is that why you took the money?"

"What money? What're you saying'?"

"I'm sorry, I don't mean it badly, I understand if it is... I saw you the last time you were at the inn. Watching the dice game. I don't know how you did it, but I know you were taking that man's winnings. A few coins here and there. He was too drunk to notice, and I don't suppose he even realised once he sobered up. I won't say anything."

"Yeah you'd best not be either!"

"Really, I won't. I just wonder if you did it 'cos he makes you?"

"I ain't got no other way of getting money, or food, we ain't all got friends what can help us. I've been doin' it too long now. No one'd give me work, even if I begged, it's 'ard enough finding places I can go without bein' recognised. I guess the inns off the list now an' all."

"Well... Maybe I could help you? I could get you some food

at least."

"Why?"

"You shouldn't have to steal, not to eat, not for him. If he's making you do it then maybe we should stop him. "

"Yeah right, me and you, go stopping that one when the guards 'ave been tryin' fer years. He'd slit yer throat, and that'd be nice compared to what he'd do to me."

"Well, maybe not that then, but I could still get you some food. At least that way you wouldn't be so tied to him. Are you hungry now?"

"Yeah, I could eat. But if this some trick mind I'll skin ye."

The day was set to be a busy one. Lana would make her way to the Tay's palace again, this time Tinnion and Selene would accompany her. Brighid and Laywyn had already made their way over to the arena, Brighid wanted to do some light practice before the tournament began in the afternoon. Once the Tay had seen them Lana, Tinnion and Selene would head over to the arena to give Brighid their support.

They were shown to the Tay's personal chambers at the side of the hall where he held court. There, he invited them to sit and offered them a drink. Once they settled and Lana introduced her friends Tay Gathwyn told them of his thoughts.

"I'm afraid I have Both bad news and good, Lana. I think it would be better if I started with the good, do you agree?"

"Yes, my Lord, if you believe it best."

"Very well. I wasn't sure how much I could help after we talked, but I understand your pain and I understand your concern for your family. So, in light of needing to look into the situation further, I decided I could, at least, do something small to help in the interim. I dispatched two of my personal guard with men and a letter to Gesith Heriloth. They have been instructed to see that your family is safe and to ensure they come to no further harm. I cannot order their release, as there will need to be a trail for that to occur. A trial I'm afraid you will need to be a part of."

Lana listened in silence, chewing on her cheek as she heard the news.

"That aside, it is clear to me now that the best way to handle this situation is to petition the queen. She will be coming here, to the city, for a celebration of the harvest. I will stand for you and make your case. The truth is, Lana. If I could, I would simply send a troop of sheriffs and remove Heriloth from his manor. He is someone I have always held serious doubts about, but he was popular with the old king and it is only the queen who can now order his dismissal."

The Tay took a drink and watched Lana carefully. She was quiet and calm and appeared to be waiting for more to be said.

"Lana, I can imagine your thoughts must be of returning to Butterholt and seeing your family. But I would advise against that. My sheriffs can make sure your family is not hurt any further but I could not protect you were you to return. It is best that you stay here in Southport, wait for the queen and stand with me as I present your cause to her. Then we can act to prevent Heriloth enacting any plans of revenge he might have."

"Thank you for sending your sheriffs, My Lord. That helps me at least to know my family will be safe now. I know you're right about staying here, but I really miss them." Tears rolled down Lana's cheeks as she spoke, she had held them back as long as she could but the damn was now broken and her emotions took hold. Tinnion and Selene both placed their hands on Lana's arms and comforted her as she cried.

"Forgive her, My Lord. It has been an emotional journey and a hard one for our friend."

"There is nothing to forgive, Selene. What Lana has experienced would bring tears to the most hardened soul. It makes her journey here that much more remarkable."

30. SUPPORT

The arena was full, every bench was crowded. Brighid had arranged a bench at the very front for her friends, a much sought after place to be during tournaments such as this. You could feel the excitement rise around the stadium as the time approached for the games to begin. A loud roar echoed through the district when the gates opened and the first warriors entered the arena.

Tyik, the giant, hammer wielding human limped into the centre of the sand filled battlegrounds. His leg was still bandaged, his nose spread across his face. He would start the day's events by fighting Saevel.

The first two days of the tournament would be fought using sparring weapons with blunt edges. Each warrior had the choice of fighting with swords, axes, or staffs. There were one handed or two handed versions of the edged weapons and shields available for those that wanted to use them. Tyik chose to fight with a two handed battle axe, Saevel picked up a hand axe and a round shield. He knew Tyik was stronger than him and that if the giant man landed a blow with the axe it would most likely end his fight there and then.

As the fight started Saevel focused on getting behind Tyik and striking at his injured thigh. Using his agility to outmanoeuvre the giant man. As he moved forward, Tyik raised his battle axe in preparation to meet his foe. He was within two feet of Tyik when he darted to one side, ready to round him and strike. Sadly, for Saevel, Tyik had already started to swing his long handled weapon. Saevel knew his side step had taken him just out of range, but he hadn't expected Tyik to let go. The battle axe spun and the end of the hand grip hit Saevel square on the jaw. He lost his balance and stumbled forward. Tyik launched himself at the smaller man and tackled him to the ground. They wrestled and rolled around the floor, landing punches and striking with their knees.

The crowd jeered as the warriors struggled to get the better of one another. Saevel was fighting in an attempt to make enough space for himself to get back on his feet and retrieve the weapon he had dropped. Tyik fought to keep him on the ground and pin him, his plan was to beat the smaller man into submission.

In the end it was Tyik's strength that won out and Saevel submitted, the following day's contest on his mind. He was bruised and his face was bloody, he had been shocked by Tyik's willingness to sacrifice his weapon, and he never recovered. He would learn from this.

Lana wasn't enjoying the display; she found the violence upsetting and the Tay's words were still echoing around her head. If Brighid hadn't been competing she would have left the stadium and returned to the inn, she wanted to spend some time alone in her room, some time to think about her choices.

She barely noticed as the other competitors fought. She was thinking about the first time she had been brave enough to approach a cow, as Tola beat Hauk into submission. Her father had held her hand as they got close and then stood behind her, ready to whisk her away if she became too scared, or they startled the cow. She imagined him holding her again now, giving her the strength to keep going, to survive without her family.

Wren was too quick for Ethrok, the noam, she dodged his blows and landed her own in a match that Lana completely missed. The crowd expected Yorane to defeat the second noam Matuk in the same way but the strength of the giant, red bearded noam proved to be the decider in a match Yorane lost.

The last fight of the day was Brighid against Batul. Brighid had told them all how Batul had entered the cavern beneath the labyrinth as Brighid and her friends were leaving. They told the

Searen warrior how to gain entry to the cavern above, and she had retrieved the fifth token.

Tinnion nudged Lana, bringing her out of her daydream and focussing her on the entrance of her friend.

The crowd were enjoying the day and went wild for the final match up. Brighid came out to the loudest roar of the day and enjoyed it. She was laughing as she worked the crowd, waving the twin sparring swords around as they cheered. Batul watched, unimpressed. The warriors shook hands and the adjudicator signalled the start of the contest.

Batul thrust forward instantly, looking to catch Brighid by surprise but the tuath warrior was quicker. She spun away from the attack, dropped low and swept Batul's feet from under her. The Searen fell to her back with a grunt and Brighid stepped away, giving her opponent room to recover.

Batul got back to her feet, struck her shield with her blade in recognition of Brighid's sporting behaviour and started circling to her right. Brighid nodded and smiled then moved forward cautiously like a cat on the hunt. Both warriors made testing strikes, watching the others' reactions, gauging their strengths and then Brighid struck. She lunged to the left with her right-side blade crossing her body, Batul moved her shield across to block the strike but it was a feint. Brighid was spinning, her left arm raised. She brought the blade down with the full force of her momentum and her strength, Batul recovered enough to catch the blow on the edge of her shield but it sent her backward and the top half of her shield splintered. Brighid didn't stop, she thrust with her right blade as Batul stumbled. The Searen managed to parry the attack but it drove her further off balance, and she found herself back in the sand. Again, Brighid moved away with a smile.

Batul got to her feet and started a run toward Brighid, her shield shedding wood as she went. Brighid crouched low, watching and waiting. As Batul grew closer she launched herself forward, matching the speed of her opponent the distance between them grew short. Batul raised her blade above her head and shouted a battle cry. Brighid leapt high into the air. Batul just managed to get her shield up in time but it did her no good. Brighid brought her right blade down on the shield and her left blade cut in from the side, striking Batul's arm. What was left of the shield fell, only one panel of wood and the leather straps remained. The force of the blow on Batul's blade arm made her drop her sword and the weight of Brighid forced her back once again. Brighid played with her prey, a flurry of blades tapping at arm, leg and torso, driving her back further and further.

When Batul fell for the third time her right arm went up, the three fingers of submission held high. The crowd took to their feet and chanted Brighid's name. She took a slow walk around the arena, smiling and waving her blade in the air. When Brighid reached the section in which her friends sat she bowed to them and then laughed a great laugh. Her blades fell to the ground, and she held her arms out, then she jumped, catching the top of the barrier and climbing over to give her friends the kind of hug a bear gives.

It was clear by the end of the second day's events that Brighid and Wren were the favourites to win the tournament. Neither had been defeated and both had won their match ups with style and ease.

Lana had passed most of the day's events in her own head again, reliving moments with her family rather than watching the fighting that was taking place below her. She did watch both Brighid and Wren fight though and was in awe of their abilities. Despite using different weapons they shared a certain style in their approach. Brighid seemed to always know what her opponent would do next and used that ability to dance around them. She never struck with great force except when she was aiming to strike their shield or defending blades. When she made a genuine attempt to strike the person she used quick, light movements. With a true blade they would cut and cause her opponent to bleed until they made a mistake and opened themselves up to a devastating strike.

Wren was similar in that she too danced around her opponents, her staff was a blur as she parried and struck. Unlike Brighid she didn't appear to have a sense of what her opponent would do, she relied on her speed and agility to stay out of danger. Lana thought a fight between the two might never end, they were so skilled at staying away from their opponents' weapons.

The girl was back in the inn's hall as Lana and her friends sat down to eat. She was sat by the fire, her tankard filled with cider, eating the bread left over from somebody else's plate. Lana smiled and waved as she noticed her, gesturing for her to come over. She didn't seem keen but in time she did.

"We're about to order food, why don't you sit with us and I'll get you a plate?"

"I don't know as yer friends would like my company. And ah don't much like bein' some kinda project for bored people to meddle wif."

"Don't be silly! I told you I'd get you food and I meant it. Come on, sit beside me and enjoy some food and company instead of just watching people eat."

The girl sat and pulled back her hood to reveal her deep auburn hair, unkempt and ragged. Dirt covered the freckles on her face and her brown eyes darted from person to person anxiously.

Lana introduced the girl to her friends. "This is Caitlin, you've probably seen her before, but she's shy. She lives in a kind of shared house in the alleys, but she hasn't got much, so I promised her some food."

The group welcomed her with smiles and shared their meal with her. They gave her short versions of their stories and asked about hers.

"I'd quite like a word with this man that runs that house of yours. I think he might have some things that belong to me." Laywyn was smiling but his tone was cold.

"I doubt you'd want to meet him; he isn't the nicest, and

he's a temper on 'im and hands like shovels."

"He'll have less chance to use them next time we meet. How about you take me over there with you and I'll make sure his temper never bothers either of us again?"

"I reckon you'd try all right but it aint that easy. He ain't no pushover, and he's got lots of friends that'd hate anything to 'appen to 'im."

"I've got friends too. Tell me where I can find him, that's all you need to do."

"Leave her be, Laywyn. She's scared, and she doesn't know us well enough yet to know we won't turn out as bad to her as him."

"Aye Lana's right, Laywyn. Give the lassie some space, she'll dae the right thing when the time comes." Brighid smiled warmly at Caitlin and poured more ale into her tankard.

The conversation turned back to merriment and talk of the tournament and Caitlin seemed to loosen up a little more as the evening went on. Talking more freely and joining the conversation as if she had known them all for weeks. At the end of the evening she slipped away into the alleys of the city but Lana had a feeling she would be back again soon.

Brighid joined her friends in the stands on the third day of the tournament. Her victories made her immune for this round which would see two warriors leave. Wren, Yorane and Matuk sat close by too and Brighid introduced her friends to them.

They watched on as the other six warriors fought for the right to continue. Laywyn and Tinnion were caught up in conversations of movement and weapon skill with Brighid and were laying bets with each other on the fights as they went on. Lana and Selene sat much quieter, talking, when they could hear one another, about the temple Tinnion had discovered in the forest.

There were jeers from the fae warriors as Tyik won his place in the final rounds and Wren took issue with Brighid's smile at the news.

"Why are you so happy? I thought you despised him as much as we do?"

"Oh aye, He's a vile creature, but this way one o' us gets tae make him eat his words."

The rules of the tournament changed on day four. The match ups would be selected at random, the warrior's tokens pulled from a chalice in pairs. At the end of the day the victors would progress and the losers would not. There would be no more sparring blades either, from this point on the warriors used their own weapons with the victory decided by submission or an inability to continue.

Lana found it impossible to watch. The violence of the fighting before had been tempered by the bluntness of the weapons. Any injuries sustained would heal in time. But this was different, the warriors fought with real weapons, real blood was being spilled and the strikes were aimed to incapacitate. She cuddled with Selene and the pair of them spent most of their day with their hands covering their eyes. Tinnion and Laywyn laughed at the pair, mocking their fragility with friendly jibes.

At the end of the day Brighid and Wren came out of their contests unharmed. Their skill in avoiding the weapons of their opponents meant that they had barely been touched during their fights. Yorane beat Batul in a well fought contest, but he had picked up a few cuts along the way, including one to his brow that bled quite a lot and looked nasty. None of those fights ended too badly however. The defeated opponent wasn't so badly hurt that they would not recover quite quickly and all ended in submission. Tyik's fight against the noam Matuk was a very different tale.

The pair both wore heavy armour and took the arena like knights. Tyik was known by now to have a bad attitude toward fae but during this fight it became clear that he harboured a real hatred. The pair circled one another trading blow after blow until Tyik got lucky with a blow that sent Matuk to the ground. At this point it was normal to give your opponent time to submit or to signal their intent to continue. Tyik didn't give Matuk that chance. He stood over the noam and continued to rain down blows on his defenceless opponent beating him badly, until Ethrok, Brighid and Wren intervened. Matuk was taken to the medic, his misshapen armour removed to reveal a body bloody and blackened with bruises.

Brighid's next fight was against Tyik and she relished the opportunity to make him pay for his behaviour. She stood opposite Tyik watching him closely. He was still limping and his face was bruised, but he didn't appear to be too worried about the fight. He was shouting at Brighid, inviting her to attack. His armour had been beaten back into shape overnight and would limit the effectiveness of Brighid's fighting style. On the other hand, she wore leather armour, it helped her to move with ease but wouldn't help her at all if he landed a strike. All he had to do was land one blow.

The crowd were chanting Brighid's name, encouraging her to attack. She moved forward cautiously never taking her eyes from his. He waited, swinging his war hammer nonchalantly as she approached. He didn't notice the subtle dip of her shoulder or the placement of her foot. His hammer was in front of his face, halfway through its arc, as the knife left Brighid's hand. By the time he realised what was happening the brass pommel of the blade struck him square between the eyes. Dazed, his eyes were only closed for a moment but when he opened them Brighid was gone.

He felt the blade slide into the muscle of his shoulder, she was behind him, the joints of his armour were exposed to her. He had to turn, to face her and to land the strike that would end this, he felt the warmth as his blood soaked into his tunic and the sharp sting as her second blade slashed the tendon behind his knee. Tyik felt the tendon run up his leg, the pain froze him. His leg gave way and he fell to his knees. He had to drop the hammer to prevent himself from landing face down in the sand. Brighid's arm wrapped around his neck, her knee in his back.

She tightened the hold and closed it with her other hand. He was red in the face, and then purple. Struggling to breathe, his mouth started to froth, the phlegm flying as he spluttered and wheezed. He raised his arm, his fingers held high, he wanted to submit.

The fight lasted less than a minute. Brighid pushed him to the ground, his purple face flat in the sand. The crowd was silent. Brighid pulled her blades from the sand and walked toward her friends. A large part of the crowd started to chant again as the shock from the speed of the fight wore off. Her name rang through the stadium. Tyik didn't move, he had to be carried from the arena. Brighid had cut him twice and with those cuts she ensured that he would never fight again. His arm would never recover enough to lift a weapon, his leg would never hold his weight and his reputation was destroyed.

Lana saw a sadness on Brighid's face as she approached them, and she reached her hand down to her friend. A gesture of comfort that Brighid gladly took before heading back into the rooms beneath the stand to ready herself for the final match.

It ended the way Lana had expected it to, with Brighid and Wren dancing together on the arena's sand. There was a strange sensation in the centre of Lana's forehead, a tingling, a feeling that all of her blood and energy was suddenly flowing into a deep well that stretched from her skin to the back of her mind.

The castle was burning, the Dryad screaming as the flames engulfed them. Noam struggled to hold back the tide of humans that crashed against their ranks, eroding their numbers. Slowly but surely reducing them to dust.

The sylph on the northern and eastern wall had taken the assault to the human lines. Gliding down to their positions, their spears and arrows filling the air before them. On landing their blades flashed, cutting circles in their formation before succumbing to the humans numbers.

One remained, one that had travelled further than the

others, she had glided to the back line of the human army, to the banner of their leader. They danced together on the ash and dirt that used to be a forest floor. The soldiers formed a circle watching them, waiting to see whether human or fae would take the victory.

The warriors fought, a lunge, a parry, evading one strike after the others the speed of the sylph matched by the skill of the human. A thrust, a side step, a spin and a block. The fight went on, but no one was injured, no one was cut, no blows landed. On and on they danced, the fae and the human, a dance that lasted a thousand years, a dance that would never end.

And Lana felt a surge around her, the wind picked up speed, the sky blackened and a crash split the heavens. A flash of light broke the darkness striking the ground sending ash and dirt and sand into the air. The fae and the human fell, knocked back by the almighty force released and the fighting stopped. For a while at least.

Dirt and ash settled once more; the warriors lay on the ground. The crowd let out a gasp, and then fell into silence. The human army, coughing and spluttering formed up their circle again as the dirt settled.

No, not the dirt and ash, the sand. She was in the arena, not in the Heartwood. Brighid was fighting Wren, not to kill her but to win a tournament. Lana closed her eyes and shook her head. The tingling faded, the sensation of energy flowing through her head ended. She looked down to the sand, to her friend.

Both Brighid and Wren were sitting, the sand between them black and charred, they were fine. Thank the gods. Lana jumped over the barrier and dropped to the floor below, she ran to the centre of the arena. Guards ran into the arena and chased her, she shouldn't be in there, but she ran. She dodged as a guard lunged at her and switched direction quickly as another tried to cut her off. In a moment she was at Brighid's side, helping her friend drink from the flask she carried.

In the end there was very little choice, the fight couldn't

continue. The crowd were chanting for a draw, the warriors were both in shock. There was a girl running around the arena making the guards look like fools and giving water to the fighters. The sun was close to the edge of the stadium and the skies were dark. Sir Reynard, flanked by a troop of The Silver, made his way onto the sand and announced the draw. The two warriors would share the prize.

The crowd erupted in cheers. They stamped their feet in rhythm and started chanting the warrior's names. A celebration began that would continue throughout the district well into the morning. Brighid and Wren were taken to the medic to be checked for wounds and concussion. Lana was escorted back to her friends; they left the stadium and made their way back to the inn once Lana assured them that Brighid wasn't hurt.

31. CALLTAIN

At the edge of Tinnion's camp there was a hazel tree, it was tall and the branches reached out to touch and mingle with the surrounding trees. It was Lana's favourite place to sit when they went out to the forest to visit Tinnion.

The hunter was preparing rabbits for their dinner, something she insisted on doing alone. Brighid and Laywyn were sparring, they said it was the best way to stay in shape but Lana thought there must be better ways, ways that didn't involve so many bruises. Still, they seemed to enjoy it, so she didn't question them too much.

She would greet the tree with a hug each evening as they returned from their hunt and ask that she be allowed to sit beneath its branches, against its trunk. Her friends were used to her behaviour by now and no longer mocked her for it, they accepted it as part of who Lana was, and they loved her for it.

It was a lovely samhradh day and the sun was warming the ground quickly. Lana sat, watching Brighid dance with a sword and a knife. Spinning and turning, leaping and twisting, her blades sometimes whirling, sometimes still as she moved. Lana's mind wandered back to the Stead and the hours she had sat watching Aeloth spar with his master, she had thought then he would grow to be a strong swordsman, a true warrior, but Brighid was different. She was a master with her blades, much more dangerous than Aeloth or his master, she didn't fight with a sword, she fought with her whole body, her mind raced ahead as she danced, watching the moves of others and planning her next strike, she had balance and fluidity.

But the thing that struck Lana as the biggest difference

was that she never tried to impress, she never looked angry, she never let emotion overcome her when she fought or practised. Aeloth had let his emotions show as he fought, his anger, his lust and his need to impress, it had always been clear on his face.

She found her hand going to her shoulder and rubbing the scar there as she remembered those days. The look in his eyes as he attacked her. His initials carved into her skin, his brand of assumed ownership that would never leave her. But he was dead, no longer a threat to her or to anyone else. His anger and his lust had ended his life that day in the field and Lana now felt her anger drain away. She couldn't have justice for the things he had done to her, she could never see him behind bars or punished by the Queen, and she knew her anger toward him was doing nothing but eating her up and causing her pain.

She still wanted justice, she still needed help, but it was to save her family, to save the Stead from the anger and behaviour of the Gesith. His son was able to hurt her, to hurt Ara and to kill Ara's father because the Gesith had let him. His father had taught him he could do that, that the people of the Stead were beneath him and to be used. The Gesith had to be confronted and punished for his treatment of the people under his care, for his behaviour when the crimes of his son were reported.

She looked up again at Brighid, and she felt her understanding grow, she hadn't been thinking about justice on her journey south, she had been thinking of vengeance. She would never find the help she needed if she was blinded by the pain and hatred that had built up inside her. She had to be like Brighid, she had to put her feelings aside, she had to do what was needed, not what she felt she wanted. Lana leaned back against the tree and her body began to tingle.

An idea struck her. She knew that Tay Gathwyn was right, she couldn't return to Butterholt, it wasn't safe. But what if she could go back to the Heartwood? What if she could visit the tree-line on the edge of the pasture, hidden from sight but seeing, just as Daowiel had done with her? Maybe that would give her some peace of mind?

She broached the subject with her friends as they were finishing their meal.

"It might make you feel a little better, or it might make you feel a little worse. What if you get there and can't see anybody? Or you see them, but they're in need of help somehow. Could you stand there and watch without trying to help? Anyway, I don't think we'd be able to get there and back before the festival." Tinnion was right, of course, if she travelled the normal way there would be no chance of getting there and back in time. But that wasn't her plan.

"I think that I might be able to get help to go there faster."

"You mean travelling hard? You'd have to have fresh horses twice a day. That's a lot of work and a lot of coin, Lana." Laywyn shook his head as he joined the conversation. "I honestly can't see a way that would work."

"No, not that. I was... Well, you remember during the fight we had in the woods. How I got behind the men? I think that I went through the trees like the Dryads do. I felt really strange and then it was like... well it was like walking in a pond but all muddy. Really slow. And then I was there. Like when the princess took me to the palace."

Tinnion looked at her a moment, her eyes never moving from Lana's as she spoke.

"You mean it, don't you? You really mean it. When we talked after the battle I thought, well I thought you were just in shock. But you really believe you travelled through the trees?"

"Yes, I do. I did it before with the princess, Daowiel. I don't know how I could have done it on my own but I think, maybe, the trees helped."

Tinnion and Laywyn fell silent.

"Lana, hen. If ye could travel like that, then maybe it would be possible. But we cannae and I'm no about to let ye go running off and putting yersel at risk all alone."

"I don't think I could do it on my own Brighid. But maybe I could get the princess to help me? Maybe if I asked the trees to find her and ask her to come?"

"I've seen fae do some strange things, hen. I've no doubt if ye were one o' 'em ye could do that. But I've checked yer ears and yer not."

"I know. But I'd like to try... tonight. I just... If it works, if she came, then I would go for a little while. I'd come back... I'd be back long before the feast. I just think if I don't try, I'll feel bad."

"Ye don't need ma permission, Lana. Nor any of ours. If ye feel ye need tae give it a go I'll dae what I can tae help."

"Thank you, Brighid." Lana smiled sweetly at her friend. More confident now than she had been when she brought the subject up.

"You know I'll help you, Lana, whenever I can." Laywyn nodded to her.

"Well, if you're going to be calling on a princess, we should tidy up the camp a bit. It might be an idea to tell her you're not alone too. I wouldn't want a startled Dryad to deal with." Tinnion smiled reassuringly but Lana wasn't convinced she believed her.

She felt her mind reaching, stretching, flowing through the tree, reaching its branches and its roots. Snaking through the earth beneath her feet and further. She closed her eyes and held her breath and stretched out even further, she felt the city fall away and pushed her mind on.

"Daowiel. Daowiel, hear me and come." She spoke the words under her breath a whisper on the breeze, her closed eyes tightened, creasing her face as she stretched out even further, her body aching and shaking.

"Daowiel. Please. Hear me." She reached out with her other hand and pushed it to the tree, leaning forward, almost falling. And then, emerging from the tree itself, another hand. It grabbed on to Lana's arm and pulled.

"Where have you brought me, Ògan?" Daowiel's eyebrow was raised and her voice more serious than usual.

"This is the forest on the island of Southport, Princess."

Daowiel placed her hand back upon the tree and another hand caught hers. In a moment Lothalilia stood in the clearing too, her spear ready to launch at any one of the humans in the camp.

"Who are these people you have chosen to expose me to?"

Lana introduced her friends and the Dryad princess, she assured Daowiel that she was safe and that none of her friends would speak of this meeting. When Tinnion assured the princess they wouldn't be interrupted by other humans they sat together and a cask of wine was opened.

Lana shared the stories of the journey with Daowiel once the formalities of the meeting were over.

Brighid and Tinnion occasionally interrupted to add a bit of colour to the tale and share some embarrassing moments that Lana hadn't wanted to include.

"We went bathing in the river you see, and you don't bathe clothed, do you? So, there we stood, splashing the water on us to get used to the chill and there were bubbles in the water in front of us. We hadn't realised someone had beaten us to that part of the river! You ought to have seen the look on her face as Laywyn came up from the water, naked as the day he was born. She was redder than an apple, and we could have roasted our dinner on her cheeks!"

They all laughed, though Lana's cheeks had reddened a bit again.

When Lana had finished her story Daowiel turned to Lothalilia and smirked.

"See, Lo'. Our sapling has grown into a bear killer and Dryad avenger!" The warrior laughed and slapped her thigh enthusiastically.

"I am most proud of you, Ògan. You are showing the strength and character I believed you to have. Though, perhaps not the wisdom you need. In the morning you will return to the Heartwood with us and you will learn, what we can teach you, of this gift you have been given."

"Ye'll keep her safe and well..."

"Of course, tuath. She has as much of my heart as she has yours. No harm will come to her in our home."

They were on the bridge again, the glow of the moss at either side stretching out into the distance. Daowiel stood in front of her, Lothalilia at her side.

"You are learning Sapling, but are you ready for the lessons to come?"

"I need to be, I want to be… will you teach me?"

"A little… yes. But my mother wishes to speak to you again first. Come."

With that they set off across the bridge and Lana scrambled after them. When they reached the other side Daowiel stood and smiled.

"Well then, Sapling, can you take us home?"

"Me?" Lana's voice rose in pitch as she questioned the Dryad.

"You have done it before, moving from Ash to Oak, do it now. Reach out and take us there."

Lana placed her hand upon the wall in front of her and let her mind flow to the Dryad Palace. When she felt that giant tree she locked it in her mind and pushed. Her mind and her body lurched forward, and she stumbled onto the platform at the base of the Dryad's home. It was only a second later she heard that familiar laugh, and she picked herself up from the floor.

"You did well Sapling, though you need to learn not to push so hard that you fall."

"Well it's not like I've had lessons." Daowiel smiled and shook her head then walked away toward the palace.

"She's full o' surprises oor little Lana eh?"

"Yes, it seems she is, Brighid. Though I understand, a little more, her reckless charge to protect the Dryad that night."

"Oh? They made an impression on ye then?"

"I've spent my life in the forests of Mortara, Brighid. I know more about our woodlands than most. To see a person *OF* the forest... That is something very... It is unique and, yes, beautiful."

Brighid smiled. She hadn't seen Tinnion so emotional about anything before. She would tease her, for certain, but it would be done with love and respect for her feelings.

32. SISTERS

"Please, sit. I'm pleased you could both make it. There is a lot to discuss." Sir Reynard was dressed in the silver and blue tunic of the Queen's Private Guard.

"As you know, I am the commanding officer of the Silver. I take care of the Queen on a daily basis. Ensuring her safety wherever she may be. There are times, however, when her safety depends on things away from the palace and the city. Times when the silver aren't able to take direct action and occasions when it's not in the best interest to send, more formal, troops." He paused here to see how Brighid and Wren would react to the information he was giving them. Both took on a serious demeanour and nodded.

"In these instances, I need a select group of warriors I can rely upon and place my trust in. People who are able to follow orders and yet think on their feet when needed. The kind of person who excels in both combat and tactics. They need to be able to work in a team as well as to stand on their own against the odds. The two of you have shown that ability."

"yer looking for people that can end bother afore it starts, and without too much fuss. Is that it?"

"That is the gist of the matter, Brighid, yes. As long as the crown has been on a human head there have been thirteen Feannag. Thirteen men and women that were trusted to what was needed. At the moment there are eleven. Each made a Thegn, each has a house and a purse from the Queen. Each keeps the existence of their unit quiet. The Feannag answer directly to the Queen herself. They are outside of the normal command structure."

"And if it all goes wrong? We dinnae exist?"

"Yes, that is the way of it. I need your answer and your oath within twenty-four hours. I need your guarantee of silence before you leave here."

"So, all this time the best o' the trials have been doin' the queen's bidding on the hush. No one knows who they are or what they're up tae. It seems a big risk, and a sacrifice tae match. Is the purse in balance?"

"I don't believe you would be disappointed."

"Well, I'll happily give ma word o silence. So yer men there can put their bows down. As for ma decision? You'll have it on the morn."

Sir Reynard nodded. " And you, Wren? You've been very quiet."

"I always hoped to have a nice property of my own and a purse to retire with. This though, seems like an invitation to a job with no retirement."

"Some have fared well, others not. That is life as a warrior."

"I shan't speak of it, except to Brighid. I would like to share our thoughts before making a decision."

"Aye, we can do that. I think an ale or two would be in order to properly consider it anyway."

"Agreed. I take it we are free to leave now?"

Sir Reynard nodded his approval. "Tomorrow then."

"Aye. Tomorrow."

It was learning to use the staff that had given her the most difficulty. She had spent the first few days in the forest walking the bridge, practising the coming and going between trees. She learnt she could travel to any tree she knew. The further away the tree was the more it tired her. But, no matter the distance, the bridge was the bridge and the journey took only a moment.

She travelled to the Apple tree she used to climb, down by the pasture, sticking her head out, hoping to catch sight of her brother or father but never seeing them. She travelled to the Rowan tree on the western edge of the heartwood and drank from the stream. On the third day she travelled to the Oak through which she'd appeared behind the attackers that had ambushed them on the road. The bodies were gone, the clearing was peaceful, no signs of the battle remained.

On the fourth day she realised that as she placed her hand upon the far wall she would get a sense of who and what was on the other side. It was as though the tree was describing the surroundings to her. By the end of the week she understood that the image she sensed was skewed by the tree's feelings. If a Dryad was on the other side of the bridge wall she would sense a gentle, calm green outline of a person. When it was Daowiel or Erinia the green was richer and there was a sense of awe.

She discussed this with Daowiel and asked what sense the trees gave of her. Daowiel laughed at the question. "You, dear Ògan. Have changed as you have grown. When I first learned of you the sense was pink and fuzzy, shrouded in puzzlement and curiosity. The feare are red and hot if they carry metal. So pink was an interesting colour, it showed they couldn't decide whether you were dangerous or not."

"And now? Am I not pink anymore?"

"Now you are Ògan, there is no way to explain that sensation. You are unique, a human that travels the bridge and the trees have their own sense of you."

Lana wanted to know more, her curiosity had been piqued, but she felt Daowiel was being vague on purpose and that asking would only get her a more cryptic answer.

In the evenings Lana would sit with Erinia, the princess was highly skilled in wood shaping and was patiently teaching Lana the ability. In some ways it was like travelling, except that, instead of reaching out through the tree into the branches and roots around it, you reached inward. Touching the wood's heart, its soul. Wood, she discovered, retained memories of its life as a tree. It had a sense of being, and in order to shape the wood you had to shape its sense of self. Gently moulding and pushing with your mind as you pushed with your hands. Talking to the wood, explaining what you wanted it to be and convincing it, or asking it, to be that. Some woods, oak in particular, were stubborn. They had their shape and felt that everyone should be grateful for it. Willow was easier to shape; it was excited and enthusiastic about exploring other forms.

Lana enjoyed those lessons, she started by shaping a simple bowl and it took her so much energy and concentration she thought she would never progress. Now though she was working on a gift for Queen Olerivia. A pendant that resembled the one she had been given on her first visit to the palace. But with a twist. A sapling grew beside the great palace tree, a sapling that she thought would make the queen laugh.

Then came the decorative handle that Daowiel had gifted her. An ancient Dryad staff. In order to extend the staff to its full length you had to shape it. But this wood was more stubborn than oak. It had the same temperament as the bull in the manor stead. She asked, she pleaded, she begged at one point, but it wouldn't grow. She tried threatening and bribing to no avail. And then she got fed up.

"You're my staff. Daowiel gave you to me, so it's no good sulking about it. Now behave!" The sudden growth of the staff from the handle almost caught Lana's forehead. From then on out it, begrudgingly, did as it was told.

Brighid had spent the last four years of her life competing in tournaments and taking small jobs to pay her way. She had built her reputation across the northern taydom and now she was a named champion of Mortara. The offer made to her was one she had, unknowingly, fought for and won in her own right. It wasn't being handed to her as a Gesith's child.

She knew she would be welcome back home and could spend the rest of her days as the daughter of the Gesith and clan chief. She'd be married to someone important and be expected to bare children, it wouldn't be a difficult life. In fact, being married and raising a family were things she looked forward to, in time, but this wasn't the time. She was, perhaps, the best warrior in Mortara and giving that up to go home now felt wrong to her.

She hadn't wanted to join an elite and secretive group of soldiers but now that the offer was before her the idea appealed. Being made a Thegn in her own right and having a manor and a purse to match was a great incentive to accept. Brighid was tempted.

"Do you think they would have shot their arrows, Brighid?"

" Aye, I reckon they would have. This isn't the kind of information they'd want getting about. If the thirteen are made up of tournament winners they're doin' well at keepin' their secrets. I'd imagine Reynard's pretty sure o' the answers he'll get too, or he'd not have asked."

"You're intending to say yes then?"

"I dinnae think I'm ready for the life I'll have if I say no."

"I feel the same way. I have achieved what I set out to achieve with this win, can I now go back to sparring with farmers and part-time sheriffs? Knowing you would be standing beside me would remove any doubt. I would know the best warrior I have ever seen would be with me, rather than against me."

"Aye. It seems to me that we're in bar the swearing. Should we make him wait til morning?"

"I think we should. It will do him good to be uncertain for a while."

Lana was exhausted, each day was a trial, each hour harder than the one before. And now she stood, hiding behind a tree, not knowing where Daowiel might appear from, not knowing if the blow from her staff would come from the side or behind her. Behind her? A noise. She spun. A deer running through the trees. A family of birds, startled, taking wing. There. Just beyond the second tree. She raised her staff, ready.

And then her vision blurred, she felt her eyes roll back and the feeling of the void filling in her head.

Two women sat beneath a tree on the lake shore. More real than it was possible to be and yet removed from reality. One of the women reminded Lana of Queen Olerivia, her hazel skin and dark green hair matched those of the queen. Were it not for the glow that emanated from her Lana would believe she was seeing Olerivia in her youth. The other woman had skin that shimmered in the light, neither green nor blue, neither red nor brown. Her long hair was streaked with blue, white, brown and green all separate and yet somehow all one.

"The humans have built a dam across the river. The lake will dry and my children will weaken. Soon they will put the forest to flame. The time to decide is upon us."

"Would we not serve our children better by ending this war? It would be a simple matter to destroy this human threat for all time."

"No, Kaoris. We have long known of the human's and our fate. These things cannot be changed. The future of this world belongs to them, we cannot stop that. In time there will be a human that lives in nature, without fear or hatred of our children. A human that can carry our essence and bring true peace to our people."

"You have seen this, Ophine? You are certain of this human?"

"I have seen what is destined to pass now and what might be. I have seen the destruction of this world and I have seen how it might be saved. Our family is divided. Solumus and Chaint have drifted away from us, in time they will make war on one another. Ulios has withdrawn, he does not believe the matters of the earth concern him or his children. Khyione has deserted you, his children and yours are no longer linked. How long will it be, do you think, before you two are at war?"

"So, it is us, we who created this world, that will destroy it?"

"In the future without humans it is our differences that destroy our home. The future in which we depart, our children scattered and without hope, sees the humans slowly poison our creation. In saving the core of our people and leaving a fraction of ourselves behind, our world will live on until the sun itself dies."

"And what of us sister? We will be weakened and banished from our own home."

"We will live as we did before this world, in the void. There, we will either regain our strength and begin again or fade. That will depend on the faith of our children."

"Then we must gather our family and do what is needed. Will you send out the call?"

"I will. I have secured the future of the Nymph in the north, the land is uninhabitable by humans, they will be safe. You must take this time to secure the future of your Dryad."

Lana's feet were pulled from underneath her and laughter floated on the breeze as she fell on her behind.

"You need to stay awake if you want to win, Ògan!"

Lana cursed as she got back to her feet.

"I want to try again. I was... thinking about stuff that time, but I will get you!"

33. HOW THE OTHER HALF LIVE

There were three manor houses on this street, one on either side and one at the end of the road. Brighid took the manor on the northern side while Wren moved her belongings into the southern manor. The buildings were identical and the grounds the same, at least in size. Each had stables and a carriage house to their sides and a courtyard with a water feature to the front. At the back of each manor were the gardens. The manors themselves had plenty of space below for the working rooms and the staff quarters. On the ground floor there were reception rooms, a game room, a library and a dining hall. On the upper floor there were six suites. The manors were luxuriously furnished and decorated and their grounds meticulously maintained.

Laywyn was the first to be employed by Brighid, she made him her house carl and put the protection of her property into his hands. He was both thrilled and relieved at the appointment. Relieved that he now had employment and a salary, thrilled he would remain at Brighid's side. His feelings for the tuath had only grown during their time in the city, and he ached when she was not around.

Kaorella was the next to come to the manor. She had been reluctant to leave the inn but the opportunity to run a Thegn's household was too good to turn down. This would enhance her growing reputation further and, having spent so much time in Brighid's company, she knew how to keep her new employer happy. It wasn't long before the house was fully staffed and Kaorella had the place running smoothly. Messages were left at the inn for Tinnion and Lana to join them when they returned to the city and Selene had been given an open invitation.

It was late into the evening when the messenger from Sir Reynard arrived. Brighid and Laywyn were sitting in front of the fire in the smaller reception room enjoying a bottle of whisky from Lochmead. Brighid's face took on a stern look after reading the note.

"You look troubled, Brighid. Is everything okay?"

"I'm afraid I'm going tae have tae leave the city for a while. I'll be going in the morning, hopefully I'll be back before the festival. If I'm not, would ye give a message tae Tinnion and Lana for me?"

"Of course. Though if something is wrong shouldn't I come with you?"

"No. I made ye ma carl so as you'd be here tae look after ma house when I'm no around. Besides, I ken how tae look after massel, so I'll be fine but if Kaorella has nae one tae cook for she'll go crazy." Brighid gave a broad grin as she mentioned her house manager and Laywyn laughed.

"That's true enough. But if you need me I'll be ready, my leg is stiff but I'm no cripple."

"I'm well aware. I should get myself tae my bed, it's goin' tae be a long day tomorrow I imagine. Feel free tae have another glass."

"Thank you, my lady. That's very generous." Laywyn smirked as he poured himself more of the dark spirit. "Sleep well."

It had occurred to Lana that if all the trees of the forest were joined, and they all had a sense of what was around them, they ought to be able to help her find Daowiel. The princess was hiding somewhere in the forest, playing her favourite game. Hunting. They would hide out in the forest, taking at least three bridges to a location they felt secure. From there they would hunt each other down. Once they met, they would spar, and when one of them was on the ground the other was named winner. The loser would have to serve the winner's evening meal.

So far Lana had yet to win a round but was determined today would be her day. Daowiel wasn't mean with her victories, but she did fully enjoy having Lana at her service.

Her eyes closed, her hand upon the bridge wall, she pushed her thought into the forest. 'Show me Daowiel'. Her mind raced through branch and root, every tree and every flower, every blade of grass. The forest was there, in her mind, in her sight. There, among the trees by the north-eastern stream was Daowiel. Lana pushed.

Daowiel had moved when Lana reached the stream but was quickly found again and Lana had a plan. She reached to the tree behind her friend and tapped her on the shoulder. As the princess turned she caught her feet in Lana's staff and tumbled to the floor.

"Gotcha!" Lana pounced from the tree and onto her friend, straddling her. She flicked Daowiel's nose lightly and laughed. "Tonight you serve me pudding!"

There was a groan from the Dryad and then a question. "Wait! How did you get here? I've never brought you to this side of the forest before. You don't know the trees here."

"The trees were bored with your gloating, so they helped me." Lana laughed, hiding the excitement of her win with some difficulty.

"What do you mean they helped you?"

"They showed me where you were and how to get to you. The flowers helped too, but they were more interested in a bee that was hovering than in you."

"The flowers...!?! Lana, that's not possible."

When they finished eating, Daowiel turned to Lana, a question on her lips.

"What's it like out there?"

"Outside the Heartwood? It's big and everywhere seems different. The towns are really different to the Stead. They all use coins to buy things and people don't seem to share much or even know each other very well. I thought the one I went to was really grand and amazing, they had big flat stones on the ground to make a path and the houses were big. But then we got to Southport and that city is giant! It's like ten towns all in one place. Everyone seems to be so busy and distant. It's as though they all live in little worlds that spin around their heads, and they don't notice the other people around them unless they need to. Some of the people are very rich and live like gesiths and ladies in really big houses, bigger even than the manor in the Stead and much prettier. But there are others that are really poor, and they sit on the side of the road and beg for food. It makes me sad, but there are some lovely things too. There are lots of woods, I think you would like those. And the ocean. That looks really, really big, there are waves too, that's when the ocean looks like it has big hills 'cept they move! Like the ripples on the lake but much bigger. Much higher than me even and so loud. People all talk differently too. Like Brighid, when she says roll she makes the r much longer and funny sounding. And the people in the city they can't say 'ing'. They just miss the g sound and you just have to know that it's s'posed to be there."

Lana stopped for a breath and Daowiel took the opportunity to interrupt her.

"Are there other fae? Is it just humans in the cities?"

"Oh. No, I've seen sylph, and noam too. Brighid knows two sylph warriors, they were in the tournament together and there are others around the city. I saw two noam too, they were fighting in the tournament too. They look very strong."

"Are there other Dryad?"

"Well I did see that one, the one that died. I'm sure there must be others too but I haven't seen any. That one, she gave me this..." Lana looked in her purse and pulled out the Dryad seed. "I think you should have it really. I know it must be important but I don't know what to do with it." Daowiel took the seed and carefully examined it.

"Thank you, Lana. It means a lot that you took care of this for her. I will arrange for it to be planted. Who was it that killed her?"

"It was a priest, Tinnion says he was from the 'circle of light' and that they hate all the fae. They come from a country a long way away, and they only have one god. They aren't nice people, more of them attacked us later on too. There aren't many of those people though, at least not in the places I've been to."

"So, the other people don't hate the fae?"

"No, I mean most people don't. I know Brighid and Tinnion and Laywyn and Kaorella don't. Some, stupid people do, but I think that's just because some people aren't nice to anyone."

"Do you think it would be safe for a Dryad to leave the forest and go to the city?"

Lana nodded. "I think so. I mean I don't think it would be any more dangerous for a Dryad than it is for me. The people in the city probably wouldn't even notice."

"I do wish that I could see it. I have always wondered what it would be like to explore outside of the forest."

"You could come with me when I go back! We all sleep at an inn and I have an extra bed in my room, you could sleep there. It would be good; all of my friends would be together."

"It wouldn't be possible, Lana. As much as I would like to, I must stay here in the forest and protect our borders. Maybe in time that will change but for now it has to be. I will accompany you as you return to your friends of course but I cannot stay."

PART FIVE
The Plot

34. THE CAT BURGLAR

Caitlin was being followed; she was sure of it. She had seen the same man behind her numerous times over the last three days. Something about the way he looked was wrong, as if his ragged clothes had been deliberately ripped, his walk was strange too, though she couldn't say why exactly, it just stood out as being forced rather than natural. It had to be one of the city guard trying to find Keikon's house. They did this every few moons, send someone out in an attempt to infiltrate the family or follow one of them back to their home. It never worked though, the entrances moved, old ones were sealed, new ones opened up. Every day it would be different. No one but Keikon and his bitch of a wife knew in advance where it would be, so there was no way to get the information from one of the kids. Poor little blighters. Caitlin was getting too old now, too big to be doing the jobs Keikon wanted her to do, so she was on a longer leash. She could operate on her own as long as she paid her dues at the end of each moon. Gods, it was almost time to send him his cut again, and she had nothing to give him. She'd have to pull something off in the next few nights and hand all of it over, or he'd turn on her. That'd be all she needed, the family on her back and the guards too. Life wouldn't be worth living.

She skipped down the alley and made her way past the dilapidated old houses to the shop on the corner. Rusty old nails sat in boxes on a trestle outside, there were hammers with broken handles and knives that wouldn't cut through soft butter. She opened the door and a bell above her rang. The breeze picked up dust and dried dirt from the floor and formed a cloud that made her cough.

"Tom! You 'ere?"

A dirty face appeared from behind the counter. Tom looked as though he hadn't washed for a month and his stubble was almost a beard.

"Where else am I gonna be, Cat? Not like I get to wander round the city doin' as I please like you do. You always were 'is favourite."

"Yeah, whatever. Listen I ain't been home for a few days. Got some tin head followin' me about. Can you get a message to 'im? Tell 'im I'll be by with 'is share once I've led this'un a merry chase."

"He'll be well angry. You know 'e don't like it when you miss a date."

"Yeah, well, tell 'im I'm happy to lead the whole bloody guard to 'im if he prefers. Not like 'es gonna be overly happy with what I've got for him anyway. Been a rough moon."

"That's twice now innit, Cat? You'll be wishin' the guard took you unless you start pickin' up again."

"Just let 'im know, Tom. I'd best be off before you get a visitor an all."

She looked down the street before stepping out of the shop, the man stood in a doorway at the other end of the block. He was trying to look casual but that was the door to the house of one of Keikon's women and anyone from this part of town knew not to be hanging around it. He'd be lucky not to end up taking a dive off the cliff if he stayed there too long.

Caitlin wandered slowly out into the middle of the street and then around the corner, making sure to be seen and followed again.

The thief led the guard around the city for another two days, stopping off at random shops and houses along the way. In the end she led him down an alley with a dead end and doubled back along the rooftops. She dropped down behind him and drew the knife from her belt before tapping him on the shoulder.

"You lookin' for me, tin head?"

The guard spun quickly but Cat was quicker, she held up the knife to his throat.

"Now, now. You don't want to be gettin' all jumpy. You might make me nervous, and then who knows what might 'appen?" She pressed the blade against his skin as if to prove a point.

"Thing is I'm gettin' a bit bored o' your company and I've stuff to be gettin' on with. People to meet, that kinda thing. So why don't you just hop on back to yer captain and let 'im know I lost ya? Be better for your health in the long run."

"We could pay you; you know if you just told us where to go. You wouldn't have to be there."

"You ain't got enough money to make it worth it! He'd skin us both alive. You've no idea what you're dealin' with or who 'e is."

The manor house was quiet, it had been for a couple of nights now and Cat was sure she had found a way in. There was a loose window that would drop her into the kitchen in the basement, she could make her way through the house from there. She circled round the house to the back, checking in each of the windows for signs of life as she went. The kitchen was empty, the fire was out, so she prised open the window and dropped down onto a countertop by the sink. She was almost silent as she moved through the rooms in the basement, taking what she could find of value, a brooch, a letter opener and a couple of country bronze coins. Not a lot and certainly not worth the risk yet, so she quietly climbed the stairs into the main house. Were there anything of value in the house at all it would be up here.

A couple of silver candlesticks from the dining room, a golden inkwell and letter opener from the study, a string of pearls from a guard box in the bedroom. It would be enough to keep Keikon quiet for another moon, but she had hoped for more. The manor was the home to an elder lady of the Tay's court, surely she must have some riches here, somewhere.

She was about to give up when the floor boards under her feet shifted slightly, curios she got down on her hands and knees to check it. It took a little convincing with her knife and the less ornate letter opener to lift the board but what she found underneath was her dream come true. If she was careful, if she was patient and took things slowly, this find would see her living well for the rest of her life.

She called in to see Tom who, after a bit of grumbling about being stuck in the shop, gave her the name of the entrance being used that day. It was out on the other side of the inn the do-gooder and her friends were staying at. She didn't want to bump into that one while carrying a sack full of stolen items. She didn't really know why but there was a sense of shame when she thought about the woman and the meals she'd bought her. Perhaps it was just that they had eaten together, that she had invited her to her table and to meet her friends. Whatever it was, Cat felt that it was important not to be seen stealing by her.

She dropped a coin to the ground and followed it as it rolled to the entrance, making any of her movements explainable if any one was watching. She pulled aside the barrel hiding the doorway and, once she was sure there was no one looking, slipped into the passage that would lead her to the home.

She didn't like going back to the home, there were too many bad memories. Beatings and hungry nights where she was refused food for failing to steal enough. Keikon and his missus had found her begging on the streets after her mother died and taken her in, promising a bed and food, they did that with any stray they found. Once she was there though they never let her go. They had people throughout the city, watching and working, if any of the children tried to leave they were soon found and brought back, beaten and punished before being used for more stealing. Cat wanted out, she wanted out badly. But even though she no longer lived in the home she had to come back every moon and pay her dues. He'd send people out to drag her to him if she missed one.

She came to a junction in the tunnel, heading to her left would take her to a blocked up entrance by the library in the central district. Going right would take her under the main wall and into a sewage pipe that spilt over the cliff a bit north of the bridge. That entrance was sometimes used by smugglers, but only by arrangement, a rope on a pulley had to be lowered. A pulley that was easily unhooked and taken back to the house. She continued going straight on, it wouldn't be long before she was there. Hopefully Keikon would be out, she'd leave her haul with the counters and leave as soon as they handed her the thieves token. She approached the opening to the home and heard talking. Three men by the sounds of it, one was Keikon for sure, the other two she didn't recognise they had strange accents and spoke hesitantly as though not in their own language. She paused, and listened. It wouldn't be a good idea to interrupt the giant leader of the house doing business and, if she managed to hear what was being discussed without being found out, it might come in handy.

The men were paying to be allowed to operate in the city. That was normal, visiting thieves would always pay respect to the local house. But these men were handing over a purse of country gold. That was far too much money for any thieving they could do in Southport. Keikon was explaining some of the ways the thieves got about the city without being seen, he gave no details of course, but he was making sure they knew he could get them where they wanted to go.

"When are you wantin' to get in there then?"

"Zer is a feast soon, a feast at which ze queen will speak, no?"

"Yeah, the 'arvest feast, wot of it?"

"We must be able to access ze palace and ze courtyard as ze feast is taking place."

"All right then. That's no bother, I'll make sure we've got it all sorted for you. Are you wanting to use the same way out or do you need a different escape?"

"Zey won't be leaving. Zer is no need for a way out."

Keikon laughed. "Do they know that?"

"Zat is not your concern."

Cat had no idea what she'd missed in the conversation, but she was sure it wasn't good. Whatever these people were paying for was big, huge. Arranging entry points to the queen's feast and not expecting to get out made the whole thing a lot worse. This suggested a lot more than a theft, after all, when you steal something you need to get whatever it is out of wherever it was. She needed to do something about this. Petty crime is a fact of life, some people can't afford to buy things, but she couldn't live with the thoughts that were swirling around her head now without doing something.

An arrow whizzed past Lana's head as she emerged from the tree, and she called out.

"Tinnion! It's Lana!"

The hunter stepped out from behind a tree, an arrow notched in her bow.

"Good to see you again Lana, and you, Princess. "

Daowiel appeared behind Lana, she was wearing a dark green set of leather armour and carried a longbow, her staff shortened and hanging at her side. They sat together and shared a drink as they caught up with each other's events.

Tinnion had stayed out in the forest hunting since the night Lana had gone into the tree. She was building up a decent stack of furs and had done some exploring in the temple they had found. She had discovered a few ante chambers, there were some ruined manuscripts and furniture in the rooms, a few bits of worked metal but nothing of much value. Selene had asked that she take anything interesting to her so Tinnion had gathered a few bits in a sack to take back to the library. It meant nothing to her but maybe the brains at the library would get something from it.

It was late, and they had shared enough wine that it made more sense to stay in the camp for the night than make their way back to the city.

When morning came, they packed up camp and Daowiel said her goodbyes. Lana promised she would return to the Heartwood soon and spend time with her again. Once the princess had disappeared into the tree again Lana helped Tinnion carry her goods back to the city and the inn.

It came as a shock to find that everyone was gone, the owner handed Tinnion a letter, muttering about losing his best manager and clients under his breath. Tin read the note with a smile.

"Well, wouldn't you know it? Brighid's only gone and won herself a mansion for us all to live in. It's up in the central district, Kaorella and Laywyn are up there with her already. We should head over there; a life of luxury sounds fun."

It was as they were about to leave the inn that Lana caught sight of Caitlin. She insisted on going over to talk to the girl and when Lana insisted it was easier to follow her than argue.

This was the issue with being brought up by the head of the thieves' family in Southport, the people you knew were all in his pocket and scared of him. You couldn't go to the guard either, they'd just lock you up, and in Cat's case probably have a party. She had built up quite a reputation. There was one person that might help, the do-gooder from the inn. If nothing else she'd be able to talk to her, the warriors she hung around with might keep Cat safe for a while as she figured it out. She knew the retired soldier, at least, wanted to get his hands on Keikon.

She waited outside the inn for three days without a sight of the red-headed girl or any of her friends. Asking around she found out that she hadn't been seen for a couple of weeks, her friends had all gone too including Kaorella, the inns head housekeeper. There was a bitterness about their departure that suggested she shouldn't keep asking.

Giving up hope she sat at a table and ordered a jug of ale. She wouldn't normally drink anything other than the soft cider in inns, she preferred to stay sharp and ale dulled her reactions, but she was hoping for dulled thoughts at that point. Halfway down the flagon and lost in her own head, she didn't notice the women enter the inn. It wasn't until they were in front of her, the red head enthusiastically saying hello that she snapped out of her malaise. She jumped up and exclaimed as she grabbed Lana in a hug.

"Thank the gods you're here!"

35. A PLAN

Tinnion listened intently at Cat's description of secret tunnels running through the city and plots being made by criminal masterminds.

"So, you're telling me there's one man in the city that organises every burglar and cut purse roaming the streets?"

"Not so much organising them all, but they all work in his name. Anyone stealing without his say so gets run out of the city. If they're lucky. He doesn't tolerate crime that doesn't end with something in his purse."

"And this is the man that attacked Laywyn?"

"It sure sounds like it, Tinnion." Lana was shocked at the way Caitlin had described the punishments that were handed out if children refused to do the man's stealing for him. It made her angry to think someone like that could be hurting children every day. Children that had already lost so much.

"I think we should tell Brighid and Laywyn. I think they'd be interested in hearing this. Laywyn would certainly like to get into that man's house and with Brighid's new position she could certainly bring it to the attention of the Tay. One way or another this Keikon will end up in hot water."

The three women made their way up to Brighid's new manor, Lana and Tinnion were looking forward to catching up with their friends and finding out more about Brighid's turn of fortune. It was a young man that opened up the door, he invited them in and showed them to one of the reception rooms.

"If you would kindly wait here, I will tell master Laywyn that you have arrived."

Lana laughed. "Master Laywyn?" There was something about the title that was funny to her. She had seen Laywyn covered in mud and had heard him pining over his feelings for Brighid. Just like she never thought of Brighid as the daughter of a Gesith she couldn't get her head around Laywyn being the master of a manor.

"Brighid had to leave, something about going up north on an urgent task for the queen. She wouldn't go into details but Wren, the sylph, went up with her. I've been spending most of my days with Wrens brother Yorane. He wasn't keen to be left behind either and is pretty much alone across the street in her manor. He's a good man and a very good swordsman. It's easy to see why he was selected for the tournament."

"Damn, we could have done with her new influence, and maybe her blades too."

"What's that, Tin? What's going on?"

They sat a while and shared the story Caitlin had told them. Laywyn, as they had predicted, was very interested in the news that the young thief was ready to give up her boss's location.

"There's no point in trying to go to the Tay with that story. The chances of him believing a well-known thief with so little information isn't great. We'd need a lot more to go with. Or, we could just go and beat the plot out of this Keikon fellow."

Lana coughed loudly, drawing attention to herself. "I know you want to go and get your revenge on Keikon and, quite frankly, from what I've heard of him he would certainly deserve some sort of punishment. But, I think we need to be a little more careful." Tinnion looked at Lana, her eyebrows raised.

"Go on, Lana."

"Well, if Caitlin can recognise these people, even if it's just by their voices, we could follow them a bit and see if we can find out more. After all, we have the best hunter in Mortara and a girl that knows her way around the city better than anyone else. If we can't find them then no one can. Once we have a better idea of what's going on we can decide what to do about it."

"You're making sense girl but you're spoiling my fun." Laywyn looked a little disappointed at Lana's thoughts.

"How about you talk to your new friend Yorane and the two of you go to the north side of the outer district, go to the inns and taverns and see if you can find any funny talking people. You can have a drink or two while you're there and have a little fun. Me, Tin and Cat can go to the south side. We'll have more chance that way."

"The inns and taverns are full of funny talking people, at least by sundown anyway." Laywyn joked.

"You know what I mean!" Lana gave the soldier a playful slap on the arm, and he feigned being injured.

The three women were back at the manor long before the men arrived. They hadn't found the foreigners but Caitlin had pointed out some passages used by the Keikon family and shown them places they could hide out or gain access to rooftop pathways. Tinnion had been fascinated as they walked around, noting everything she was shown and asking a lot of questions, some of which Caitlin politely refused to answer.

When the men did arrive they staggered through the door to the reception room smelling of ale and burnt grease.

"You look like you've managed to have fun then Laywyn! Did you find anything?" Tinnion asked, smirking.

"Oh. Oh! Yes. We found people. Didn't we Yorane? We found them. Tell them, Yor. Tell them what we found."

"He's right. They were all at the inn, all of them, the funny talking ones and the..." Yorane fell back into a seat grabbing Laywyn's arm and dragging him down as he lost his balance. They spent a few moments stumbling around and by the time they were both up and sat properly he had lost his train of thought.

"Laywyn?" Lana's voice was soft, and she was smiling as she spoke.

"Wha?"

"You were telling us what you found."

"Oh yes. Falcon islanders, them. They were at the inn."

"Do you remember which inn?"

"Course I do! What are you suggesting? Eh?"

"Which inn was it?"

"It was. Wait. We went to the old lead bucket but there was no one there, so we just had one jug. Then we went to the White Mare, and we thought we heard someone foreign, so we stopped there for one, but they were just people from over by Eastwood."

"No. Laywyn. No, we had three there. It was the black stallion we had one. You remember when you said that man with the beard was cheating at dice."

"Oh yes. Yes, you're right Yorane, three. There was three of 'em. And they were from the falcon islands, and two of them were staying there and one wasn't. And that one was all dressed in black and had his hood up the whole time. But the other two. They weren't."

"So, they're staying at the White Mare?"

"Yes." Laywyn nodded.

"No." Yorane shook his head and slapped Laywyn's chest. "No, they are staying at the Black Stallion where we had that fight with the big ginger bearded man that won all your money."

"Oh yes, that's right. He was cheating."

Seeing there was little use in carrying on the conversation Lana announced she'd be going to bed, and they could talk about it all in the morning.

A young maid showed her to her room, and she lay down on the soft mattress, her head sinking into the down pillow. It was so soft and warm that it took very little time for her to fall asleep.

The temple candles threw shadows, dancing and flickering across the floor. The floor stones were highly polished and glowed orange, reflecting the flames and warming the room.

"The circlet is beautiful, Qura. But what help will it be to our children?"

"The stone holds memory, thoughts and knowledge. It will enhance the mind of the one that wears it."

"And who will that be?"

"The chest will open for one that has our true soul, the stone will join with their mind and can only be worn by them."

The goddess of the skies placed the circlet within a chest upon the altar. She took her brother's hand and together they sealed the box. To be opened again only by one created by them, a child carrying a piece of their souls.

"And now?"

"And now we leave this place to time. Our children are safe and far from here. Our time in this world is close to its end. It is time to join our family."

The candles dimmed, their flames growing small, the floor stones turned back to their grey. As the gods of the sky flew from the temple the earth shook and the temple was swallowed by dirt and rock.

Caitlin announced that she wanted to visit an old friend in the commercial district; she explained that he might be able to give them more information on the Falcon islanders and what they were paying Keikon for. She thought it best to go with Lana rather than the warriors as the farm girl would fit in better and look just like another street urchin if she wore her old clothes. Lana agreed and, having fastened her belt under her blouse, she followed Caitlin to a shop in the southern portion of the outer district.

The shop was down a small side street close to the harbour road and Lana felt lost, she'd never seen this part of the city before and was shocked by how dirty and run down everything was. There were shutters hanging off buildings and doors with holes in, the path was covered in dirt and dog faeces. Lana was forced to look where she was putting her feet rather than where she was going in order to stay as clean as she could.

The shop itself was no better, the door was barely on its hinges and the floor seemed to have never been cleaned. The objects being sold were old, often partially broken or in need of a little care. There was a man sitting on a countertop, he was a little older than Lana and Caitlin and was dressed in holed and torn clothing, the type that would have been worn by a lord many years before but had been discarded due to their condition.

"Watcha, Cat! 'ows tricks?" The man's voice was low and gravelly his accent was thick and difficult for Lana to understand.

"Yeah good thanks, Tom. Just thought I'd pop by and see if you 'ad anything might be useful."

"Well, that kinda depends on what it is yer lookin' to do dunnit? Who's yer friend?"

"Oh, just some country girl, came to the big city to see the streets o' gold an' that. You know the type, sweet but a bit... slow. Takin' 'er under me wing a bit, showin' 'er the way of it 'ere."

"Very kind o' yer Cat." The man let out a short chuckle. "An' what's yer name them, country girl?"

"Ara." Lana looked down at her feet as she gave her friend's name. She didn't want anyone in this part of the city to know who she was and while lying felt wrong to her, she felt it was the wiser choice.

"All right, Ara. I'm Tom, you could say I'm Cat's big bruvver, or close enuff to it."

Lana smiled at him, then wandered over to a bucket full of rusty old swords and pretended to be looking through them.

"I was hopin' you could tell me what the big score is Olly? I saw the old man with some strangers and I wants in. If there's summit to be 'ad I want my share of it."

"Funny you should mention that Cat, the old man's been looking for ya. Offered a city bronze to them what knows where you are. He seems a little upset with ye Cat, says he doesn't mind if ye've a few bruises when 'e next sees ye."

Tom jumped off the counter, grabbing a short knife as his feet touched the ground.

"I'd rather not hurt you though Cat, you know, for family's sake."

"Run! Lana!" Caitlin drew a couple of knives that had been hidden in her blouse and faced her old friend. "I'm not so sure you wanna do this Tom. I'm a little quicker than you now."

"Being quick ain't gonna 'elp ya when there's nowhere te run now, is it?" He gestured to the shop door and the three burly men making their way through it, cudgels and staffs in their hands.

Lana pulled one of the rusty old swords from the basket and held it up between her and the men.

"I'll never forgive you this Olly." Caitlin leapt forward toward him ducking and rolling past him as he swung his knife at her.

Lana ran forward to the closest man, he was bigger than her by half and carrying a club that he swung at her head. She blocked his blow with the sword but it snapped as the club hit it, three-quarters of the blade landing with a clatter on the dusty floor. She reached down to her belt for her staff, tearing the seam of her blouse in her hurry. The big man laughed at her as she swung her hand forward.

"Wha's that little fing gonna do?"

His legs buckled beneath him as the tip of the Dryad staff struck him hard between his eyes. His friends pushed him aside and ran toward Lana. She took a stance she had learned from Daowiel, one she had been shown to use when fighting against more than one person. Her left hand raised, her left leg forward, the staff balanced in her right hand. She waited until one of the men was within striking distance and stepped forward, swinging the staff around and striking at his knees hard, both hands behind the blow. He stumbled forward and Lana stepped aside giving him room to fall before pushing at his back to help him on his way.

Caitlin was behind Tom again, crouching on the floor, a smirk on her face. He spun and lunged at her, she rose, quickly dancing to one side and dragged a blade across his cheek. He groaned as the blood dripped from his face and turned round to face her again.

The third man had his own staff and launched it towards Lana, who parried it and struck back. He had clearly fought with a staff before though and blocked her effort. They swung and blocked, parried and stepped, their staffs clashing together with force. It was a misstep that gave Lana the advantage and led to the last of the big men falling. Lana had turned her staff swinging in a wide arc above her head, and he stepped back to avoid its force, tripping over the unconscious body of the first man and on to his back. Lana stepped forward bringing the tip of her staff down onto the soft belly of the man, winding him badly.

Caitlin had disarmed Tom now, a deep cut marked his forearm, but he wasn't ready to give up and swung wildly, angrily at the girl he had called sister. She spun on her heel and landed a kick to his jaw, sending him unceremoniously to the ground with a thud and a cloud of dust.

"We'd better get out of here before more of them come."

By the time they were back on the path, the staff was once again a handgrip and the knives that Caitlin had produced were hidden. They ran out of the district and back to Brighid's manor.

36. SHADOWATCH

T welve warriors in black entered the town of Shadowatch as the moon rose. The tall tower on the edge of the cliff was dark and the buildings below it were closed up, storm shutters covered the windows and the doors were tight. The wind howled and the roar of the waves, striking the granite rocks far below, filled the air.

Brighid pulled back her hood. "Something's definitely wrong here. The inns should be open at least, even if they're windows are shuttered."

"Aye it looks all wrong." The deep voice came from a tall man on the horse at the lead. He pulled back his hood to reveal a short, grey beard and cropped sandy hair. His accent gave him away as a tuath, a native of the northern lands like Brighid. "I've ne'er known a tuath too feared o' a bit wind to forgo a tankard of ale."

They rode over to the inn and tied their horses to the rail out front. The man climbed the three steps to the door and rapped his fist against it.

"Hallo in there! Are ye no taking travellers these days?"

"Who are ye?" It was a woman's voice that answered, a shout that was muffled by the door and blown on the wind.

"Ahm Eoghann MacCathbharra, ma friends and I have ridden up frae Langa. We're wanting beds and ale. A bite tae eat and some warmth."

"How many are ye?"

"A dozen. All famished and wi a mighty thirst."

The door opened a crack. "Show's yer coin."

Eoghan took the purse from his belt and pulled it open showing the city silver inside. The door opened up fully, revealing a stout looking woman with red hair tied up. Her tartan skirt and white blouse covered by a well-used apron. Behind her half a dozen men sat around a table by a roaring fire, their plates and tankards full.

"Ye'd best be comin' in then. You'll leave yer weapons by the door though or ye'll find it closed on ye."

The warriors removed their weapons each laying them down on a bench by the door and entered the hall. The smell of cooking meat and fresh ale making their stomachs grumble. Brighid walked to the fire and warmed herself before sitting down at the table to eat. She was pleased to be back in the north, she missed it whenever she was away, but the bitter winds had her wishing she'd spent a little longer in the luxurious comfort of her new manor.

Brighid was woken by the sound of the blacksmiths hammer, the sun was still low in the east and the sky was red. She splashed her face with water and dressed in her casual clothes, leather trousers and a light blue tunic. She was a lady now, but she never felt it or dressed in a ladylike manner. Brighid felt the day would come but for now she was a warrior and warriors don't wear fancy dresses and frills.

She made her way down to the hall and ordered up some food for her breakfast, it wasn't long before the others joined her and the room was filled with the buzz of meaningless chatter.

"Yer blacksmiths up and working early eh?" Brighid asked the maid as she placed the breakfast plate down on the table.

"Oh aye, he's the busiest man in town these days. The only one making money, ma says. He's had tae take on another apprentice just tae cope wi the sharpening o' blades, let alone the forging."

"Why's that then? What's the need for it?"

"You mean ye have nae heard? There's war comin' sure enough. A moot's been called fer and there's nae doubt the clan chiefs'll all be calling in their men."

"War against who?"

"That deasin that calls hi'sel Tay. He's decided the clans are awa much o' a problem for him, so he's gathering his army to end us. He'll no find it easy though, we've men enough tae defend our towns."

"There's nae doubting that. But I've not heard anything of the Tay calling his thegn's in. Are ye sure you've heard right?"

"Oh aye. It's oor lords ain men that brought the news. There's nae doubt in his mind. Then there's those circle priests, sniffing around. There's nae one o' the clans that'd hold wi them, as you well know, but they're all over the country. Some say there's even ships frae the falcon isles off the west coast. We've no seen 'em up here but it lends weight tae the issue."

"Aye that's troubling right enough. When's the moot tae be held?"

"It's set for the full o' the moon, up at the tower there."

"And all the heads'll be here?"

"Aye, those that aren't selling out tae the Tay at any rate."

"That's good tae know, so."

With that the maid smiled and walked back to the kitchens. The warriors fell silent for a moment and looked to Eoghann.

"We'll finish up here and head off down the cliff, it's too long since I've felt the sea spray on my face."

They all nodded and sounded their agreement before tucking into their food.

37. AMBASSADOR

The ambassador from the Falcon Isles was a short man with long grey hair, in his day to day life he wore an ornate robe and was accompanied by a large, muscular guard with more knives and swords than Lana had ever seen any one person carry. Tonight though he wore plain brown clothing and a ragged grey cloak, his cowl pulled over his brow. Tinnion followed along the rooftops as he walked the streets, his guard nowhere to be seen. Laywyn and Caitlin were a few minutes behind him, making sure his guard had really been left behind. As he entered the Black Stallion he walked past the table that Lana and Yorane sat at, a jug of soft cider sat half full in front of them. The two strange sounding men Caitlin had heard were sitting at the back of the hall beside the fire and the ambassador joined them.

In a few minutes Laywyn, Caitlin and Tinnion entered the hall and sat on the other side of the door to their friends. They ordered drinks and sat, waiting and listening.

"Ze men are paid, ze way is open. We have nozing more but to wait, and it will be done."

"You were careful as you paid? Zer is nozing to show our hand in zis?"

"Ho, Yirema. Of course, we are careful. Zer is no way to trace zis back to us. It is not like zis is our first time."

"It is ze first time wiz such a target. Ze investigation will be more zorough zan any ozer task you have done."

"It is only ze zief zat has seen us. He will be silent, his loyalty is bought. Ze men he has hired know nozing of what we are doing, zey know only zat zey must do it or die in a hole."

"Here zen is ze knife. Zis will point to ze noam, zen we will have planted ze seed, succeed or fail."

Ambassador Yirema drained his tankard and left the inn, Lana and Yorane followed. The other men stayed and ordered more drinks so Laywyn stayed in the inn to make sure they didn't move on while Tinnion and Caitlin left and took to the rooftops to find their friends and follow.

The Broken Anchor was a tavern on the mid level to the harbour. It was a dirty, rough place that made Lana's skin crawl. The stench of stale ale was strong and the floor was strewn with straw, covering gods knew what. The ambassador was sitting in a nook with a large, rough looking man. Yirema was trying to keep the volume of the conversation down but the bearded giant had a bellowing voice that carried through the room.

"Aye the ships ready. Yer men are aboard and grating on me lads' nerves. They'll not be a bother, but they'll celebrate hard when yer dress wearing zealots are ashore again."

"And ze skiff?"

"It's where you want it. When I gives me word I keep it, no matter the temptation. Lucky for you."

"You'll be rewarded well in your new life."

"I'd better be or me and me lads'll be knocking at yer door. You can count on that."

"I'm sure." The ambassador threw a bronze coin on the table. "Drink yourself to sleep Xentan. Be ready when I call."

Tinnion and Caitlin arrived as the ambassador left, they sat with Lana and Yorane for a moment and then the four of them made their way to the nook and stood around the sailor.

"Your friend there might be more trouble than he's worth Xentan."

"You'd know all about that Cat. What's it like havin' a price on yer head from both sides o' the law?" The man smirked.

"Well I've always been popular, Xen. You know that." She winked at the pirate.

"Reckon you've not long left now Cat. Shame, you were

good at it and not a bad type really."

"Aww, did I win that stone you call a heart Xen?"

The sailor tilted his head to the side and smiled "Why's that, Cat? You so desperate for friends, yer offerin'?"

"Oh, I've got friends, Xen." Caitlin and Lana sat down opposite the sailor, Tinnion and Yorane stood behind him.

"This one?" He pointed at Lana. "This is what yer counting on to keep you safe? A skinny wench, a sky fairy, and a wood cutter's bitch?"

"He's not very nice, Cat, are you sure you want to talk to him?" Lana's face was screwed up. She looked as though she had just taken a large bite out of a lemon.

"He's just showing off. Give him a minute and he'll soften up. Least that's what I've heard, right, Xen?" The sailor scowled at Caitlin then leant back in his seat and nodded toward the door.

"How 'bout you and your friend here come out back an I'll show you?"

"How 'bout we all go out back and you tell us what you're doing for the Falcon lords?" Caitlin's response was quick and the playful tone had gone from her voice.

"Falcon Lords? yer messed up girl. I aint doin' nothing for them. It's those religious nuts I'm taking outta here."

"What would circle priests need with you Xen?"

"I don't know. They say they're taking some great treasure outta the city and need to be outta Mortaran waters fast. What's it to you anyway?"

Caitlin leaned across the table, lowering her voice to a whisper. "I saw 'em pay their dues, Xen. A purse full o' gold. You know as well as me there ain't no treasure in Southport worth that. If there were, Keikon'd have it in his vaults already."

The sailor paused for a moment, his brow creased. "That why you're on his list then?"

"That and a little tiff with Tom." She nodded.

"He still alive?"

"Yeah, and he was already ugly, so I might even o' helped

him out." There was a smile on Caitlin's face again and it seemed that the momentary seriousness of the conversation was over.

The sailor laughed. A laugh that seemed to come from the depths of the earth and echoed around the inn.

"You know I've got to tell him ye've been asking about the priests." The laughter was replaced with a sigh as the sailor spoke.

"You don't want to do that Xen, it'd hurt my feelings."

"Tell you what, yer friend here comes down to my ship fer the night and I'll forget all about you by morning."

"Can we not go now, Cat? He's told us what we need, and he really isn't being very nice."

Caitlin ignored her friend and continued taunting the man. "What'd be the point o' that, Xen? You've not gotten to full mast in years according to the harbour girls."

"You know there's a bonus for each o' yer fingers? Maybe I take a couple now..." Lana couldn't tell if the sailor was joking again. It seemed to her that given half a chance he would actually cut off Caitlin's fingers right there; that only the fact he was surrounded prevented him from trying. He had said it with a smile on his face though and that made her wonder.

"Maybe I end you even tryin' with the girls, Xen. How's that sound?"

Xentan rolled his eyes. "Sounds like you weren't here, Cat. You or yer pretty friend."

"I always know where to find you if I hear otherwise, Xen. Remember that."

Caitlin stood up and started to walk away, Lana quickly followed.

"If ye ever change yer mind, red, I'll be happy to show ye me main sail."

Lana gave him a slap across his cheek and walked away.

"So let me get this straight. You say there's a plot by the ambassador from the Falcon Isles to kill the queen and a bunch of priests from the circle of light are going to steal something really big and leave the city on a pirates ship?"

Captain Terrin was a middle-aged man, his stomach was too big for his uniform and his hair was little more than a circle, like a brown and grey crown around his head.

"And you got all this information from the cat? A thief that's been a right royal pain in my arse for the last ten years."

"It's not a pirate ship, it's Xentan's ship."

"Xentan. Big man. Bushy beard. Laugh like thunder?"

"Yes, that's him!"

"Xentan the pirate king of Karos, that no one's ever seen and most sailors reckon is just a myth."

"Why won't you listen to me? They're plotting to kill the queen and you're acting like I'm telling a fairy story in an inn."

"Why don't you try that? I'm sure someone there'd listen to you."

Lana wasn't getting anywhere with the captain; he was mocking everything she said.

"Now how about you tell me why you've been spending time with a known thief?"

He nodded at the guard by the door. Lana turned to see the guard taking a chain and cuffs from the wall.

"I haven't done anything wrong. You can't arrest me."

"I'm the captain of the guard and you're acting suspiciously with known criminals. I can very definitely arrest you."

"Please don't come near me." Lana pleaded with the guard, her hand reaching to her staff. "I can't stay here, if you won't listen to me we'll have to stop them." The guard opened the cuffs and held them up.

"Take her to the cells, we'll get the location of the cat from her in no time." The captain was worse than Lana had thought, she had to get out of there.

"I don't want to hurt you." She looked at the guard, her eyes narrow, her voice pleading.

The captain laughed and the guard reached out for Lana's arm. The staff sprung to full length as she spun, striking the captain across the head and knocking him to the ground. She pivoted, placing her weight on her front foot and kicked back. The guard dropped the chain and grabbed his stomach, and she turned back to face him, her staff hitting the back of his knees. He fell to the floor with a groan.

"I'm really sorry. I didn't want to hurt you but I have to get back, so we can stop this."

The coin Keikon had offered to his family on finding Caitlin had increased to a country gold. The terms had also changed. She was to be taken to him alive and bound but a bonus bronze would be paid for each finger she was missing. This news made Caitlin nervous. Keikon's family was large and loyal to him, or at least scared enough to ensure they wouldn't betray him. The only reason Xentan hadn't gone straight to him was that the sailor was head of his own family and Keikon's equal. It was the morning of the feast; the evening would see the full moon rise and everything was about to get terrible. Lana and Tinnion were meeting with Selene at the feast, as the Lore Master's aide she had been invited to attend and had managed to obtain two extra tickets. Caitlin would make her way to the harbour with Laywyn and Yorane and wait for the circle priests and whatever it was they had stolen.

As they made their way through the city streets, by Tom's run down shop, a group of men blocked their way; weapons drawn.

"You aint gettin' away this time, Cat." Tom stepped out from between two burly men armed with clubs. There were ten of them all together, each armed, each eager to take the bounty on Caitlin and take her place as Keikon's best. She turned to run back up the street but ten more men stepped from the doorways to block her escape. Laywyn and Yorane drew their blades and Caitlin pulled her knives from her belt.

"I'll kill you for this, Tom. I'll cut your throat from ear to ear." She launched forward toward her oldest friend, a tear in her eye.

"Go help her, I'll hold these men off." Yorane clapped his

hand to Laywyn's shoulder and turned to face the gang of men approaching from the rear.

38. THE QUEEN
OF MORTARA

The afternoon started with a formal presentation for the Queen's welcome to the city. Tay Gathwyn presented her with an elaborate, ceremonial, corn doll. In turn she announced the celebrations would begin and that a donation would be made to the workers of the Tay's hold. Once those formalities were done the Queen, the Tay and all those invited took their places. The queen and her party were sat on a raised platform on the east of the courtyard, their backs to the palace wall. Next to the queen was her daughter, Princess Eleassa. The ambassador was 3 seats from the queen, next to the lady Aelwynne, the Tay's daughter and Queen's Voice. Behind the Queen, dressed in ceremonial armour, was a tall, dark-haired man. His clothing showed no sign of his rank though he wore the Queen's seal and was clearly a trusted and respected man, he was addressed only as Reynard or Sir and Lana recognised him as the organiser of the feannag tournament.

Once everyone was seated, and those with invites were in the courtyard, the gates to the palace district were closed and the offerings began. Everyone there brought food or coins to be distributed later to the poorer people of the Southern Hold, they piled them up against the platform with words of thanks to their Gods and to the Queen. Most of those donating money would take a coin or two from their purses and hold them up with an elaborate gesture before placing them carefully into the small box provided and giving a short, but loud speech praising the queen and asking for her continued support. Lana's turn came, and she walked to the growing pile of donations by the stage. Her pretty stones safe in a separate pouch she took a purse from her belt. She took a city silver, holding it in her left hand and placed the rest of her purse beside the money box, which was too small to contain it. She looked up to the Queen and the Tay and quietly thanked them for her invitation before asking that some of the money donated be used to provide shelter for those living in tents on the edges of Shorebridge. The Queen nodded and smiled.

It took a while for each of those in attendance to make their donation and Lana counted four people wearing the ceremonial robes of the Circle of Light. A whisper from Tinnion confirmed they were all Falcon Islanders and had all been seen during their search for information. When the donations had all been made and the nobles in the courtyard were satisfied their charity had been properly observed a parade of entertainment began. There were jugglers and acrobats, animal handlers and dancers. Musicians came and played songs and tunes hoping for the patronage of a noble house. It was fun and at times Lana lost herself in the revelry, forgetting the danger they were there to prevent. She thought the animal handlers cruel though and expressed her feelings loud enough for those around her to hear. The use of sharp sticks and whips appalled her, and she refused to acknowledge their performances, sitting in silence alone as those around her cheered and clapped.

As the sun began its downward arc the entertainment stopped and a dance was called. Those at the long table were escorted to the clear area in front of the platform where they took a partner and began a dance. The Queen and Tay danced one tune together as a symbol of unity between the governance and the crown and then returned to their seats to watch as the entire courtyard filled with music and dancing. Some dances were traditional and familiar to Lana from the Mabon celebrations in the Stead. Others, though, confused her, and she found herself spinning aimlessly more than once, unsure as to where to put her feet or whose hand to hold. During one of the dances, the

Lady Aelwynne leaned into her and whispered the steps as they went along. Lana was grateful for her help and tried to stay close to her as much as possible.

During the next dance, she was paired at times with the ambassador, he took those moments to comment on the generosity of her donation and to express his desire to hold a private discussion with her at some point, going as far as to invite her to his official residence once the celebrations were finished. Lana graciously declined his 'kind invite' stating a prior engagement as an excuse. As she danced with the man she looked around for Tinnion, hoping she would be close. She found her, eventually, beside the flower bed, a cup in her hand and a large grin on her face.

As the afternoon wore on and the skies darkened, Lana became more anxious. She knew something was going to happen, and she started to wish it would happen sooner so that she could go back to a normal life and relax.

When the last chords of the following dance struck Lana was opposite a rather plump man with a red face and grey hair. He was breathing heavily from the activity and sweating rather a lot. He put a hand on Lana's shoulder and one on his chest, leaning forward and putting a lot of his weight on her while muttering about how he used to dance like an acrobat through his panting. Lana tried to hold him upright and comfort him as he coughed and wheezed. Then a loud bang exploded close by, echoing through the courtyard. Everyone turned to look as fireworks lit up the darkening sky with their multi-coloured rain. The entire crowd were oohing and ahhing with each explosion and display of light and so it was that few people turned their heads as the cries came from the platform where the Queen was sat.

Lana took the plump man's arm and sat him down, then turned to run back through the crowd to the platform, Tinnion was already halfway there. Reynard was fighting off a half dozen men, dressed in ragged, dirty clothing. They hadn't been part of the festivities but had managed to get into the courtyard despite the closed gates and guards. These must have been Keikon's men. Each of them was carrying an old sword and trying to get past the heavily armoured knight. Tinnion leapt up onto the platform and launched herself over the table to Reynard's side. It took Lana another moment to catch up, by which time two of the men were on the floor clutching at different parts of their bodies and moaning in pain. Lana's staff sprung to life as she joined the fray and struck out at the legs of one of the would-be assassins. As he tumbled to the floor she swung her leg, striking him square in the jaw and sending him into unconsciousness. Faced now with three opponents, two of the remaining men threw down their weapons and surrendered, begging for mercy. The third turned and fled, running toward the northern wall.

The Queen was safe, Reynard and Tinnion were tying the hands of the attackers and questioning them about their plot and alliances. Lana was checking on the Queen, ensuring she hadn't been hurt in the commotion and Lady Aelwynne was making her way through the crowd with Selene. Tay Gathwyn was shouting at his own guards, organising them to pursue the fleeing man and find out how the attackers had gained entrance to the courtyard. There was panic in the square as the crowds fought with each other, some tried to get to the platform and the queen's graces, some tried to get away from it and shouted about the possibility of further attacks.

The chaos continued for some time. As well as the information Tinnion already had she and Reynard discovered that the men had been promised extra money if they managed to kill anyone at the main table. They were reporting the information to the Tay and the Queen when Yorane burst through the crowd and ran to the platform. The guards moved to block him, but he slipped by them and grabbed Lana's arm.

"We have to go; Cat's been taken and the circle has the princess. Come on. Now." He started pulling Lana away from the crowd around the Queen and shouted for Tinnion to join them.

The guards, however, had organised themselves and stood in their way.

Lana turned back to the Queen, shouting over the chaos.

"Your Majesty, please, we need to leave, we have a hope of catching them. But I have to leave, now."

"Bring them here." The Tay's voice was hard and serious. The guards reacted quickly, grabbing Yorane and Lana's arms and marching them back to the table.

"You are the girl from Butterholt. What is your concern? The queen is safe, and we are grateful for your help."

"If I may, My Tay?" Selene's voice was calm and raised only enough to be heard through the commotion.

"We have known for some time that a group of men were plotting against the Queen and would be acting on their plans today. It was our concern that the guard was not prepared, that led my friends to take precautions. They have assisted here but it seems that this attack was not designed to succeed. The Circle of Light has another plan and the princess is in danger."

"If you've known about this, why have I not known? Why didn't you inform my guard."

"We tried, my lord. We told Captain Terrin about it, but he tried to arrest me because I learned of it from a... beggar... Please, my lord, the circle has the princess. Let us go, and we'll save her."

"My Tay?" a voice rose from one of the guards watching over the captives. Lana looked around and saw the young guard she had knocked to the floor.

"This Lady did come to the guardhouse with information, but Captain Terrin told her she was being conned by the Cat."

Tay Gathwyn took a moment to consider the young guard's words before he spoke again.

"You can go. Selene, you will remain here and tell us more about this threat. Don't make me regret this." He gave Lana a nod "Guards, release them."

"I won't, my lord. I promise." Lana nodded and pulled herself free of the guard.

As Lana, Tinnion and Yorane ran from the courtyard they heard the Tay order a small group to follow them.

39. A MURDER
OF CROWS

Brighid waited anxiously as the clan chiefs of Fearann a Tuath gathered in the town of Shadowatch. Her father would be amongst them and it had been four years since they last saw one another. She had much to tell him. It was, however, the request she had which made her nervous. The Feannag needed to know what was happening at the moot and as the daughter of a clan chief she had been tasked with joining her father's party.

Cohade MacFaern was a tall man, his red hair was long and braided, his beard was its equal and tinged with grey. He had been a muscular man in his prime but was now best described as stocky. His eyes lit up as he saw his daughter standing on the steps of the inn, and he pulled his horse up to greet her.

"Ho, daughter! Have you come all this way to see your father?"

"In a manner, father. Aye. Can we talk?"

Cohade dismounted and headed into the inn's hall with Brighid, they sat at the table and ordered a jug as they gave each other news.

"Ye ken this is nae right, father. The Tay might be a deasin, he mightn't understand our ways fully, but he'd never go against the Queen, and she'd never sanction an attack on the tuath clans."

The clan chief looked around cautiously.

"Are these yer friends, daughter?"

"Aye. They can be trusted, father."

"Well then, between us I'd say this. I'm no convinced that the Tay has any idea of whits happening here. I've a hunch it's more likely ol' Ruairidh MacKenna has his eyes set on making his hold a wee bit bigger."

"Can I join you, father? At the moot? We've tae figure this whole thing out a'fore it ends bad for all."

"Aye, lass. Ye can come in wi me. But yer friends'll not be admitted. There'll be the two o' us and Angus."

Brighid nodded her agreement, at least she'd be able to see first hand what the plan was and get an idea of the truth behind the rumours.

The seven clan chiefs sat around a large table in the tower's main hall each with his retinue stood behind him. Some had two men, some had three but Ruairidh had a half dozen men scattered around the hall with another dozen in various places between the door and the tower exit.

The host welcomed his guests and ordered up ale, then set out his thoughts. Describing the Tay as an ambitious warrior that had taken the north and pushed the clans back to the west of the taydom. He talked of the Tay's apparent belief in the one god of the circle and his affinity with their priests. He called upon his fellow clan chiefs for reports on the growing number of circle clergy in their holds and of falcon ship sightings to the west. Finally, after a long narration he called out for the pride of the tuath to be shown.

"We'll no wait for the deasin tae bring his armies through our holds and tak our lands. No! We'll tak the fight tae his door and make Northfort oors again!"

A cheer went up from the chiefs and their men. All except Cohade and the clan MacFaern.

"Ye dinnae seem eager Cohade, are ye ties tae to the Tay so strong?"

"I've seen nae proof of what ye speak MacKenna. I've heard nothing but rumours and whispers put forward as facts. I've nae desire tae mak war wi a man unless he's sure tae cause harm."

"Ye stand alone, MacFaern. It's no a good place tae be."

The others turned to Cohade, Brighid and Angus and tension filled the room. Angus put his hand to his blade hilt and Brighid moved aside a little into space.

"We all stood together and swore an oath to the Queen, MacKenna. Whether ye like him or no, the Tay is her man. If he brings an army tae ma hold he'll pay dearly but I will nae break ma oath."

"It's a case of attack wi us or defend against us, MacFaern, and I'm eager tae hear which yer choosing."

Cohade turned to look at his daughter and the warrior beside her. Brighid looked around the room. There were twenty-four warriors staring at them, their hands by their weapons. She looked at Angus, a man as broad as he was tall, he carried a blade at his side and a war axe on his back. She knew him to be a capable warrior but could he handle the odds against them? Brighid looked to her father and smiled, giving him a nod.

"I'm assuming I'll no get a chance tae leave the room without an answer then."

"Aye. You'd be right."

The clan chief of the MacFaern's stood and drew his sword.

"Let's get this over wi then."

Eoghan and the Feannag stood around the base of the tower pretending to browse the stalls or talk to one another. Their attention though was firmly on the main door to the Gesith's keep and the guards on duty there. A crash came from above and the Gesith of Langa, followed by a hail of glass followed. The sound as he hit the stone road made a number of the local stall holders sick. The Feannag reacted in an instant, rushing the guard and heading into the tower.

They were greeted by a dozen men, all heavily armed and ready for a fight. They weren't prepared for the Feannag though and the battle was over in moments. Wren was the first one through the door of the main hall, what she saw there was carnage. Brighid and her father stood back-to-back, eight warriors surrounding them. Three Gesith were standing at the back of the room, four more warriors to protect them. The rest of the room was littered with the dead.

Cohade was injured, his side bloody and Brighid had a cut to her arm. Wren launched herself into the fray, striking down the man ahead of the Gesith and putting herself to Brighid left.

"Good tae see you Wren."

The sylph smiled. "I heard you were trying to keep all the fun to yourself. I couldn't have that."

The room soon filled up with the Feannag and things looked to have turned. The warriors that had been so sure of victory against the loan Gesith and his daughter fell back. Forming a semi circle around their allies.

Ruairidh smirked and stepped forward. "Did ye truly think I'd no recognize ye Eoghann MacCathbharra? I was wondering how long it would take ye tae find yerself here."

"I wasnae expecting it tae be like this, cousin." The old Feannag sighed.

"Aye it's a shame tae end yer line like this Eoghann, ye could always walk away and let me finish what I started."

"Ye know I cannae, Ruairidh. But you can tell yer men tae put their weapons away, and we can end it all peacefully."

"Maybe ye should be looking behind you cousin. We're no alone."

A half dozen more warriors had entered the room as they talked, dark skinned fae dressed in black leather, blades drawn.

"Shadows!" The cry went out a moment before the blade cut Eoghann's throat.

40. KEIKON

Stealth and subtlety weren't things Laywyn was good at, he was a man used to fighting heavily armed warriors in the open. He had cleared the way so far but not without injury. Bruised and bloody from a dozen small cuts, his body ached, but he was determined. When he burst through the door at the end of the corridor he found himself in a room full of older children and a large man. Cat was on the floor, tied and cursing at her former keeper.

Keikon smiled. "You have a new sword then I see, it will go nicely with the one I already took from you." The large thief drew Laywyn's old sword from his side and walked forward.

The two men clashed with a flurry of swords, and the injuries Laywyn had gathered on his way through the maze of the thieves' house limited his movement and drained his strength. He found himself outmuscled and surrounded, but he was a soldier with years of experience, he had fought many men, and he recognised that the thief was not used to using a blade.

He waited for Keikon to lunge and dropped his shoulder, moving aside just enough to evade the attack. Then he brought up his sword with force, slicing through the large man's gut. As the thief fell Laywyn brought his sword around and brought it down across the back of his neck, taking the big man's head.

Laywyn let out a cry as the head hit the floor, a challenge to the thieves that were watching them fight. Not one accepted that challenge.

In a moment Cat was free and shouting orders to the thieves. Laywyn was in a chair, being bandaged and a dozen of the older children were hunting the streets for Keikon's widow.

Caitlin had always been popular amongst the family members. She had spent time with the younger children as they were brought into the family and many of the older children had grown up with her. The few adults that were part of the family ily generally liked her, they had turned on her only because of their loyalty to or fear of Keikon. The demise of the family head had changed things dramatically, a lot of the adults had fallen in the street battle and more on Laywyn's journey through the secret passages of the home. Caitlin was now one of the eldest members of the family and many were looking to her now to see how they should react to the situation.

By the time Adney, Keikon's wife, was brought into the hall Caitlin had secured her position as the new head. She had made promises to those there that their lives would change for the better. What they had would be spread amongst them fairly and that as long as things were going well no one would go hungry. Something that didn't happen under Keikon and Adney.

As for Adney, she was very unpopular amongst the children. Her initial kindness and motherly behaviour, shown to entice them into the family, was quickly replaced with cruelty. Her sadistic pleasure at handing out punishment had earned her a reputation to match that of her husbands. It was because of this she was now bound and bruised, on her knees before Caitlin.

"Cat, dahrling! Thank the gods you're here. Let me up, would you, sweety? There's no need for all of this."

"Dahrling, is it? Sweety? You've spent the last fourteen years of me life takin' everything I've got and tellin' me it's not enough. You've starved me and beat me and locked me in a cell. But now it's sweety? I reckon you know if I let 'em, your 'children' here'd tear you apart!"

"Honestly, sweetheart, I had to do all that. I had to do what Keikon said, we all did. You know that."

"I know that you whispered in Keikon's ear whenever a child stood before him. I know you smile whenever a beating is handed out and you get off on watching or doling them out."

Caitlin looked around the room, a lot of the older children were rubbing their hands, looking forward to getting a chance to pay the woman back in person. The younger children looked scared, holding each other and whispering, tears in their eyes. Then her eyes landed on Laywyn. He sat quietly, watching her closely. As her gaze met his, he raised his eyebrows in a way that showed his interest in her actions. A year ago the man's opinion wouldn't have mattered to her at all. But he had risked his life for her, fighting a gang in the streets, fighting his way through the passageways. He could have left her to Keikon and taken his own revenge at any time.

"Would you be prepared to help me again, Laywyn?"

Laywyn simply nodded.

"Could you escort our old keeper to the guard house? I could have Wes here show you a way through the passages. I'd go myself but I doubt I'd leave there."

"Aye. I can do that for you, Caitlin. I'd like something from you though too."

"What's that, Laywyn?"

"When the current situation has settled you'll come and meet with us. I want to speak with you."

"I'd be happy to!"

41. A BOAT RIDE

It was clear Yorane was holding back as they started running through the street and Tinnion knew it would be quicker for her to run the alleys and rooftops she had learned from Caitlin. She paused for a moment to catch her breath and called out.

"You go on ahead, no point in holding back waiting for me, I'll go my own way and catch up."

Yorane nodded then looked to Lana who laughed. "I'll race you, Yorane!!"

As they started their sprint away through the city streets Yorane was shocked to see Lana keeping pace, her long red hair flowing behind her like her cloak. Lana was ahead of the sylph as they approached the long steps down the cliff face to the half level platform of the harbour. The look of surprise on his face was replaced with fear as the drop of the steps grew closer. He pulled up, stopping as quickly as he could.

"Lana! Stop, you need time to..."

He watched as she leapt from the top step, the fear on his face growing. Then he sprinted forward, as quickly as he could, and dived from the edge, hoping to reach the platform before Lana and somehow soften her fall.

Tinnion watched from the roof top as her friends leapt down the cliff, her mouth agape. She jumped from the roof top using her cloak to slow her descent and ran down the stairs. When the three friends met at a wooden jetty, Lana was already sitting in a skiff, a look of concern on her face.

"Come on! We've got to get out to that ship before they set sail."

Tinnion looked to the sylph as they pulled at the oars. "What were you thinking? Letting her get ahead of you like that?"

"Your friend is full of surprises, huntress. I allowed nothing; she is simply faster than I. Though I don't understand how that is possible."

As they approached the ship they heard cries to pull anchor and away. Lana scrambled out of the skiff and grabbed the anchor chain, climbing up it as nimbly as a Dryad in a tree. She reached the top of the chain and clambered up the rest of the way to the deck, digging her fingertips into the prow of the ship. She looked through a gap in the railing and after checking it was clear pulled herself through and onto the deck. Within a moment she peeked her head over the side and lowered a rope to her friends. Tinnion went next, followed by Yorane. They were at the back of the ship, hidden from the sailors behind barrels and crates of supplies. The deck was a hive of activity and the companions knew it wouldn't be long before they set sail.

"I guess there's no way to do this without a fight. I wish Brighid were here." Lana closed her eyes and took a few deep breaths, then she felt a hand on her arm.

"You'll be fine, Lana. We've done this before. Aim your strikes low, make them think twice about getting back up and everything will work out. I'll keep my eye on you and stop anyone that gets too close." Tinnion's voice was low and sure, her smile was warm and reassuring and Lana felt a little less scared.

"Thank you, Tin."

"I will go to your left, Lana. I'll give you room to fight but I'll stay as close as I can."

Lana looked to the sylph warrior as he drew his blades. "Try not to kill them. Please. They're just sailors doing their jobs, they aren't to blame for what the priests are doing."

"As you like, Lana. I'll keep my strikes in check."

"Tin?" She looked at her friend.

"Yeah. No problem, Lana. Let's go."

Yorane stood and crossed his swords, letting out a cry

that drew the attention of every man on the deck. Work stopped and everyone turned, picking up whatever weapons they could grab. Most had knives, one or two had swords, the rest grabbed whatever heavy object was close to hand.

"If you would like to surrender now it will spare you a small amount of humiliation!" He started a slow, confident, walk from behind the crates but his words met with laughter and jeering from the crew.

That laughter ended suddenly when an arrow bit deep into the thigh of the loudest man there. Tinnion stood atop one of the crates, a second arrow already notched and aimed.

"So, what is it to be then? Will you fight or lay down your arms and let us pass so that we might take out our anger on those to blame?" Lana stepped out from her hiding place and stood beside the sylph, her staff ready in her hand.

"Two little girls and a fairy? Kill zem!" The voice was foreign, the accent thick. Lana recognised it as being the same as the envoy she had danced with. A Falcon Islander, she looked to the front of the ship and saw a priest of the circle in the doorway to the quarters.

The sailors started to move forward, spreading out across the deck, and then, with a cry ran forward.

Tinnion aimed for the thighs and arms of the sailors, trying to disable rather than kill them and two fell before they came close to meeting the other companions. Lana worked her way around them, striking as often with her feet as her staff, she broke through their line quite quickly and was able to strike from behind as the sailors were occupied with the onslaught of Yorane's blades.

The ship rocked gently on the waves, swaying side to side, but Lana danced as she had seen Brighid do. Her staff whirling through the crowd in front of her, finding soft flesh, creating bumps and black bruises. There was no escape from the companions, as the sailors moved to avoid Yorane they were met by the crack of Lana's staff on their fragile bodies.

It wasn't long before the deck was clear and the sailors

subdued. No one died in the fight, though a few men were sense-less or unconscious on the floor. They took the time to tie the sailors together as Tinnion stood guard. Once they were sure there would be no pursuit from the men, they made their way to the cabin and the maze of rooms below deck.

Tinnion led the way from here. Moving through the ship quietly and deliberately, her long bladed knife drawn and ready. Quickly taking down anyone that showed themselves as the ship rose and fell on the waves.

It didn't take long before they were standing outside of the captain's cabin, the door was barred and heavyset they could hear the priests inside arguing with Xentan. Yorane took a few paces back and launched himself at the door, it didn't move at all however and his face showed a momentary glimpse of pain.

"That door is way too solid to force open, we will need an axe and a good few minutes to get through it." He rubbed his shoulder as he spoke.

"They'll be on us long before we get through, we can't risk that if they've got the princess in there with them." Tinnion sounded concerned and looked to Lana. "What do you think?"

"Give me a moment... I'll.... Back up a bit and stay quiet."

Lana reached out and placed her hands on the panelling of the door then took a sharp breath and closed her eyes. She stood for a few minutes before taking a step back and kicking out at the door. Her friend's mouths dropped as the door splintered into a million shards at the strike of Lana's foot. In a moment an arrow flew past Lana's ear and into the chest of one of the priests as they looked up from the table at which they sat. In another the companions were inside the room, weapons drawn and ready.

"Ah, the red head. You came for me after all! Gimme a moment to clear this lot out, and we can get to my bed." Xentan laughed.

Lana looked at him and screwed her face up in disgust. "I think I'll decline, Xentan. Though I'm happy to slap you again."

"Aye. Fair enough. Listen, I reckon you and these frock wearers have stuff to talk about, how about I get out of your way and let you get on?"

"Why don't you turn the ship around and head into the port Xentan, that would be a help."

"Well, you see, I can't really do that on account of me being wanted in Southport and me ship bein' known. I can stop her going anywhere though. How's that?"

"I suppose it will do."

The pirate captain made himself as small as his bulk would allow and quickly walked round the friends and out of the cabin. Lana turned her attention to the priests.

"It's over, you know. You can't escape the room and you've no help coming. Let us take the princess back and you can go. No one has to get hurt." Lana was no longer nervous, she was strong, showing a commanding presence her friends had never seen in her and calmly setting out the terms for surrender. She knew a fight would end quickly, but there would be a risk of the princess being harmed if it came to that.

"You dare to speak zat way to a priest of ze Circle?" It was the same priest that had ordered their death that spoke up now and Lana was irritated by the arrogance in his voice. He reminded her of the sheriffs that had come to take her back in the Stead. "Do you know what we are, child?"

"You're four men, in frocks, that will die if you don't do as I say." She mimicked the pirate as she spoke.

Tinnion chuckled as her friend spoke.

"You are no longer in Mortara, child. You are in open water, and we are ze Circle, we are in control here." The man smiled and turned to the priest on his right. "Go to ze princess, if they move forward, cut her, deep."

The priest turned and walked to the corner of the room, he sat on a stool beside the cot, blade in hand.

"Now, leave the room or you'll watch as we carve up your princess."

Another arrow flew through the room and pierced the

throat of the man holding the knife.

"So, about that surrender?" Tinnion asked as she drew another arrow.

The talkative priest looked to his companions and growled.

"What are you waiting for? Kill zem already!"

The fight didn't last long at all and unlike the sailors on the deck there was no thought of keeping the priests alive. Blood spilled on the cabin floor and Lana launched herself at the leader of the group.

"Wait!... Wait. She'll die if you kill me." The priest had lost his bravado and was shaking as he spoke.

"What do you mean? What have you done to her?"

"She's been poisoned, I'm the only one that knows the antidote. If you kill me she'll be dead by morning."

Tinnion walked over to the cot where the princess lay and checked her.

"She's barely breathing and has a fever. What did you give her?"

A smirk spread across the priest's lips. "You won't find zat out until I'm free."

Lana turned to Tinnion.

"Take the princess and go back to the skiff, get ready to leave. I'll get the antidote from him once he knows you're gone."

"Lana... I do not think that is a good idea. We can search the cabin for it and take her now." Yorane's eyes darted between Lana and the priest, his head moving side to side as he spoke.

"No Yorane, he's right. He has the Princess's life in his hands, so he's in control, take my staff and go, get ready. I'll be fine."

"Well isn't that sweet? ze child gives herself up as a hostage." The priests laughed as Yorane helped Tinnion carry the princess from the room.

"Now, we're alone, I'm not armed, there's no threat to you. Give me the antidote and you can go."

Lana joined her companions back down in the skiff and gave the bottle of antidote to Tinnion. As the Princess came round they could hear the anchor once again being hauled up to the ship deck and the shouting of orders to set sail.

"So, we're just going to let them get away then?" Yorane sounded confused.

Then it started, a quiet creaking at first barely noticeable above the sound of the sea slapping at the sides of the ship. In a few moments the creaking turned to a groaning sound as wooden panels shifted and turned. Tinnion grabbed her oars and started rowing away from the ship. A loud cracking was heard, louder than the explosion of the fireworks from the festival, and echoed through the air.

The main mast buckled and fell, taking the smaller mast ahead of it down as it tumbled to the deck. A panel from the side of the ship shot free and landed ten foot away sending water spraying into the air. Another crack and another panel sprung loose at one end, sticking out beyond the bow of the ship. Yorane grabbed an oar and helped his new friends row.

Within moments half of the ship was exposed. Panels splitting and tearing their way from their bindings. The sea was full of wooden debris and the contents of the cabins now open to the elements. The companions watched as the sailors, now free, started jumping from the deck and into the sea below. Another priest followed, leaping from the shattering turmoil around him. An arrow pierced his chest before he hit the water. Tinnion smiled.

Back in the captain's cabin the hands of the talkative priest were enveloped in the wooden arms of a chair, and he was screaming as the wall beside him tore away and plunged into the sea below. In a moment the floor beneath him gave way, and he too plummeted into the choppy waters.

Lana turned to her friends. "I suppose we should go back to fish him out and take him to the Queen. I'm sure she'd like a word with him."

Xentan floated past on a cabin door as they pulled the priest from the water. "I don't know what the hell happened up there but you owe me a ship girl!"

42. CEREMONY

When the companions returned to the dock they were greeted by Lord Reynard and a dozen guards. The priest was taken into custody and the companions were encouraged to return, with a guarded escort to Brighid's home. They were subsequently ordered to appear at the Tay's palace the following morning, an escort would again be provided.

Selene and Laywyn were waiting for them at the mansion, with hot wine freshly made and ready to serve. So, despite the fatigue which had grown over them they sat together and drank a cup or two.

They listened with great interest as Laywyn told them of his encounter with Keikon and how Caitlin had taken charge within the family of thieves. Lana was relieved to hear she had ordered the woman that had tormented her taken to the guards rather than allowing her to be killed. She was also thrilled when Laywyn told them Cat would be visiting them in a few days.

Once he had told them his story Laywyn asked what had happened at the feast and listened as the story unfolded.

"Wait! Is no one going to ask about the ship? How did you do that?" Laywyn asked, rubbing his chin.

"Honestly? I asked nicely. The wood was just happy to be rid of all the iron within it. Once a few bolts were torn away the rest happened naturally."

"You learnt a fair bit while you were with the Dryad then Lana?"

"A little, Laywyn. Though I wasn't so sure what I had learned would work the way it did tonight."

"You've grown a great deal, Lana. You took control of that situation in a way I would never have expected. I have to admit, I'm liking the direction you're going in. Going back for that priest wasn't something many would have done. It showed a great deal of wisdom as well as a little mercy. Continue like that and you'll make a great leader."

"Do you think so, Tinn? I was trying to be like you and Brighid, calm and sure."

"I do."

Lana's cheeks reddened, and she smiled at her friends. "I'm sorry my friends, but I'm so tired. I'm going to need to go to bed if I'm going to get up in the morning."

There was a murmur of agreement, and they all went to their rooms while Yorane and Selene stayed in the guest rooms of the large house.

A crowd had gathered in the Tay's courtyard, which appeared to Lana to be as busy as it had been at the festivities the day before. The queen sat on the raised platform beside Tay Gathwyn as she had during the dance. Beside them stood Aelwynne and Sir Reynard and at the back of the platform a number of maids and guards ready to attend the queen's needs. The companions were given seats within a few feet of the platform, behind them a line of guards held the crowd back in place.

Once the companions were seated Lord Reynard shouted an order and the guards all crashed their lances to the floor in unison, the crowd went silent. There was a momentary pause before Tay Gathwyn rose to address those gathered and it seemed the entire city held its breath.

"Last evening, as the city celebrated the harvest, Princess Eleassa was taken by priests from the Falcon Isles. These men poisoned the princess and took her to a pirate ship in the harbour. Their intent was to return to the Falcon Isles with our princess and use her captivity as leverage over our Queen."

A groan grew through the courtyard as the crowd reacted to the news of the kidnapping.

"In the interests of Mortara the ambassador from the Falcon Isles has been detained and is being questioned by the royal guard. A priest involved in the kidnapping has also been imprisoned. He has confessed to the crime and told of the plot. The Princess is now safe and well and the Queen was unharmed in the attempt. For these things we are grateful."

A cheer replaced the jeers and the square rang out with a joyous roar.

"It is with great relief that we are gathered here today to hear the words of Queen Rhiannon."

It took a while for the crowd to settle again and silence to return to the square. Once calm returned the Queen stood and addressed the crowd.

"The people of Mortara are strong, we do not bend to extortion, we do not surrender to those that wish to control us. We stand as one against those that would hurt our country. And we stand victorious.

It is with great pride that I stand before you today, as a diverse group of Mortarans came together, in an unusual circumstance, to defy the priests of light and deny them the hold on our country they desired. Warriors, hunters, fae, city dwellers and a country maid. These are the people to whom we owe our thanks today.

Each of these Mortarans placed their lives in danger to protect our country, to protect my daughter and for that I am grateful. And so today I will show my gratitude and reward those that came to my aid in a moment of need. It is to them I dedicate this day and this feast.

Let the celebrations begin!"

The celebrations continued into their second hour and those on the platform went back into the palace halls. A soldier, dressed in the silver armour of the queen's personal guard approached the companions and invited them to follow him back into the palace to meet in private with the Queen. An invitation they were happy to accept.

Once inside they sat around a grand table, large enough to seat twenty or more. On one side sat the Queen, the Princess and Tay Gathwyn and all of their retinue. On the other the companions. Lana was given the seat opposite the queen and her wide-eyed look gave away her nerves.

"Let me start by giving some assurances." The Tay spoke with a low, soft voice. The kind of voice that could lull you to sleep but would be impossible to ignore giving an order. "The priest and the ambassador will remain here in custody, a number of their companions have also been arrested and the threat, as far as we can tell, is over."

Lana smiled and clapped her hands before turning bright red and lowering her head as she noticed no else had joined in.

"Tay Gathwyn and Lord Reynard have both told me some of your stories. Yorane, your achievements at the tournament were impressive. Lord Reynard and I agree that we would like to invite you to join the silver. I understand the life of a guard is somewhat different to that which you have lived thus far and I want you to know that no offence will be taken should you turn the invitation down."

"No, Your Majesty. It would be an honour to wear the silver and to serve you." The sylph had a smile on his face so wide Lana worried that his jaw might fall off.

"Selene, I understand that your part in this was small, but your explanation at the feast gave us understanding. I have spoken with the Master of Lore this morning and you are to be officially named his personal aide. I hope in time you will show yourself a capable successor."

"Thank you, Your Majesty. I will do my very best."

"Laywyn, former captain. I understand you carry an injury that rules you out of rejoining my guard?"

"I have the will, Your Majesty. Sadly, however, my body hinders my abilities."

"And yet, from what I understand, you are responsible for ridding this city of the thief Keikon and bringing his wife to justice."

"I had a little help, Your Majesty."

"Indeed. As a soldier you swore an oath to the crown. Are you willing now to swear to me directly?"

"In a heartbeat, Majesty."

"Then you will leave here a Ser and you will be granted a purse."

"I am honoured, Majesty." Laywyn bowed his head.

"Your 'helper', should you meet her again, will also have the opportunity to swear her allegiances and give promises. In return for which we would be willing to forgive her past... indiscretions."

"Should I see her again, your Majesty, I will be sure to let her know." Both the queen and the old soldier smiled.

"Now, Tinnion. Selene was kind enough to tell me a little of you as you were rescuing my daughter. A hunter with great ability and a finder of hidden temples. You came here, in part, to pay the debts of your father and redeem your family name. Would you too swear an oath to serve me?"

"I would, your Majesty."

"Then you will join Laywyn once we are done here and be named Thegn."

Tinnion bowed her head, her cheeks a little red and Lana wrapped her arm in hers, giving her a hug.

"And finally, the farm girl. Between your friend Selene and Tay Gathwyn, I feel I have been given a reasonable account of your journey to Southport and the reason behind it. I am left to wonder though how a young milk maid, barely a woman, finds it within herself to lead the rescue of a princess? There is more to you, I am sure, than the story told.

You will ride to Butterholt in the morning, accompanied by Aelwynne and a guard. Heriloth will be ordered to release your family and acknowledge your innocence. Of which I have no doubt. Once your journey is completed, I invite you to return and join us in the palace, as a lady in waiting."

"Thank you, Your Majesty. I don't really know what to say... Oh, but I do have something I was asked to give to you or the Tay. May I?" She reached into her tunic and pulled out a letter.

"Of course." Lord Reynard reached over and took the paper from Lana, then passed it onto the queen.

There was silence as the queen read the letter she had been presented, Lana sat with her hands between her thighs and her head down, waiting quietly to see what the letter she had carried was about.

The queen put the letter down and then looked intensely at Lana. It seemed at that moment the room and everyone in it held their breath.

"I may need to rethink my plans for you, Lana Ni Hayal." Lana was struck by the serious tone the queen had used as she broke the silence. All of a sudden she felt a little uncomfortable and shifted in her seat.

"I'm afraid I will have to insist on your return here to Southport once your family is safe and your reputation clear. This letter has taken that choice from you. I assume you are capable of delivering my reply?"

"Yes, your Majesty."

"Then I would like you to tell Olerivia, Queen of the Dryad, that I would be happy to meet with her and agree to her terms."

"Yes, your Majesty."

The jaws of those on the queen's side of the table fell open at the mention of the Dryad queen. They all looked at Lana again with curiosity and a little suspicion.

"Tell me though, Lana. Are you aware of the terms presented?"

"No, your Majesty. I was just asked to carry the letter."

"Then I think we shall have to spend a little more time together when you return from Butterholt."

"Is something wrong, your Majesty?" Lana chewed on her bottom lip as she waited for the answer.

"No, Lana. Just very strange." The queen smiled. "There's no need for you to worry, I'm simply puzzled by this unexpected turn. It's not often I find myself surprised by people but you have managed it twice in two days now."

43. AELWYNNE

L ana woke early, she had found sleep quite difficult that night as her mind wandered. She thought of her family and her friends in the Stead and how good it would be to see them again. She thought of how the Gesith might react when instructed to release them and accept Lana's innocence in the death of his son. She wasn't sure he'd be too happy with the situation but with the voice of the queen there and a guard as well as the sheriffs the Tay had sent previously, he would have no choice but to accept.

Lana wondered what the Dryad queen's letter had said and how it had changed Queen Rhiannon's mind on her future. She wondered what her family would say when she told them about her journey and that she had been ordered back to Southport to spend time with the queen.

The queen! She had dreamt about seeing the queen as a child, catching a glimpse of her walking the streets of Southport. It had been a daydream she never imagined would happen and yet here she was. She had talked to the queen, she had helped rescue the princess, she was going to be spending more time with the queen in the future. The life she was leading now was beyond her dreams and yet it had been so full of difficulties and horrid experiences. Bad things that had scarred her, physically and emotionally. She reached up to her shoulder and touched the crude 'A' that had been cut into her flesh.

She had spoken to her friends and Tinnion was eager to come with her to Butterholt. That made her happy. The most amazing thing about her journey had been the friends she had made along the way. She felt a love for Daowiel, Tinnion and

Brighid that was similar to the love she had for her family. She felt that in Selene, Kaorella, Laywyn and even Caitlin she had made friends that would be with her throughout, and help shape her life. Thinking of her friends made her think of Leuthere and Allric the soldiers that had died protecting them. She had only known them a short time, but she had come to like Leuthere, his laughter had been contagious and filled her with happiness. Poor Allric had been so young and his obvious love for Tinnion had made him so endearing. Their loss had hurt her, it had shown her that the world was hard and unforgiving sometimes.

When the first rays of light broke through the window of her room she jumped from her bed and dressed. She had put her belongings into a bag the night before which she grabbed on her way down the stairs. Kaorella was preparing a special breakfast for the group and Lana was excited to tuck into it.

Tinnion walked Lana through the city to the Tay's palace where they met with Aelwynne and the four soldiers that would be accompanying them to Butterholt. Eight horses had been readied for their journey; Lana had been given a chestnut mare with a little white star on its brow. She stroked the horse's nose and scratched her ear before mounting up and whispering in her ear. "We're going to have so much fun riding to the Stead. It's such a beautiful place, full of fields for you to run in."

They walked their way through the city and over the bridge before allowing their horses to run along the road a little once they had cleared Shorebridge. The day was clear and the road was quiet, so they travelled a good distance, passing fields and a copse or two of trees. When they stopped for the night Aelwynne pulled Lana aside to talk.

"How are you feeling, Lana? Are you excited to be going home?"

"I feel excited to see my family and for them to be safe, it's going to be such a wonderful thing. I'm just a little nervous about the Gesith and how he'll react to it all."

"That's understandable, I hope you know I'm here to support you as much as to ensure the queen's orders are observed. I'm hoping to get to know you as we travel, the queen is very intrigued by your relationship with the Dryad."

"Oh, well, Daowiel, the princess, she used to watch me sometimes, and she always laughed at me. She says that when I say thank you to the trees for letting me climb them or for letting me have their fruit it's funny because humans can't talk to trees. Then when I ran away from the Stead the queen wanted to speak to me, cos I was in their forest, so they let me in the palace, and we spent some time together. Then I went back because I needed to know what was happening to me and the queen knew, and she told me the first time that I would go back, so she wasn't surprised, but I was. And that's when she gave me the letter."

"Woah, slow down. Take a moment and breathe. So, you say you went back to find out what was happening to you?"

"Uh huh. It was confusing and I was a bit scared. The first time it happened I thought maybe I was going mad but then I realised it was what the Dryad do. That's when I understood the queen could help."

Aelwynne smiled and placed her hand on Lana's arm. "Don't be so nervous, Lana. Start again and tell me from your first time in the palace."

Lana took a deep breath and started to tell Aelwynne her story. Taking her time and letting her know everything she thought was important to know. The moon was high when they finally turned in, Lana was tired and her mouth was dry from all the talking she had done.

44. BACK HOME

The journey was peaceful, a far cry from the journey Lana had taken to Southport, and she found she was spending a lot more time talking and answering questions as they rode than she had before. Aelwynne was really curious about Lana's journey and her time in Southport and seemed to want to know every little detail, so she asked a lot of questions. She didn't answer so many though and Lana felt she was being interrogated at times.

She did learn a little about her new travelling companion though. Aelwynne was the daughter of Tay Gathwyn and had been the queen's emissary for eight years. She was eight years older than Lana and had grown up around the palace in Southport and the royal family. She was often called the Queen's Voice and held a lot of power around the country; representing the queen when she was unable to be involved herself.

Lana found Aelwynne to be rather formal initially and that made her uneasy but once they had spent some time together the formality dropped and they grew closer. She was very intelligent and attentive, listening to everything Lana had to say, even during her long rambling stories. But she was also friendly and showed a lot of empathy, the details of Lana having to leave the Stead shocked her. The burning of the house and killing of the blacksmith, the cruelty of the punishment given to Ara and of course the attack on Lana and her family. A hundred years ago those things would have happened without comment from the royal house but things were different now. Queen Rhiannon had changed a number of laws since inheriting the crown from her father. She believed in justice for all of her subjects. Of course, Aelwynne explained to Lana, it is only possible to change a law and enforce it where you have representatives. But if those people you trust fail you, it is almost impossible.

"Could you show me how you travel in the trees, Lana?" They were camped in a copse of trees by the side of the road and Aelwynne seemed hesitant to ask.

"You have to know the trees before you travel." Lana explained as she placed her hand upon the trunk of the tree next to her.

She closed her eyes and reached out, then she heard the sharp intake of breath from Aelwynne as she disappeared into the tree. She was gone a while and Aelwynne was left astounded when she re-appeared carrying a skin of wine and a roast chicken on a skewer.

"Where on earth did you get those?" Aelwynne's eyes were wide.

"Oh, I popped out of the tree behind the 'Old King's Dog' and ordered them for us." She panted a little as she spoke.

"So, you could just go and get us food whenever we wanted?"

"Well, it's not as easy as that."

Lana went on to explain how travelling by the bridge worked, explaining how tired it made her to travel distances and how you should be sure it was safe before popping out into an area. Aelwynne leaned forward, her head tilted toward Lana as she talked and Lana was sure everything she was saying was being noted and kept in the emissaries' mind.

It was the day of the first quarter moon when they arrived in the Stead. The sun was bright but gave little warmth and the trees were shedding their leaves fast. Lana stopped as they approached the square of the stead, tears in her eyes. Her home had been burned to the ground, Only the stone foundation remained. The square, normally a place of meeting for the Stead folk was empty and the doors of the surrounding houses were closed. She climbed down from her horse and ran into the square toward the small house they had built for Thenra and Ara. She called out to them as she knocked at the door, but she got no answer. The shutter on the window to the side of the house was quickly closed with a clatter and Lana cried.

"Ara, please. It's Lana. It's safe I promise, I'm here with the queen's men. Please, come out."

The door opened a little and Ara poked her head out. She stared at the soldiers, at Tinnion and Aelwynne. Seeing the fear in her friends' eyes Lana introduced them to her. And called them over to show they posed no threat. The door opened fully and Ara stepped out. They sat on a bench beside the well in the centre of the square and Ara explained that the Gesith, annoyed at the presence of the Tay's men had become as hard as he could within the laws of the land. He had set curfews and made it a crime to gather in the square. The rents he was charging to remain in the Stead had risen, and he took a greater share of everything they made. Life had become miserable and hard. Thenra had passed recently, hunger and an early cold had overwhelmed her, and she passed in her sleep.

Lana held her friend close and they cried together.

"Things will change now." Aelwynne looked to Lana to sign what she was saying to Ara. "I am the Voice of the Queen and I will put an end to the hardship you have suffered. You have my word."

The party took a drink from the well and rested a little before mounting up and heading up the path to the manor. They had all felt pity for the people of Butterholt and their faces were stern as they rode.

One of the silver sounded a horn as they approached the manor gate and the party stopped, awaiting a response from inside. The gates were open and Lana watched as panic filled the square, pages ran to and fro, sheriffs and courtiers ran to the manor, closing the doors behind them. The first to walk through the gates were the Tay's men.

"Ho! It is good to see you, Lady."

"And you, Captain Crurith. Though I have been deeply saddened by everything else I have seen since my arrival in this holding."

"My Lady. You will find no dissent of your opinion from me or my men. We do what we can for the people here but sadly we cannot challenge the Gesith's law."

"I Understand, Captain. Where is Heriloth?"

"He is within the manor, My Lady. I fear he finds our presence rather irritating."

"Well if he will not observe proper protocol and greet us in person then we shall have to make it impossible to ignore our presence."

With that the Tay's men stepped aside and allowed the party to ride into the square.

"Form up!" Captain Crurith ordered his men, and they fell in beside him, their armour and weapons readied.

"Stay at my side, Lana." Aelwynne reached out and squeezed Lana's hand reassuringly. "Would you mind taking my left, Ser Tinnion?"

Tinnion smiled and took her bow from her back. "Of course, my lady."

Together they entered the manor and its hall. The Tay's men initially ahead of them and the silver behind. As they entered the hall the Tay's men moved aside and allowed the women to walk forward unhindered.

Gesith Heriloth sat on a grand chair at the end of his hall, his face was red and had a look of thunder upon it. He turned from shouting at a page to face the oncoming Lady.

"Lady Aelwynne. What can I do for you?"

"You can begin by standing and greeting me correctly, Heriloth. I am not some common courtier to be welcomed in this manner."

The Gesith stared in silence for a moment, his eyes tight and his brow creased. Aelwynne smiled sweetly. Sensing his moment of defiance should end he stood and bowed.

"Lady Aelwynne, my apologies. Welcome to my hall and my hold."

"You almost managed to sound sincere, Heriloth. Well done."

"To what do I owe this honour, my lady?"

"You have in your custody a family of stead folk, Hayal's kin. You will release them and compensate them for their imprisonment."

"I shall not. They are held for assaulting my sheriffs and protecting the murderer of my son."

"What happened to your son, whilst I'm sure difficult to bear, was an act of nature. You cannot enter a bull's territory without precaution."

The Gesith looked at Tinnion and Lana for the first time and showed recognition.

"I see you have the murderer here with you. Sheriffs!"

Two men stepped forward, their hands on the hilt of their swords. Tinnion raised her bow, an arrow notched in a blink of the eye. The silver and the Tay's men drew their swords in unison, sending a haunting sound through the hall.

"You will stand down." Aelwynne commanded the sheriffs who looked to the Gesith, confused.

"This is my holding, child. You cannot come here and order me like some peasant."

"I am no child Heriloth, I am the Queen's Voice and I command all in her name. It is our Queen's will that this family be released and compensated. This woman has been found innocent of any crime in the court of Tay Gathwyn and will be untouched by you or your men."

"And what compensation am I to provide exactly?"

"Their house will be rebuilt and you will give a purse of one city silver in value to each."

The Gesith choked, a look of despair changed to anger in a flash.

"Bring the prisoners up." The command was given with a

scowl. The two sheriffs that had been ordered to take Lana left the hall.

"I am afraid my house is full, Lady. I will be unable to house you or your men. Your father's men, I fear, will also need to vacate. I am sure you will find shelter on the road back to Southport."

"Do not presume we are finished Heriloth."

45. GESITH

When the sheriffs returned to the hall, they led Lana's family, still chained, thin and pale. Behind them followed a half dozen more sheriffs armed and wearing their armour along with an equal number of courtiers each with swords at the ready. The prisoners were pushed to the floor at the Gesith's feet. The sheriffs, now outnumbering their visitors, emboldened and cruel. Gesith Heriloth gave a thin smile.

"Cut them free." He commanded his men as he took four coins from his purse. He threw the coins at Lana's family, never taking his eyes from Aelwynne.

"As ordered, My Lady. Now, I bid you farewell."

Lana ran to her family, helping each to their feet and hugging them. She looked at the Gesith, her eyes swollen and red.

"You should be ashamed." Her voice was quiet but cutting. She walked her family back to the safety of The Silver.

"We will speak in private now, Heriloth. Your men and your courtiers are dismissed."

"No, My Lady. They will remain here with me. I will not be alone with you and your guard."

"Very well. I had thought to spare you the shame, but if you wish they may stay." Aelwynne paused, giving the Gesith time to consider and change his mind. He remained silent, staring at the queen's voice with disdain.

"I see. Then we shall continue." Aelwynne took on a note of formality.

"It is by order of Queen Rhiannon the first that on this hour, you, Heriloth of Butterholt, are relieved of your duties. Your title and your privileges removed. You will be allowed to retire with whatever money you have in your purse now. Though you may take nothing more and may not remain in Butterholt. Your sheriffs are relieved of duty and the hold will be placed into the care of an administrator, all lands and property reverting to the crown."

The atmosphere in the hall grew static, swords were drawn and angry exclamations shouted. Lana took the handle of her staff from her belt and readied herself to defend her family.

"You are dismissed, Heriloth. You must leave this hold now, never to return."

"Kill them! I'll reward any man that takes her head with half the hold!" Heriloth spat his order, his face bright red and his mouth frothing. He ran to the wall behind his chair and took down a broad sword before turning to face Aelwynne again.

An arrow pierced his left eye.

The ex Gesith's men stood, still as statues. Their leader fallen; their titles removed. Considering their futures carefully they dropped their weapons, one by one, and took to their knees.

Aelwynne walked to the fallen man, she bent down and removed his purse and the ring that was his seal of office. She sat in the tall backed seat and addressed his men.

"Take his body, give him a proper burial. You have until the full moon to vacate your properties and leave the hold. I am sure some of you will find employment with another lord."

"My lady," one of the sheriffs spoke. "We followed orders, no more, please have mercy on us."

"It is because I choose to believe this that you have the chance to leave here today. You each drew your swords against the queen's emissary and for that you could be executed."

The men stood and left the hall, four of them carrying the body of their lord.

"See they cause no trouble as they leave, Captain," Aelwynne ordered the Tay's men, and they followed the former sheriffs.

With the manor cleared of its occupants Aelwynne took the Gesith's room and had others prepared for Tinnion and Lana's family. The guards took residence in the Gesith's men's barracks. Meals were prepared and served to the temporary residents in the manors dining hall and the staff expressed their relief at the day's happenings.

Lana sat between her parents, holding their hands and hugging them in turn through the evening. She told them of her journey and her meeting with the queen, asking repeatedly if they were okay and if she could do anything for them. When she finished her story her mother, Ellie, looked concerned.

"Is it true, Lady Aelwynne? Will you be taking our daughter away from us again?"

"I am afraid your daughter must return to Queen's Island with me when we leave, yes. Whether or not that means you are separated again is a decision for you all to make. There will be options for you all, I am sure." Aelwynne smirked and Lana thought she recognised a glint of mischief on the emissary's face. She knew more than she was saying, Lana was sure of that.

"Now, it has been a long and eventful day. Tomorrow will likely be just as challenging, so I suggest we retire to our rooms and try to sleep."

Aelwynne revealed more of her plans as they ate breakfast the following morning.

"Might I count on your assistance today, Hayal?"

"Of course, My Lady. Anything that I can do to repay you."

Aelwynne's smile was wide. "The stead appears to be in disarray, your friends and neighbours scared and, honestly, I know little about farming. I wonder if you and Andel could head down to the Stead and let everyone know what has happened. I would like to invite everyone in the Stead to a meal here tonight."

"Yes, of course, My Lady."

"Lana tells me you made the most amazing treats when you were head of the kitchens here Sera?"

"They were certainly sweet enough to keep a growing girl happy, My Lady."

"Might I ask you to go back to your kitchens and prepare a feast for the stead?"

"It would be an honour, My Lady."

Aelwynne turned to Ellie then. "Ellie, dear. Lana has been such a great help; she has a bright future ahead of her and today she must deliver my queen's message to another queen. Beautiful though she is, her clothing is far from appropriate. I wonder if you can find her something a little better in the rooms upstairs?"

"M'lady." Ellie nodded With a smile.

"Well, Lana. You aren't going to let your mother do all the work now are you?"

"No, Lady Aelwynne. Of course not."

Once Lana's family were all on their way and occupied, Aelwynne turned to Tinnion.

"So, Tinnion. What do you know about farming?"

46. ANSWERS

The Dryad throne room filled quickly when news spread that the Ògan had returned with a message from the human queen. Murmurs followed Lana as she walked down the aisle toward the throne, whispers of future visits to woodlands far and wide. Her forest green dress, a hint of future earrach in contrast to the golden browns and reds of the late foghar forest. She curtsied as she reached the queen and the room fell silent.

"Welcome back, Ògan. I hope you are well?"

"I am, Your Majesty, and I bring word from the court of Queen Rhiannon of Mortara. May we speak?" Lana's voice was stiff, uneasy, with the formalities she had been instructed to use.

A familiar giggle came from the side of the room and Lana turned quickly to Daowiel, sticking her tongue out.

"I hope the news is good, Ògan?" The queen was smiling, her eyes glistened.

"I think so, Your Majesty. Queen Rhiannon has asked me to advise you that she accepts your proposal."

"That is wonderful news. And your family? They are now free?"

"They are." Lana's smile was wide and bright.

"Will they return with you to Southport, or remain in the stead?"

"That hasn't yet been decided, Your Majesty."

"But you will return to Southport?"

"To the Queen's Isle." Lana nodded as she spoke "She wishes to find a role for me in her palace."

"Then I think we should continue our talk in private, Ògan. There will be questions and it's time you had some answers."

"The lake was dry, the forest burned, the fortress of the gods lay in ruins. A dozen Dryad families had been taken to the world tree, Kaoris' home, now the Dryad palace. A safe haven that lies half within this world and half without. The Gods had made their children safe before leaving the world to mankind.

The humans had no interest in the old fortress, their king was in the south, his lords had castles in the north and east. And so Mortara's heart was left. Seeds that had fallen found their feet in the soil. The damns, built to destroy the nymph's home, eroded and the river returned. The lake reformed around the fortress ruins, creating islands of the higher land.

And then a child came. A child that talked to trees and held no hatred for the fae. The child placed her hand upon the elemental stone and the essence of the gods was freed.

You, Ògan are that child. You hold within you a fraction of the old god's abilities. Dryad, noam, nymph and sylph, you have the abilities of all, though you must learn to use them. More than that, it seems your abilities are pure, undiluted by the centuries that have separated the fae from their gods.

You are capable of doing things we can no longer do.

I do not know what your future holds Ògan, I do not know if you will unlock your true potential. I do know, that in time, you could be capable of things this world has not seen for a thousand years. Stay true to your heart and those things will be great.

I have faith in you, Ògan. I will help you where I can. But I must ask for your help also and that brings us to the condition of my agreement with Rhiannon. You are to be there as we hold our talks. A human that is loyal to her kind and a trusted friend of the Dryad.

Daowiel will accompany you. I know she wants to explore the world outside of our forest and this appears to be the right time to allow that."

Lana smiled at that news.

"There is one other thing you should know. The soul of the fae is undying, when our bodies betray us our spirit is reborn in another, in another time, another place. But if we betray our word our spirit dies. Your soul is fused with the souls of our gods. I do not know how that will affect your spirit upon death. Were I you, I would not give my word or swear an oath I could not keep."

"Thank you for your advice, Your Majesty. I'll keep that in mind."

Daowiel paused when the time came to leave the shade of the trees. Lana turned to look at her friend and smiled, she held her hand out to the princess. "We can take a moment, if you like?"

Daowiel nodded. "I've never been in a place with no trees, even in the clearings of the forest there is a canopy. Knowing that I will be stepping out into that world now is strange."

"When I left the forest and made my way to the road south I didn't know how far away things were or what towns would look like. It was all new to me, and I was nervous. But my friends helped me and I knew it would be an adventure. You met Tin, she's here too."

"The huntress?" Lana nodded.

The princess took a deep breath and held Lana's hand then walked onto the path beside the pasture.

The two friends laughed and talked as they walked to the manor, keeping Daowiel's mind from her nervousness and her eyes from the endless, leafless skies above. Once inside Lana made introductions and took Daowiel to her room to get ready for the feast that had been arranged.

47. RELATIONSHIPS

T he feast was going well, Lana sat with Aelwynne to her left and Daowiel to her right. Her family sat opposite and were enjoying the evening. They were beginning to look like their old selves again and that made Lana happy. What thrilled her though was the sight of Ara and Andel sitting together and holding hands beneath the table.

When the sweet buns were brought to the table Lana dived for the platter and took two. She picked at the first, pulling small pieces from it and eating it slowly, enjoying each piece as much as possible before swallowing it.

"These are the best! I have missed your treats so much Sera!"

Before Sera could respond Aelwynne stood and called the courtyard to pay attention.

"I am pleased you have all taken the time to join us here. As you must know now, a lot has occurred since our arrival in your stead. The Gesith of old is dead, his sheriffs and courtiers gone. They will harm you no more. This was done, in the name of Queen Rhiannon, to free you from the burdens of an unreasonable Lord."

A cheer spread around the courtyard as Aelwynne spoke. She paused for a moment and waited for it to die down.

"An administrator will be appointed to the holding, a person trusted by the queen to carry out her instructions, rebuild the Stead and create a better life for you all. She will need your help and your support as they rebuild and reorganise the hold. I know I can rely on you all.

Would you like to address the stead, Tinnion?"

Lana's jaw dropped as her friend stood. The news came as a true surprise and left Lana feeling torn. She was happy for her friend, to be rewarded in this way, given the chance to have a holding of her own, that was wonderful and Tinnion deserved it. She was happy the hold and the Stead in which she grew up would be in the hands of a practical and kind person, someone she knew would keep the people safe and well. But at the same time the news cut her. Tinnion was her friend, they had grown so close and now, just as she was reunited with her family and another friend was joining her, she would be leaving Tinnion behind. She wanted so desperately to have her family and her friends together, in one place, safe and happy but it seemed life would not allow her that.

When Tinnion finished speaking Lana got to her feet and hugged her tight.

The surprises continued the following day as Tinnion held her first court as Administrator. The first petition was from Andel. Lana had spent some time with her brother the previous evening, and they had talked about things in general, what they thought of Tinnion's appointment and how they felt their lives would progress. He had told Lana he was happy, and he would consider his future once he had talked to their parents.

As he stood Lana could see he was shaking, his nerves getting the better of him.

"My lorrr, err, m lady." His face turned bright red, and he wiped his brow on his sleeve. "Sorry, my lady. I would like to ask your permission, if it's something that I can do to... Well, I realised when I was locked in the cell that I missed my sister and my job and good food but that the thing I missed most. I mean, the person I missed most, was Ara. And I wondered if it would be possible for us to be hand fast?" Sweat was pouring from Andel's head by the time he finished staggering his way through his request. He turned to Ara and smiled, a nervous smile.

"I take it that Ara wants to be married too?" Tinnion asked him, with a smile.

"Oh yes, m'lady. Yes, she does."

"I'm afraid that I can't give you permission without Ara's word of acceptance, Andel."

Lana's brother panicked "Well, she... I mean, she would m'lady but..."

Tinnion laughed. "I'm sorry Andel, I was just teasing. I didn't mean to panic you. Of course, you can marry. On one condition."

"What is that m'lady?"

"You allow us to hold your ceremony here before Lana returns to Southport."

"Oh yes, m'lady. Of course! I would... that is, we would love that... Wouldn't we Ara?"

Ara nodded; her face bright with joy.

When everything was over and all the Stead people's petitions had been heard Aelwynne called a private meeting. She requested Lana, her family, Daowiel and Tinnion to be there. Everybody else was dismissed.

The participants sat around the table in the dining hall and Aelwynne opened the meeting.

"Lana, Daowiel and I will need to leave the Stead by the full of the moon, we have things to attend to in Southport before moving on to the palace on Queen's Isle. In the meantime, we will do what we can to assist in the transition towards Tinnion's administration of the hold. This is why I have called this meeting. I have information that may shape your futures and the future of this stead.

Lana's appearance in Southport and the events that have happened since caught the Tay and the Queen by surprise. A surprise further compounded by the letter of the Dryad Queen. We knew little of Tinnion or Lana and there was concern over her future. I was instructed to get to know you all, and I was given authorisation to present you all with opportunities should I deem them appropriate.

Tinnion has impressed me, and I was convinced she was

the right choice to lead this holding. That leaves me with choices to make with you all. Princess Daowiel aside.

It is my hope that you will become my aid, Lana. You will learn from me and work with me. You have a lot to learn about protocol and etiquette but your heart and your head are, without doubt, in the right place. Your beliefs, so far as I can tell, align with mine and our queen's.

Should you accept my offer you will be housed in the palace, Princess Daowiel as well. Your family then would face a choice. Employment is available on the Queen's Isle, and employment brings with it accommodation. Each of your family would be welcome.

Alternatively, I know Tinnion would also like to make your family an offer."

Tinnion put down her tankard and coughed, placing her hand on her chest. "Mmhmm. Yes, I know how to set up communities, how to ensure everyone has what they need. As a hunter, travelling the country and meeting with others to follow our prey's migration we frequently do this. But I am a hunter, what I know about farming is limited. I am going to need help. Having you here would make things better, easier. With you helping me to rebuild we could make the hold a happier, more productive place a lot quicker and with fewer mistakes. The stead will be rebuilt, making the homes there more comfortable, you could choose to live there or to stay here, in the manor."

Once the meeting was over the previous day they had found a quiet corner of the manor and discussed an idea. Something Lana believed would make the changes and rebuilding of the hold easier for all. Once they had come to an agreement between them that they believed would work they spoke with Tinnion and Aelwynne.

"We've been talking, and we think we have an idea that can help. You're going to need wood to rebuild things and to keep the fires going, so I asked Daowiel if we could find a way to work with the Dryad instead of destroying their home and hurting them. There are trees that are dying, or dead, trees that would provide wood to build or burn, and they're scattered throughout the forest. If you promised to let the Dryad plant some new trees along the border in the pasture. It wouldn't take up much space but it would help them. Then in return we could arrange for people to be escorted to trees that can be used without hurting the Dryad, they could chop them down and bring them to the Stead to use. Then everyone could be happy."

Lana watched as a smile grew on Aelwynne's face. "What made you think of this, Lana?"

"Well it just makes sense, doesn't it? I mean the trees are there. I know that the Dryad are really nice, but they get upset and angry with humans 'cos we go and chop down their trees all the time. If we only chop down trees they let us take, and we let them plant new trees then we could all be friends, like me and Daowiel."

"It does make a lot of sense. The choice is Tinnion's but the idea has my approval."

"It sounds good to me, if it can be agreed with the Dryad Queen."

"I'm sure my mother will approve. Lana and I will go and talk to her tomorrow."

The following day saw the manor courtyard a hive of activity once again. People coming and going decorating the square for the joining of Andel and Ara. Meanwhile, Lana and Daowiel travelled to the Dryad palace once again, eager to share their idea.

The smile Lana had seen grow on Aelwynne's face was reflected in Queen Olerivia's. She asked a few questions, wanting to know more about Tinnion and how many people would have to be allowed into the forest. It didn't, however, take long for the agreement to be finalised and a promise was made to have three Dryad warriors escort two woodcutters to their first tree on the following day. They would meet on the edge of the pasture as the sun reached its peak.

When they returned to the Stead the manor square was set and the Stead folk were gathered. Lana hurried to see her brother and Ara, hugging them briefly and expressing her happiness at their decision to join together. She had hoped this would happen for such a long time and was sure they would make each other so very happy.

As the Lady of the holding Tinnion performed the ceremony, she was a little nervous at speaking in such a formal role in front of the entire stead, but she managed to make it a touching moment.

"When you choose to bind with another it is your souls and your hearts that join. Your minds, your bodies may follow but it is love that leads the way. It is an honour today, to bind Ara and Andel in love and to watch as their souls join. I see the strength of love this couple share and it fills my heart with joy that I am able to help them to a life they desire and deserve. May your love and your happiness last throughout your lives."

Their wrists were bound by the cords of family and love and the couple shared a kiss as the square erupted in celebration. Another feast was served and an evening of enjoyment lay ahead.

"Lana, pet. We've talked about this a lot since yesterday, and we think we should stay here. Help the lady Tinnion with the hold and look after baby Ranya while Ara and Andel work. We know you have friends and a life in Southport. We know Lady Aelwynne will take good care of you, and the life you will have there will be better than the life you could have here." Ellie held Lana's hand as she spoke, her eye's welling up with tears.

Lana threw her arms around her mother's neck and held her as she cried and Hayal joined them, wrapping his daughter and his wife in his arms.

"I love you, mam and dad. I don't want to lose you."

"You won't be losing us, pet. We're here, and we're safe

now and well. You can come to visit us anytime you want. Besides, you're going to be so busy with learning from Lady Aelwynne and spending time with your other friends. When you come home it will be special, you'll be here just for us."

Lana stayed with her family throughout the evening, holding one hand or another as they celebrated.

They stood on the edge of the pasture. Lana, Tinnion, Daowiel, Aelwynne and two of the men from the Stead. The sun was at its highest, and they were waiting for the Dryad warriors that would escort the men through the forest to the nearest of the trees that could be felled without harm.

The first to step through the tree line was Daowiel's friend, Lothalilia. They greeted each other with a nod and a smile, the warrior still a little guarded at being out in the open with humans. Next to her was a young warrior Lana had seen in the palace but had never spoken to. And then came Princess Erinia.

"Sister? You have come in person?" Daowiel's voice was higher than normal and filled with surprise.

"This moment is rather important, Daowiel. I felt it appropriate to be here and to meet the new Lady of the hold."

"Then let me introduce you to Tinnion, Lady of Butterholt." Daowiel gestured to the hunter with a smile.

"It's an honour to meet you, Princess. I hope we can make this agreement the start of a new relationship between us."

"I share your hope, Lady. Lana, it is good to see you smiling. And who is this lady?" Erinia gestured to Aelwynne.

"This is Lady Aelwynne, the queen's own emissary."

The princess and the voice of the queen shared a smile and a nod in greeting.

"A pleasure," they said in unison.

"I don't think I need to go with you Lothalilia, Cinerea, please escort the feare to the tree."

"Yes, Your Highness."

The Dryad warriors and the men left together, leaving the

princess to speak with her sister and the humans.

EPILOGUE

Fearann a Tuath

C astle MacFaern stood on an island in the centre of Loch Mead. A large, stone tower surrounded by and reflected in the deep, dark waters. A storm was picking up, the skies were dark and the water hit the rocks around the island with force, sending spray high into the air. Brighid looked out of the window to the town across the lake.

"It won't be long now before they come." Wren was holding her friend up, the bandage around her arm bright with blood.

"Aye, a day or two more I reckon." Brighid's stomach and left thigh were heavily bandaged, her left arm was wrapped around the sylph's shoulder, and she had a crutch under her right arm.

"Your father has called his men to leave at first light. It took some time to convince him to leave the hold and travel east."

"I'm surprised ye managed it at all, Wren. He's not normally one for shifting once his mind is set."

"He's a brave man."

"He's stubborn as a bull is what he is." Pain shot through Brighid's body as she laughed, the crutch fell to the floor as her hand went to her wound.

"Careful, Brighid. You'll tear the stitching. You'll need to travel in the cart, there's no way you can ride yet."

"Aye, you're right. I suppose I can sit wi a cross bow and keep an eye on our rear as we go."

They had only just escaped the tower with their lives, Co-hade had been struck about the head early into the battle and left for dead by the shadows. Wren and Brighid had managed to hold their own against the dark fae for a while. They managed to strike a few of their enemy but in the end the speed and number of their adversaries won out.

Brighid charged at the shadows line as wren and Gyrd, a large deasin warrior, carried the unconscious Gesith through the gap she created. Brighid moved to join them once her father was clear of the room. She was halfway down the corridor when the spear pierced her thigh, Wren gave the weight of the Gesith to Gyrd and ran back to help Brighid.

They made it outside and to their horses without being pursued and pushed their mounts into a gallop. Before they were out of the towers shadow an arrow pierced Gyrd's back and he fell to the ground still and lifeless. They galloped on until the horses tired and the town was behind them. Then they stopped beside a stream and Wren tended to their wounds.

Gesith MacKenna sat on his horse, an army of three hundred at his back. Beside him sat the woman that had been a maid in his home and to either side of them sat six shadow warriors.

"My clan and MacStorey's will march down the face and take Lochmead. MacTiern will meet us in the east, he's another few hundred men tae add tae our ranks." Ruairidh explained to the young woman.

"How long will it take your men to clear this fort? What are your plans if your enemy flees? Make this quick MacKenna, this campaign is not designed to feed your ego." The maids voice was commanding and filled with impatience. The Gesith simply nodded at the order, his eyes wide and a thin smile across his face. Only the shaking of his left hand belied the calm he tried to project.

He hadn't known when he made the deal with his maid that the warriors she had promised him were shadows. The children of Chaint. Faster than any fae and able to conceal themselves in the dark, the shadows were silent and sadistic killers. Preferring to infiltrate and assassinate than to fight in the open and the light.

How his maid, Caoimhe, had come into contact with these fae, who had not been seen since the Great War, he did not know. How she had come to lead them he could not fathom. But they did not question her, they did all she said, and they had wiped out all but three of his enemies in the tower of Shadowatch. MacFaern, his daughter and a sylph had crawled away, injured but alive. He had wanted to chase them down, to end it there and then but Caoimhe had let them go, sure they posed no threat. Now he would kill them in their own home, if they had even made it that far. He would kill their family and raise their town to the ground. It would be an example to the other clans. You follow, you do as commanded or you and yours will die, a bloody and violent death.

She had revealed her plan to Ruairidh, though a lot of it had made no sense to him. She had promised him power, he would be the chief of all the clans. Fearann a tuath would be his to rule. *Should he manage to survive.* She had seemed certain of her success, but beyond that and the well being of the shadows, didn't seem to care about him or those that followed him.

She was weak, this new body was serving her as it should but the spirit that had owned it was hanging on. Fighting. There were moments when she could feel it, coursing through body, trying to move its mouth, trying to scream, to cry for help. She had been gone too long. Only twelve of her children remained, only one was a priest. The people of Mortara believed her dead, her temples were empty, her altars bare. Without faith, without belief, there was no power.

And yet her brother was strong. She could feel him out there, him and her cousin the god of the oceans. Ulios of course would survive, as long as there were fish in the ocean, his children would never be found. They would thrive in their home, deep in the oceans of the world. But her brother should have faded, he should be like her.

Her brother, who had left her, far out to the north, her ship no more than flotsam. Her brother who had betrayed her, who had set her ship to flame and killed her children. Her brother, Solumus. He would pay dearly.

Her mind drifted back to that day. In the Heart of Mortara, far to the south. Her cousins were charging the elemental stone with their souls. But her brother had convinced her to leave with him; to travel by ship to a land in the west. A land with no gods, the humans would have no reason to hate them, to fear them, they would be easy to enthral. With their cousins gone they would rule together. They would build their power with the faith of those humans, and they would return to Mortara to take back what was theirs.

But as their ships reached the icy north he showed his true plan. He bombarded her ship with flaming barrels destroying it under her feet, sending it into the depths. He never could share; she had known that. How could she have been so naive? How could she have trusted him?

With her children dying around her, drowning in the stormy salt water of the northern ocean, her power was fading fast. She had no choice but to hold on to the wood beneath her and swim.

There were humans on the island, fishing folk that survived on the bounties of the ocean. They hunted seals on their northern shore and that was where they had found her. They her to their village and fed her. Not knowing who she was, not knowing they were nursing the goddess of night. By the time the first of her children had washed up on the shore half the men of the village were dead.

The women, now living in fear, nursed the fae back to health. By the full of the moon there were a dozen of her children and the island was theirs. The human women kept alive to serve, the men killed, sacrificed to the goddess Chaint. She drank their blood with relish. As the humans died and the fear of her filled the island, she grew a little in strength. A temple was built and for a time she thought all would be well.

As the centuries past however the humans died out and her connection to her children grew weaker. It was known that with each generation that connection would fade, but when the fae ruled over the world the effect of this on her family was small. Now though, with only a dozen shadows at any one time it took its toll. She needed the humans to love her, or fear her, it didn't really matter as long as they served as long as they believed and worshipped her. But with her power fading once more her body was dying. She would need a new one and soon. So, she trained her children to kill in the darkness, and she brought them to Mortara.

She took this body, this human maid, she used it to whisper in the ear of the gesith, and she took Shadowatch as her own. Now she sat with the human, an army at her back, whispers of her plan running before her. Spreading through the farms and villages of Fearann a Tuath.

Soon Lochmead would fall, and with it the only clan chief that had rejected that plan. News of their deaths would spread fear through the north and as the fear spread, as the blood flowed, more would believe come to their side and her power would grow. Once the clan chiefs of the tuath and their holds were with them she would lead them to Northfort and the Tay. There she would take the castle and the Tay would die. Then she would reveal her true self. One by one the holds from the western coast to the mountains of Sgàil would fall under her command. She would rule the north, she would build an army, she would grow her power and in time, she would take Mortara. The humans would be enslaved and the fae would bow to her, the darkest of their gods. With Mortara hers she would set her sights west, to the island of falcons and her brother.

With Chaint's mind lost in her memories and her thoughts of revenge the soul of Caoimhe found strength. A cry, small and weak, escaped the lips of the body that once belonged to the human soul. In a flash, a fraction of a heartbeat the weight of the goddess bore down on the human that remained. Forcing the soul back to a dark corner of the body, taking control back once again. An echo of the cry ran through the body they shared, it's skin prickled, its hairs stood on edge.

The eyes closed and the echo stopped. Caoimhe's spirit was cowed and silenced.

"Yes. Solumus will pay. But first, this body must be mine and mine alone."

ACKNOWLEDGEMENT

I would like to take the opportunity to thank a few wonderful people that helped me during the writing of this book. They each took time to read my early drafts and point me in the right direction, as well as giving me general support and encouragement.

Allan J Hubert-Wright, my oldest friend and a constant source of inspiration.

Victoria J Price, a wonderful writer, a kind soul and a font of knowledge.

And then onto people who, as far as I know, don't have a 'J' in their names...

Ceal Madigan, though I don't know her real name, it could very well have a J in it. Her support and encouragement over email and chat was a wonderful thing.

And, last but not least, Hilary Taylor. Someone who started this journey into writing at the same time as me, whose work I enjoy and who's friendship I'm pleased to have. Look out for her stories!

All of the above are incredibly creative people and their advice means a lot to me.

ABOUT THE AUTHOR

Madelaine Taylor

Madelaine grew up in a small town on the coast of Northumberland. The chill north eastern air and grey waves of the north sea greeting her every morning.

Having travelled, and lived, across the UK and parts of Europe she longed for home, and is now back in Northumberland. There, wrapped in a warm blanket and with an almost constant supply of tea, Madelaine has discovered the joys of writing.

Inspired by the books of Pratchett, Tolkien, Eddings and Jordan; her short stories often contain elements of fantasy and humour.

Now, with the release of "The Elemental Stone", she has created a fantasy world of her own. One she intends to fill with heroes and villains, light and darkness, love, laughter and sorrow.

Printed in Great Britain
by Amazon

82805601R00173